W9-CVO-273

Random House, Inc.
201 East 50th Street
New York, N.Y. 10022

SBN 425-03664-2

BERKLEY MEDALLION BOOKS *are published by*
Berkley Publishing Corporation
200 Madison Avenue
New York, N.Y. 10016

BERKLEY MEDALLION BOOK ® TM 757,375

Printed in the United States of America

Berkley Medallion Edition, JANUARY, 1978

When the battle to be human becomes heroic . . .

Benny Beer did what every young man in the
1940's did. He fought a war in Europe and fell in
love at home. And since Benny had killed in war,
he wanted to heal in peace. He became a doctor—
the American dream.

But then Benny Beer fell in love again. And
had to fight another war in Asia.

But Benny kept fighting and falling in love,
because that was what being alive meant—until a
routine mission sent him to a POW camp and a
fight for survival more desperate than any he had
known before.

$1.00

also by Stephen Becker

THE CHINESE BANDIT

DOG TA

STEPHEN BECKE

A BERKLEY MEDALLION

published by

BERKLEY PUBLISHING COR

To Nan Swinburne
with love

In the Days
of Thy Youth

1

LIFE IS A riddle but death is no answer, and a soldier alone walks in fear because there is no one with him to die instead. In April of 1945 Benjamin Beer found himself alone and afraid on a German plain, the land stark, spring itself stunted, misborn, the sky frozen, the wind a scythe. Fear: silence and solitude overwhelmed him after months of carnage and clamor; also he was a Jew and this was Germany and he loved women, all women, deeply and did not want to die or be mutilated in a swinish land. He followed a track westward across a waste of frozen stubble and vowed never to kill again if he survived this day. He knew that he was not the first to make that vow, and that he would break it. He kept to the small groves for shelter from the wind and hostile eyes. He skirted lacy ponds, ice rimmed. Where were the birds? The rabbits, stock, dogs? He sniffled and spat.

He was twenty-one years old and wanted desperately to be twenty-two. He stood six feet one inch and was burly, almost six poods as he planned to tell the Russians when the grand meeting occurred; had black hair and vehement brown eyes. Being young and omnipotent he saw himself as a demigod, and felt that he ate barrels and baskets of meat and grain each day; drank firkins and hogsheads; sweated wine and honey; committed extravagant nuisance with extravagant pleasure; and blew his nose musically as became a fiddler. Like certain fiddlers of legend he ranked fornication above all sport. He disdained lesser pursuits like football and dancing as irrelevant, amusements for the flighty or timid but not worth the time of a serious man. In April of 1945 he had not touched a woman for four months. He would not rape, and for the time being scorned German flesh. In return for that manly forbearance he hoped, now, on the brooding and vengeful Teutonic plain, to be spared. Though he did not believe in justice, or even in God.

Prayer was something else: a useful distraction, an aspect of poetry. O God of Abraham and Isaac. Lesser gods, Johnny-come-latelies, might do for flat tires, clap and dog-bite, but in his present difficulties he preferred to deal only with principals. O God of Abraham and Isaac. O God of Abraham, Isaac and Israel, uncounted cubits tall, ordinancer and manna-maker, O God of my fathers, wake up and pluck me from this coil! God slumbered on. Benny saw him, huge, rabbinical, dandruff, a faint odor of herring.

Benny tugged his wool scarf tighter and blinked into the sun. The track was joined by another; the ruts grew deeper and wider, almost a road, and Benny was faintly cheered. He seemed to be walking backward in time, perhaps directly toward the God of Abraham et cetera, but was nevertheless encouraged by the wider ruts, evidence of bustle and humanity. Around the next bend would lie a village, a village of the thirteenth century, perhaps earlier; perhaps these were late Roman days and this was the land of the Goths. The sun blinked back, low, a mad yellow eye. Shortly he would meet a charnel cart heaped high with peasants felled by the Black Plague. And a monk driving. "Ave." "Ave." Sign of the cross. The corpses, contorted. Benny's regiment had been shown photographs. Mounds of skinny cadavers, open mouths, empty eyes. The new Black Death. It was somewhat incomprehensible. Benny himself refused to comprehend it; he grew icy and would not discuss such matters. For a day or two he enjoyed a mournful celebrity. The men of his platoon deferred to him, almost apologetic, and seemed to wonder what unique importance the Bennys of this world shared, that they must be rendered ash and clinker. And who in that platoon would be educated, ennobled, exalted by that hour of photographs? Not one.

The sight of a village roused him. His senses were congealed; he had barely the wit to feel alarm. He was muffled, deaf, blinded, hands and feet numb, nose so cold that the hairs no longer crackled. The village was all stone walls, like an ancient monastery half in ruins. There was no sound, no motion, no play now at dusk even of light and shadow, as if that plague had left the place gutted and damned; as if he might find crosses painted on the wooden doors, or hear faint plainsong from spared friars. A blind leper with a begging-bowl. Stark against the gathering night, a gibbet.

He advanced, wary but harmless. His rifle was slung, his hands too cold; more, he knew that the village was deserted. Not a man, not a rat. He imagined a tavern: a blazing fire and a round jolly innkeeper, a registered Vandal but for reasons of business only, you understand, a man must live; and a barmaid, a merry Saxon wench with fat breasts and unrelenting thighs; in the corner a drunken scholar, splenetic, wrung by morose delectation, muttering dog-Latin. Good even, master scholar. Good even, host. Come by the fire, girl, and warm a soldier. Benny would set his pack in a corner of the cozy room and they would serve him bread, cheese and ale. He would warm his hands between those thighs.

No. Not a man, not a rat, and he sensed it; half a dozen stone houses at a crossroads, and he knew they were deserted as he knew a man was dead. He had tried not to kill, not to hate, but had done both, and with some exhilaration, and always knew, surely, whether a man was dead or merely wounded: as if there were a smell or a glow or a sly wink of the dead eye. He shivered again in the wolfish light, and chose a door and broke it down.

He entered a shambles, the rude hooks hanging rusted, the wooden floor stained with generations of blood, with centuries of sheep, pigs, goats, cattle, heretics; in famine cats and dogs; perhaps babies, surely rabbis. Benny shivered again. The next two houses were dwellings, bare, inhuman, on one wall a carved crucifix, on another a rippled mirror. The fourth building was his tavern, with a table and chairs and a couple of wide benches, with a deep stone fireplace (the butcher's lamb, spitted, the spatter of hot fat, savory smoke telling travelers a bill of fare). A fire might betray, but Benny was perhaps behind his own lines and disinclined to freeze. He set down his rifle and pack, broke up a chair, shaved kindling with his bayonet, opened the ponderous, ancient draft, dumped a ration from its waxed box, set fire to the box and fed the flames with

6

care. He warmed his hands. They ached. He removed his helmet. Then he yawned. He yawned three times, great racking yawns, and hunkered himself onto a chair and blinked, thick, powerful blinks that squeezed tears from his tired, windburned eyes; and sat there like an ox. After a moment he poured water from his canteen to his cup, set the cup in the flames, and extracted a tea bag from his cartridge belt.

A tea bag. Benny was a city boy, from the greatest of them all, the heart of Manhattan, yea Union Square, and in his cartridge belt he also carried cubes of sugar. "Sugar gives cancer," a street cleaner had once confided. A little fellow all in white, leaning on the broom. In the spring of 1938, when a trip to Atlantic City would be an epic. "And furthermore I do not eat protein. No meat whatsoever," and with the sunniest of smiles, "so I am for my weight the strongest man in New York City and I don't fart." "That's interesting," Benny had said, fourteen, and sidled off discreetly. Now he was twenty-one and while preferring cities he enjoyed the countryside and scorned provincial pride; he knew that civilization consisted of New York and a few European capitals but saw no reason why men should not live elsewhere if they chose. Choice was all! Benny loved people, animals, plants, the sights and sounds of life; hearing that the Chinese spoke to flowers, he understood. He loved smells, of women, sweat, exhaust, frying onions, birdcages, his own effluvia, cigars, cheap perfume, lions in the zoo, gunpowder, tea and sponge cake; and the feel of women, rough stone walls on a summer day, the steering wheel of a jeep, rough bark, shingles, cats, subway straps, hammer handles, cosmoline, heavy wool; the taste of all food and drink (pork, yes, mussels, yes) and many flowers,

7

best of all buttercups and violets, and of course women. Women. He experienced tender affection if not carnal desire for the female of any species, drab orioles and cardinals (yes! in city parks! the '40s!), tabby cats and mallards and dugongs and vixens. One female leopard he remembered with the pangs of true heartbreak; he wondered if she were still alive, pacing her corner of the Bronx. He grew giddy in a subway car amid stenographers and salesgirls. He loved certain politicians (yes! the '40s!) and believed that even clergymen might ultimately be pardoned. He did not love the Germans and he was fighting a war he believed in.

With warmth came content. The water boiled; he concocted tea, and the first sip swirled him dizzily back to Union Square. He laughed aloud, and tasted charlotte russe; a cubby on 14th Street that sold only charlotte russe. Where else in the world? He saw girls scampering to kiosks in the opal winter light, the delectably underbred faces, a contour too little chin, a contour too much nose, shapeless bodies breathing steam. At home Benny woke to music, blindly turning a knob, lying in wait for the day's omen. Once a month it was a Beethoven quartet and he knew the girls would be pretty that day. Or the third Brandenburg; Benny was a fiddler with a fiddler's prejudices. He had begun, or been begun, at the age of five, with a half-violin. He managed somehow to star at stickball also. He did many things well. He healed wounded cats and dogs, once a sparrow with a broken wing. He forced (the power of personality) recalcitrant automobiles into life and motion. He pleased his father, which not all young men cared to, or knew how to do; even tipsy, Benny insisted on a courtly manner, emanations of Vienna, Heidelberg, Leipzig absorbed from a tailor-father five feet six who, abandoned by God, had clung instead to Trotsky and civiltà, a word learned from a Florentine buttonholer, a word he could not properly define but only surround: dignity, privacy, respect for oneself without which there was no respect for others. So Benny bore himself always (barring ultimate moments of animal savagery, when killing, for example, or struggling in sweaty agony with a late quartet) like a princeling, and Jacob Beer was proud of him. "The boy will be what he wants to be," Jacob said flatly. "A lifeguard. A cigar wholesaler. Whatever. But a gentleman." In those days it seemed to matter. "And not like your Morgans and Rockefellers, take away the gold falling out of every pocket and what's left has no brains, no class. Benny is noble." Trotsky would have shrugged in despair.

Benny the paragon sat alone, lost straggler from a lost platoon, much aware that he was in Central Europe, that a coachman bearing letters for Herr L. van B. might have paused at this very inn for rest and refreshment. He sipped at the hot tea. He prayed for strudel and none came. The fire rose; he unwound his scarf. Jacob believed in scarfs, which he called mufflers, and on a January morning little of Jacob was visible: between the fur hat and the muffler, two sharp eyes, one sharp nose. Forty years of tailoring and eyes like an eagle (iggle, really, but Jacob invested a New York Yiddish accent with royal resonances): "Aiees laika niggle," he said, "and do you know why? Because I make a point to alter the focus. Frequently. I look at a star. Or Jersey. And never never look into the sun. Alter the focus. Similarly the nose, the tongue. Once a week, Italian food. And," this impish old man,

9

"a good grade of cigar helps, and moderation in intercourse. Every man can live to be a hundred."

Strudel failing, Benny prayed for a good cigar; none came. Reviving nonetheless, he rose to be a soldier, to inspect his perimeter before eating and sleeping. Through cloudy windows he reconnoitered the road. It entered the village from the northwest and curved off to the east. The last light faded. It was so quiet, as Jacob said, you could drop a pin. He was about to turn, to leave his fate in the lap of the gods (or the Hitlers and Stalins and Roosevelts), when his eye caught a flash of white, and an explosion of fear stopped his breath. He dashed for his rifle and pressed the safety, and crouched like a lover in the flickering firelight, hot and stupendous.

The man, the creature, the moving object, approached from the east. It proceeded by jerks and lurches, like a marionette. Puzzled, elementally perturbed, abruptly at the edge of tears, enraged, Benny pressed the safety back and set his rifle against the cold stone wall.

The creature approached in zigzags and staggers. It wore a clown's suit, horizontal stripes. It was bald, shoeless and tiny, a child of nightmare. It stumbled to its knees and seemed to sleep; fell forward; lay flat. One star twinkled.

Benny stepped outside, peered left and right, and went to fetch it. He saw that it was a man, and picked it up. It weighed little more than a full field pack. Benny toted the man inside and placed him before the fire. The bald head gleamed like old ivory, yellowing. Frozen snot crusted the nose and lips. Gently Benny wiped it away. The feet were icy. Benny's ear found a heartbeat. He removed his jacket and smoothed it over the body. He wrapped the feet in his scarf. He broke up another chair and stoked the fire. He chafed the wrists; when ladies in novels fainted, wrists were chafed. He rubbed the body like a masseur. A more conscientious warrior would have owned a blanket, but Benny had tea bags and sugar, and was sorry now. He chafed the wrists again, and the forearms, and in the firelight he saw the tag on the breast of the suit: 57359.

The man remained alive. Benny quit rubbing after a time and sat back against the stone fireplace. He was hungry but had only the one ration. Perhaps the man was dying. Those photographs. The survivors in striped hats, haunted. Huge eyes. The angel of death would stride in like a knight, but only bones, a cheerful smile on his death's-head, and would stand before the fire, snobbish, wearily elegant, jaded, leaning on his pike. "Be off," Benny said aloud. The angel nodded coldly and passed along.

Nature called; Benny stepped once more outside, this time to make the village his own. The barest gleam of firelight followed him. The village was a bad dream and Benny was weary. He stood with his back to the breeze and pissed on Germany. Steam rose dimly, and two Bennys smiled in rue, sad and strange: half of him was named Hansi, illiterate, passed water in the road, loved the Saxon wench, chaffed the scholar, paid the host, sat unbathed at the oaken board and gobbled pork; the other half lay unconscious before the fire and might not see another dawn.

He buttoned up and returned to the little man, who had not stirred: only the bare rise and fall of the sunken breast. He smelled the man's barracks and saw him

11

eating garbage. The fat guards with tiny eyes and no lips. The commandant, a fantasy from the cinema, ranting in Teutonic English.

So. Now it had to be comprehended, a little at least. The camps were not off in Atlantis, with robed officials waiting gravely to set wrongs right. Benny Beer had prayed for strudel and cigars and had been sent this mummy. Benny Beer who could eat eight stuffed cabbage leaves at a sitting; who had perfect pitch; who had pleased Irene S—— four times between eleven and one, and under a stairway at that; who was a corporal, by God. And now this. This wee criminal. A Jew? A politician? A traffic ticket? In this insane country how could you know?

Benny rubbed the man's hands and feet, and sipped tea, and thought upon life and death and heaven and hell.

Later the man groaned, a birdlike exhalation, and licked his lips, and heaved a sigh, and slept. So did Benny, but lightly.

When Benny awoke, the little man was struggling to rise: on all fours, swaying, straining, staring. He hissed in horror, and wept.

"It's all right," Benny said, moved, unmoving. "Kamerad. American. Amerikanisch."

57359's lips formed words, uttered no sound. Benny stood up, and the little man contracted, and showed his rotting teeth. His ears were like wings.

"It's all right," Benny said. "Frei. Frei. Du bist frei." The little man grimaced like a cat. "Look." Benny pointed. "A fire. Feuer. Essen. Trinken." Warily the man turned to see. His eyes were tremendous, Egyptian eyes, doe's eyes in a mouse's face. He dragged a knee toward the fire, slipped sidewise; he sat facing the flame like a baby, legs apart, back hunched, hands limp between his legs.

Benny showed him the rations, the canteen cup. He filled the cup again and set it in the flames. He offered the canteen. It fell from the man's hands. Benny knelt beside him and tilted it up. The man compressed his lips and shook his head. Benny sat back, bewildered, almost angry. The little fellow's claw picked out the helmet, the scarf; Benny passed them along. A whisper: "Bitte." 57359 slipped the helmet comically over his bald head and draped the scarf upon his shoulders. He peered about him like a child and then spoke aloud. He murmured and muttered and rocked and nodded. He was thanking God and not Benny. Benny looked away.

The little fellow pinched him. Benny gave him the canteen, and he drank deep. Benny withdrew the canteen and said, like a concertmaster, "Langsam." He opened the tin and shaved a slice from the cylinder of cheese. Slice by slice he fed his charge.

"Wasser."

Benny obliged, and pointed to the cup: "Tea."

"Tee." 57359 tried to smile and Benny's heart cracked.

He fetched socks from his pack and slipped them onto the tiny feet, cursing that he had not thought of them sooner. He shaved more cheese. There were bits of bacon in the cheese. Meat and milk and not only meat but bacon. Well. The Messiah would come a day later.

57359, this newborn mouse, sipping tea, wept as if thawing. His tears gleamed like quicksilver, welled from the huge eyes and flowed beside the huge nose, dribbled from the little round chin. Fascinated, Benny crooned encouragement, recalled formalities: "Benny Beer," he said. "Benjamin Beer. Benyamin Bear. Ich bin Benyamin Bear." The survivor stuttered nods, swallowed, sighed, shook his head, pursed his lips, looked Benny in the eye and shrugged. Benny recognized the shrug: what difference can a little war make, or a little century, or a little death? A Goliath of shrugs. A Leviathan of shrugs.

In firelight the wraith licked his lips for forgotten crumbs. His vast brown eyes gleamed, a lunatic affirmation of life, appetite, hope. Again he attacked the tea, slurped, spilled, squeaked his pleasure. He published a thunderous belch.

When the sun rose Isaac gathered up Abraham and they set forth across the plain.

"Wie geht's?" Thus Benny the world traveler.

"Gut."

Big Ben laughed aloud and trudged on. A milder morn, and spring suddenly possible. In an hour they wandered two miles, three. Benny set down his burden, trotted in place, rubbed his own weary muscles. His mouse sank to the road. Benny hauled him up, hugged him, massaged him, abraded him, mauled and manhandled him; the little man warmed and smiled.

The lone aircraft flew out of the west, low, and Benny assumed it was American. Perhaps it was. When the strafing began he fell upon his friend, who wailed, clutched, scrabbled, strangled—with what secret strength? in what last outraged spasm? Benny choked, and the earth tilted and went dark.

● ● ●

Later that year Benny awoke to dancing ranks of light and the smell of vodka. He strove yet budged not, and decided solemnly that he was alive and upon earth but had lost all four limbs. With that depressing notion he slept again. Ages more, galaxies more, and he sighed, swallowed cotton, opened his eyes; a woman was leaning across him and he embraced her. "Ah non." She giggled. He had embraced her with one arm. That aroused his curiosity. "Lie still." A foreign lady. Perhaps he was abroad. Perhaps this was a grand ocean liner. Benny was agog; in his excitement he blinked furiously. "Well well. Hello there." White jacket. A ship's officer, or a steward. Yes. A steward. "Broth," Benny said. "You're all right," the steward said. "You're in Paris, and you'll be all right in time."

"Paris." Brackets on a wall; a row of lamps.

"You've had a bad . . ."

But Benny heard no more for now; he saw the beds, faces, bandages, and a swift illumination shocked him: the village, Jacob, 57359, night and morning. "Ah God. Jacob. Have you told my father?"

"I'm sure he's been told. All's well, my lad."

All's well, my lad? "These wires."

"Intravenous feeding. Do you know what that is?"

Benny concentrated. "Am I hurt."

"Six bullets, shoulder to calf. All out. Smashed shoulder blade. Smashed femur; that's your thigh-bone."

"Connected to the kneebone." Benny quaked; he had made a rare joke.

"Well, yes. And you've quarts of new blood in you."

"Type O."

15

A chuckle. "We know that now."

"You must not laugh," Benny said firmly. "Important. On the dog tags."

"I'm afraid we couldn't find your dog tags."

"Around my neck. Three two nine three two five two seven."

"Yes. You rest. We'll talk about that later."

Benny strained to think, frowned and set his teeth. "My balls," he said, "and my spinal cord. Sir."

"All there. Absolutely all right."

Benny burst into tears, and cried himself to sleep. He woke again at night, the ward silent and shadowed, and he recalled it all immediately, and smiled. "God of Abraham and Isaac," he said to the dark, to the shadows of his forgotten ancestors, "thou who never wert, I thank you. If you should require assistance in the future I hope you will not hesitate to call upon me."

"For Christ's sake shut up," someone said. "We're trying to sleep."

Benny would doubtless spend six weeks in bed. "I'll need books." The doctor was jovial: anything, everything. Red wine, in time. Newspapers. La Vie Parisienne. The doctor winked. Benny stared coldly and the doctor became busy.

They brought Benny soldiers' editions of many books and he read the glories of western literature in 12mo., paperbound. He read Greeks and Russians and Frenchmen and Englishmen. The Armed Forces Edition of the Iliad! He also read French newspapers, four or five a day, most of the political left, each with evil to say of the others, and thought that Jacob would be amused. Barring an ungrateful irascibility he was an exemplary patient, cheerful and calm, aglow and

16

moaning at the passage of nurses. In danger of bedsores he submitted to massage, humming low, eyes shut, drifting nirvanaward on waves of eastern sensuality. Madame Fribourg, Marie-Elisabeth, his witchlike specialist, was aged and bore a tufted wart, but she was all he had of houri, peri, succubus. Sexuality oppressed him; he was in essential respects hale, yet bedridden and fragile. A Mademoiselle Nattier caught his eye, and later his—ah no. Benny's is a story worthy of more than passing fancies.

Still, she was what "Frenchwoman" had always promised: dark, small-featured (something stingy there, mean), busty, her buttocks twitching neatly, symmetrically, metronomically as she walked. Allegro vivo e con amore. She smelled wrong but she loved him: at first, while he was down and out, with subtle touches of hospitality; then, when he was up and coming, with zut and oolala. Benny gave tongue to bleats of joy. His wardmates knew, approved, envied. Finally, the joint triumph of Asclepius and Eros: standing up. The leg held. All this behind curtains, in linen closets, twixt lights out and cock-crow. She improved her English: "Am I ready to be occupied by the Americans?" "Oh yes," Benny said with fervor, "oh yes." He remembered her always with pleasure and pride; years later she stirred him still, though they knew nothing of each other but flesh. Though? Perhaps because.

He wished he could forget Captain Parsons. This one came marching in one day with two lieutenants prissing along behind him, all three identical, painted by number, and they brisked a few wooden chairs Benny's way and perused his chart with earnest, forthright, wholesome menace. Having learned his name, rank, serial number, age, height, weight, religion, ailments, output of urine and talent for bowel movements, they sat down and one of them asked, "Corporal Benjamin Beer?"

They were summer fools but they were *they, them,* the eternal faceless functionary, and Benny's first thought was that they brought bad news about Jacob; but he revised that at once, realizing in a paroxysm of joy that he was about to be given a medal. "Yes. That's me. Three two nine three two five two seven."

"Hmm," the captain said. The lieutenants apparently agreed. "My name is Parsons," the captain went on, "and this is Pistol and Bardolph." He did not really say that, but no man is expected to retain the names of lieutenants once the peace is signed. "We have to talk to you about a matter that may be rather delicate, and you are to consider that Lieutenant Pistol represents you."

"Represents me?"

"Yes. We're legal officers."

"Oh?"

"Now. Pay attention. We're trying—"

"Pencils ready," Benny said.

They blinked.

"We're trying," Parsons said patiently, "to piece together the day you were shot. The two days, I should say. By the way, you may have an independent witness, but it isn't really necessary. This is just questions, not under oath or anything, and anyway we have Pistol and Bardolph."

"Not under oath," Benny mused. "So you figure it's all right if I lie."

"Well," and Parsons laughed ineptly, "I wouldn't advise it. I was merely explaining the procedure."

"Yes. I see," Benny said. "I don't need a witness. I'll tell you exactly what happened."

18

He did so. The farmhouse, the mill and the small bridge. "The farmhouse was full of them. So we fell back across the little bridge and the rest hauled ass down the road while I covered our end of the bridge. But the Germans ran downstream and crossed and cut the road between me and the others. So I just tiptoed into the woods, and figured to circle around and find them later. And all of a sudden Europe was empty. I couldn't find anybody on either side." He went on: the village, the tavern, 57359, the morning's journey. They listened with identical frowns. "And that's all I remember. What happened to the little fellow?"

"I have no information about that. I'm only gathering facts."

"I'd like to find him. Will you note that, please? Corporal Beer would appreciate any information about this little civilian prisoner from some camp, number five seven three five nine. Maybe the lieutenants could note it too." They all nodded; Parsons scribbled. "So that's it," Benny said. "What happened to me afterward?"

"They pumped some blood into you and dumped you aboard a plane. Nobody knew who you were or even which side you were on."

Benny stared.

"You were half naked at the side of the road, and you had no dog tags."

"My weapon?"

"No weapon."

"I'll be damned." Much to think about. "How come they flew me here?"

"I suppose to keep an eye on you," Parsons said, "until they could establish an identity for you."

"Well what the hell," Benny said. "You know

19

now. You have my prints. I'm not a German spy or any escaping Gauleiter. So what's it all about?''

"How do you know a word like 'Gauleiter'?"

Benny understood that he was in the presence of the police, and was properly impressed. Forlornly he cocked his head at each lieutenant in turn. Pistol pinked; Bardolph was lost in thought. "It was in all the papers," Benny said. "Captain, I know about forty words of German, a couple of hundred of Yiddish. You know much Yiddish?"

Parsons crossed his legs. "None at all, I'm sorry to say."

"It's a rich tongue. How about German?"

"I have a rudimentary working knowledge."

"Acquired before the war?"

"No." Parsons was nettled.

"Italian? Did you serve there?"

"No."

"Japanese?"

"No. Why do you ask?"

"I'm staving off the moment of truth," Benny said. "I don't think I'm going to like it. I suppose the doctor told you about my rages."

"Rages." Parsons wrestled with belief.

Benny sighed. "Oh I'm in pain. Why are you here?"

"Your platoon," Parsons said, "was badly shot up that afternoon and there is some question of desertion."

Benny bawled like a bull and roared fire. "Nurse! Doctor!"

Parsons expressed dismay.

"Where's my Purple Heart?" Benny bellowed. "And where the hell would anybody desert to? Are you crazy? Who was killed? Tell me that anyway."

20

"Four were killed, two wounded," Parsons said. "I don't have the names."

Benny mourned. They were bumblers, pimply lechers, Jew-baiters, goldbricks, but they were his. He hoped Haas was not dead. He had once lifted a jeep off Haas, the poor man shrieking and blubbering; Haas had sustained minor bruises and Benny had simulated hernia for some hours, falsetto and tottering.

"Well sir," he said, "you're officers and I'm only a dumb corporal but anybody who knows me will tell you that I don't desert. It's that easy. I was a good boy and I done all they tole me and only a moron would cut and run with the war just about over. Furthermore when a man is blown to bits in action the presumption ought to be in his favor."

"That's true," Parsons said. "You command quite a vocabulary. I was a spelling champion in high school."

Benny stared again.

"Presumption."

After a moment Benny nodded slowly. "I know another one."

Parsons smiled happily.

"Tatterdemalion."

Parsons nodded. "Not really hard."

"But think of all the words you can make from it. Three letters or more."

"Good Lord yes! But perhaps later," Parsons said briskly. "We've got to take this statement."

"You've taken it," Benny grumbled. "I don't enjoy this, Captain. It's like being called a bad name." None of the three, Benny saw, wore the badge of a combat infantryman. Snob!

"I suppose it is. I'm sorry."

Benny shrugged. His anger was gone. Mugs and

shits, as an Anzac drinker had once described politicians and such. Mugs and shits and nothing to be done
about them. They were not merely an aspect of life,
they were life itself, and the rare souls who boasted
nobility and true intelligence, like himself, Benny
thought, were freaks.

The three scanned their notes. "I'm sorry," Parsons
said amiably. "I am indeed. Somebody got a bee in his
bonnet. I don't blame you for—well, for that look on
your face."

"I just want my Purple Heart," Benny said. "I
promised my father I'd come home with a medal. It's
important to us because we've been military folk for
many generations."

"I certainly won't put any obstacles in your way,"
Parsons said, bluff and hearty, and Benny remembered
someone saying, All's well, my lad. He caught a gleam
of humanity from Pistol, who immediately suppressed
it.

"I thank you for that, sir." He shook hands with
Parsons. "I do indeed. You've been very civil." He
shook hands with Bardolph. "Lieutenant." And with
Pistol, who did not meet his eye. A Jewish grandpar-
ent? "I really ought to sleep now," Benny said. "My
leg hurts."

He was not to hear from them again for some time.
But a week later a new set of dog tags adorned his hairy
chest, and when he left the hospital a Purple Heart made
his theater ribbon less lonely. That was after a day of
farewell to Miss Nattier, as she insisted he address her.
He asked her if she was descended from the painter, but
she had not heard of the painter. They clung together
and she said she would never forget him, which was
true enough; they knew that the memory would be

sweet, and warm, and outlast lust; and for the final hour
of her shift they stood at the window in harmony and
innocence while night flittered down on the chimney
pots like a flight of bats.

2

AT THE END of spring Benny Beer came home. He arrived in New York standing one meter eighty-five, weighing in at ninety-three kilos; disembarked with seven hundred others onto an empty pier, no bouquets, no brass bands; and took the subway to Union Square in late morning. Jacob Beer, custom tailoring for men. Mirages rippled off the hot tar. Benny marched up Broadway limping slightly, duffel bag perched heroically on one shoulder. Women noticed. Benny beamed and ogled. Dazzling. Downy forearms. Ambushed behinds. Benny ached. The sun lay on his nape like a woman's hand. Summer breasts. He stared, chirped, swooned. Thighs, nests. The sun slanted off cool stone sills, shadowed grooves. Pigeons paraded, flapped welcome. The smell of doughnuts, of exhaust. Shoppers, earrings, sandals. Old men, sad, canes. Benny swelled. The women were imperfect and he loved them for it: a wrinkle behind the knee, a rabbity smile, tiny eyes, faces bred to filing as ewes to wool, upswept hair lacquered stiff, hanging hems, slipping slips, faint mustaches—so? *So?* He wanted them all.

Yet he dawdled, smiling tolerantly at his own child-ishness. A policeman saluted casually, noting Benny's small rainbow of ribbons; Benny nodded, limped, al-lowed a glaze of hollow horror to dim his bright brown eyes, and moved on, stifling unseemly mirth. Were all women beautiful? He had trod God's country for an hour now and seen none beneath his notice. Once off the lugger and I am theirs! He had survived. He lived again, sap and rod rising, death and killing past. Time to rejoice. Create! Let joy be unconfined! Any race, color, creed, age, shape or previous condition of pul-chritude. Benny is home! Wearing his sex at a rakish angle.

And there he was: the doorway took him by surprise. The plaque: *Jacob Beer*. The lobby was cool, eternal, marbled. A new elevator boy, perhaps sixteen, already pinched and pale, petty thief, cigarette complexion, the *Daily News* wedged behind his Otis joystick. Benny was levitated to the seventh floor and stepped into the familiar corridor, strode to the familiar door, entered, passed through a short hallway of felt screens, and approached two men standing before a triptych of mir-rors. He dropped the bag and embraced the smaller man, kissing him once on each cheek and then on the mouth.

Jacob Beer bawled. He honored his son by bawling: stood in the presence of his client Croesus and per-formed a cloudburst. When he could speak, still in the circle of Benny's arms like a bride, he said, "My son. You'll excuse me, Feldman. My son Benjamin. Home from the war. Wounded. My son. My son Benjamin." Benny grinned at him and mussed his hair. Jacob was so small. Three cubits twelve, weight barely over a Babylonian talent. In age two score eleven. In palaver

25

English, Yiddish, childhood German and Polish, and Italian numbers, the last from haggling with cutters and stitchers and buttonholers. ("The rest, all right, but God spare me buttonholers. Specialists. Right away a buttonholer is Victor Emmanuel.") Because in the early years there had been as many Italians as Jews in the trade. An Italian Jew was the highest trump. The Beers boasted a tradition: that in the year 1400 A.D. (whose D., Jacob asked darkly) a direct male ancestor had been the Grand Rabbi of Padua. Jacob made the most of that. "Galleazo," he would say, "a buttonholer you are, the best, no question, but did you know that in the year fourteen hundred . . ."

Jacob's tears were of joy, but behind them lurked a grief and Benny read it immediately: that Benny's mother had not lived to see this day. She had not lived to see his departure either, having died of cancer when he was ten, but that was irrelevant. A moment of joy, was a moment of joy, two, three, five in a lucky lifetime, and bad enough they came so seldom without the pain of rejoicing alone. Feldman effaced himself, shaking Benny's hand and taking gracious leave. Jacob nodded gratefully and waved in farewell. When he was alone with his son he bawled a bit more. He recovered, donned his sharkskin jacket, speechless, shaking his head and gulping; he embraced Benny again and found his voice: "We'll go to Pinsky's for lunch. Wait till Karp sees you. Karp! Ha! He said everything wrong. He said Leningrad would fall. Stalin would be assassinated. Trotsky makes a comeback. Alevai, but it won't happen. Karp! Benny, Benny! How are you? Does it hurt? What's the ribbons there? A hero? You a hero?" They bustled to the door, where Jacob turned, said, "Thank God. Thank God," and flung his arms

26

again about his son. Dementedly he jigged, whirled, clapped his hands. "Benny! Have I got a flannel for you! And a Harris tweed from pre-war. And my God, Benny, I can cut a suit! For four years I haven't cut a suit. In the war I have only Feldmans to cut for. Feldman doesn't wear a suit, he wears a slipcover. Look, a waist! I'll make you a vest. With lapels. A veteran should wear a vest. Time now for dignity, something formal." They were in the elevator. "O'Brien," he said, "this is my son Benjamin. Home from the war safe and sound, and with medals."

"O'Reilly," the boy said.

"You must have big plans," Jacob was saying. "No, no, not now, you're right. Lunch, some new clothes, you can tell me your war stories, you probably have a girl you wrote to, hey?" He dug Benny in the ribs. Only in the movies, and Jacob Beer: the elbow in the ribs, the wink, "Hey, sport?"

From the doorway of the delicatessen they contemplated the elders of Zion. "All men are second cousins."

"These are the grandpas," Jacob said. "The real eaters are still in uniform. And a good thing, too, with the rationing. Pinsky makes miracles. Not little ones like Joshua but big ones, chopped liver with egg yolk and onions."

Gray heads, pepper-and-salt, brown and bald, bowed or nodding, hairy ears, hairy nostrils, pouched eyes. Scrawny arms in short sleeves. Benny heard Yiddish, German, Hungarian and was swept back in time on a flood of perfumes, pastrami and corned beef, eddies of derma and chicken soup, a ripple of sturgeon; above the flood a light mist of beer and tea. He remembered an overheated, overupholstered living room in Brooklyn, a congregation of uncles and aunts orating a lost revolution, tea in glasses, exotic names. From infancy, it seemed, he had thought of Lenin as Ilyich. The day will come! When anybody can have in a shvarzeh one day a week! When no man will worry for food, shelter, a winter coat! What would it take, two thousand, three thousand a year? Nothing. With *machines*.

Uncle Isaac: "And a pair teeth that *fit*."

Aunt Rose: "More sponge cake."

Uncle Jeremiah of the silky white mustache: "In the country. With chickens. You'll see."

All: "Herzl."

Now Pinsky billowed toward them, all two hundred pounds, all five feet eight, Man Mountain Pinsky. Benny had remembered him as a Renaissance caricature, the harvest figure, carrot for nose, raisins for eyes, apples for cheeks, melon for chin, but Pinsky in the flesh surpassed his fantasy, Pinsky was a rebus, pickle-nosed, egg-eyed, beet-cheeked, potato-chinned, pumpkin-bellied: Pinsky and his life's work were one.

Beside Pinsky he saw 57359, skin and bones, for a second only, but how real! Benny blinked, perturbed, as he and Pinsky embraced. Pinsky, merely a lifelong friend, sobbed once. "You're not hurt."

"I'm all right."

"Thank God. You've filled out on that trash they feed you. Beans. Pork." Pinsky shuddered like an aspic.

"I'm big and hard."

"Strong as ever?"

"Stronger."

"That's pretty strong. How goes it, Jake?"

28

"Benny's back. How could it go?"

Pinsky's wide eyes gleamed; he giggled and jiggled. "Benny. Have a pickle."

Benny walked forward, tall and broad among the smaller ancients; Benny immense, alien. He swiped a plate from Pinsky's counter and followed his memory, and then his nose, to the pickle barrel, the pickle barrel of myth, eternal and self-replenishing; on impulse he poured a handful of brine to the sawdusted floor: Thanks again, thou who art not. If God preferred gherkins? On such flaws and lapses empires fell. He fished with wooden tongs and landed a whopper. He knew then that he would never die, and bore it off in triumph. Jacob was seated, Pinsky hovered. "Anything you want, Benny. Name it. What you can't get at Fort Mammoth."

They ordered. Benny wanted one of everything. "There's Kantrowitz," Jacob said. Waves, gestures, smiles. On each checkered cloth stood a jar of mustard, a family of small condiments, a cruet of vinegar. No sugar. Sugar upon request. Small pools of sound shimmered and spouted, babbling and cascading from table to table, wool, Roosevelt, Auschwitz, peg pants? from my shop? California weight. Pinsky, this is honey? Real honey, fum bees? A genius, Pinsky, a genius. "Aha," Jacob crowed. "Karp, Karp, Karp. Sit." Benny reached up to shake hands with Louis Karp, a small man, bald and skinny, who could be inconspicuous in a purple rayon suit. He glowed. "Benny, Benny. You're all right?" All right. "Home for good?"

"For good. Hello, Mister Karp. You look good."

"Don't ask," Karp groaned. "I know things got to get worse before they get better. But *always*?"

"That's Trotsky," Jacob gloated.

Karp shrugged: "If the shoe pinch, fix it." He cocked his head. "Benny. You'll need clothes." Karp was ffolliott Suitings. He sat down and sniffed at the mustard. "Fresh."

Jacob exhaled a classic raspberry. "Clothes he gets from me. From you overalls."

Karp chuckled. "With your Italian buttonholes. You'll make him a balloon suit?"

Jacob smiled at Benny and tapped himself on the temple.

"What's a balloon suit?" Benny asked.

"You wouldn't believe it," Jacob said. "Wide legs and sleeves, and the cuffs tight. You never saw such nonsense."

"No thanks."

Pinsky arrived, laden, followed by Leon, also laden, and they heaped the table with herring, sturgeon, whitefish, gefilte fish, rye bread and horseradish. With cole slaw and beer. With anchovies and sardines. With carrots and parsley. "Enough," Jacob said. "Where's the wedding?"

Pinsky sucked thoughtfully at his green thumb. "Okay, Benny? To start?"

Okay, Benny nodded, dewy-eyed; his voice failed him. Pinsky saw his distress and was charmed. He and Leon retired discreetly, professionally.

The three began in silence, a sense of ceremony strong; they raised forkfuls of fish in silent salute; the horseradish was passed, sniffed, assayed with solemnity. With the salt fish Benny swigged beer; Leon brought more and said, for the thousandth time, "Sweets to the sweet." For the thousandth time Jacob acknowledge the witticism with a dry, weary, patrician smile. Leon was a refugee, a Hungarian, and could be ponderous in seven languages.

"So what will you do now?" On Karp's chin, flotsam.

"Leave him alone," Jacob said. "He's just off the boat."

Karp spelunked thoughtfully in the left nostril. "He should decide now. They'll come home thick and fast and furious, and he should do something on the ground floor."

Jacob grunted. "Pay no attention."

"I've thought about it," Benny said. "I had all that time in the hospital."

"And?" Jacob looked sly. "You'll be a ball player, maybe. With that build. A catcher."

Karp moaned. "Or the strong man with dumbbells in the circus."

"So what should he be with those muscles?" Jacob said. "A lawyer?"

"Could do worse," Karp said. "Look at Brandeis."

"I'm looking," Jacob said. "The only thing this country has too much of is lawyers. In ten years they'll be shlepping into the ocean like lemons."

The pickle was perfection; Benny bit into it with wonder, with the glorious resignation of one who knows that he will never be poor, or sick, that he has been singled out for a long and untroubled life. The Solomon of pickles. What'll you do first when you get home? they had asked, and the immediate, obligatory obscenity hooted down, they had, true Americans, shifted to mom's apple pie, popcorn, sundaes. Benny's destiny was a sour pickle.

"He'll make up his mind when he's ready. First he'll

31

sleep, and read the funnies."

"They're not so funny." Karp stood up, wincing.

"Where you going now?"

"The men's room," Karp groaned, a man afflicted, secret stones and spasms. "The Wandering Jew was looking for a men's room." He trudged off.

"A nice man," Jacob said. "The union goons beat him once."

"I know." Benny and Jacob disagreed politely on unions. "How's his wife?"

"Fine, fine. All day she plays mah-jongg. Well. You made it. For once we swindled the angel of death."

"I ran into him once." Benny saw 57359 hunched in Pinsky's munching on halvah. Jacob grew grave and respectful; Benny laughed. "Don't be silly, now. The worst time was in the hospital."

"You had pain?" Again that tone, eternal: there is no life without pain. Pain is the one sure sign.

"No. The bedpan. I was in plaster."

"Undignified." They were both thinking of Hannah, bald and raving. "Well, you're home."

"I'm home." Benny hesitated. "I think I want to be a doctor."

"Benny!" Jacob leaned toward him, fork upraised. "Benny! A doctor! Of course!"

Benny dug him in the ribs and said, "It's those nurses, sport."

Some nights they talked, and some nights Benny roamed the streets. Days were lazy; princeling, he rose late, ate well, perused reports from city and province, and proceeded by easy stages to the Polo Grounds for the vaudeville of war-torn baseball. Or walked to Wall Street, to the Brooklyn Bridge, to Central Park. His leg grew firm, his limp vanished. Scars faded. Old friends were long gone but he found a girl, black-haired, pouting, and stoked her every few days with steak, movies and rye whiskey, in return for which she consented to further stokings. She wanted to be a singer. Benny approved. Her voice was indifferent but her figure was good. "I'd like to learn Latin," she said, and Benny jumped a foot. "What for?" "So I can sing Latin-American songs." Benny told Jacob, who was reproachful: "No need to tell your father tall stories, in an age of monstrosities." Benny said, "When did I ever lie to you?" Jacob said, "You're serious. You mean this." Benny nodded and Jacob grinned in unholy triumph: "Shiksas." But Benny loved her; what else could he call it? The warmth that suffused him as he invaded her was the heat of prehistoric swamps, of ancient suns, of the primeval soup. "Don't move," she whispered. "Let's don't move for as long as we can," and for many minutes they simmered at the edge of madness, of the vast hot nothing, and slipped in and out of deep dreams and steaming landscapes; they quit time. Then she moved, or he, and they strained and burst and traveled the universe; and she liked him, and he liked her.

A hot night in early August; father and son paused for orange crush. Jacob wore a blue sports shirt, Benny a Vassar T-shirt acquired by swap. They stood at the stand. "We'll stand at the stand and drink our drink," Jacob said, and while they drank a rumor limped toward them. They sensed event. Cars stopped. Windows opened. Shouts flew. The vendor asked, "What's up?" Benny said, "I don't know. A fire?" The vendor said, "Let me see on the radio."

And so Benny heard of Hiroshima. Amid rejoicing he stood with Jacob. "A whole city," Jacob said. "What's this atomic bomb? Do you know?"

"I have an idea. A thousand tons of ordinary bombs, the man said. Einstein had something to do with it."

"That's all right then," Jacob said.

"It changes things."

"For the worse?"

"All change is for the worse," Benny said, and they laughed.

"Then the war is over."

"It must be."

"Life begins again."

"Life begins again."

Benny's singer thought it was marvelous and served them right. "Look what they did to the Jews," she said. When her husband was discharged Benny stopped seeing her. By then he was a senior at City College. He and Jacob supped off brisket and horseradish; winter winds beat at their walls and they sighed and shivered intellectually, morally, staring out at the cold lights of the capital of the world. "I was twelve," Jacob said, "and not big, naturally, even shorter than now and ninety pounds. They gave me letters for Uncle this and Uncle that, and I crossed from Russian Poland into Germany—a refuge then, you understand, a place of light and freedom—and took a boat to London. I ate like a pig, like a real pig, paying no attention to kosher. In London I delivered the letters and found that I was a courier for the socialist Bund. A labor hero at twelve. You see why I hated the goons. If the Russians had searched me I would now be sewing buttons on flies in Verkhoyansk."

● ● ●

And the war, always the war, echoes, memories. On a rainy night Benny said, "We swarmed from the hollow ships and pitched our tents on the shore of the wine-dark sea. Eisenhower king of men led us, and the wily Montgomery bided his time on the flank."

"Now what's all that? Some other landing."

"Some other landing. It wasn't bad where I was. It was worse later. Mostly dull. Except at the end. Whose plane was it? Where is that little fellow?"

"He saved your life, maybe."

"And got me shot up, maybe."

"You should write to UNRRA," Jacob said firmly.

"Yes. Or maybe no. Maybe we all go our own way, and don't look back."

"Maybe you saved his life," Jacob said. "I happen to know that according to the Chinese that makes you responsible for him."

Benny brooded. "I'll write. Needle in a haystack."

"You know his number. I'll find out, is there a newspaper for the camps, like want ads. Messages. Isaac knows these things. A fund-raiser."

"What a family," Benny said. "Everything but a black sheep."

"We're counting on you. What do they call it? A rake. Benny the rake."

"I'll do what I can," Benny said. "You're a pretty immoral patriarch, old Jacob."

"From wrestling with the angel," Jacob explained. "The angel won on a foul, so why should I be moral?"

"Impossible. Blasphemy."

Jacob snorted. " 'Touched the hollow of his thigh.' "

"A fine thing," Benny said.

"They were rough in the old days. Elijah. Killing a

hundred men just to show what a big shot. And the wives? the children?"

"I wonder what it adds up to," Benny said. "I bet you everybody killed in the whole Bible was about ten percent of the last five years."

"Progress. That's called progress. The worst is yet to come."

"Always," Benny said. "Some of these generals want to bomb the Russians. The poor god damn Russians."

"Generals!" Jacob said. "Old Mendel—you know, overcoats—*he* wants to bomb the Russians. Overcoats!"

Another night Benny fiddled while Jacob beat time with a disproportionate cigar. From a gypsy nothing Benny modulated to the sweet German dance from the B-flat quartet, and Jacob sang a sigh; the cigar rested. To this he did not whistle. Jacob whistled often but in the tuneless tradition of Russian opera, and could not believe that his melodies were unidentifiable. He loved music blindly, and deafly, honoring his own nine-tone scale so that he believed, for example, in the existence of a French composer called Jackie Bear; that anything whatsoever in three-four time was a waltz (what else could a German dance be?); that Benny was a great fiddler; and that he himself had perfect pitch. It was all heredity. "A," he would say as Benny tuned up. "That's an A."

Another night Benny said, "It was a mistake to let me see her. You should have said 'Mommy's gone to heaven,' or even Miami, and won't be back. You wanted too much truth."

"What's too much truth?"

"Too much truth is asking a ten-year old boy to share tragedy." Benny cocked a cold corona. "I should have been allowed to remember her as someone, or something, warm and soft, all food and drink and love. Not bald and delirious, not that dead-white color and arms like a sparrow. Aaah." He looked away, groped for matches.

"Yes," Jacob said. "Me too. She was so pretty when I met her, the pawnbroker's daughter. In those days a pawnbroker was a great man—possessions, money, jewels, even a metal safe. She was what I always thought women must have been like centuries ago, in the golden days. A big woman," Jacob's eyes were moist and Benny fussed with his cigar, "saftig, smelled of bread, uncomfortable even at the movies. She loved home. The opera too, but she fidgeted, looked around waiting for a uniformed guard to march her off. In a fur coat she was an impostor."

"I remember the time she lost a ring. It was the first time my feelings were hurt."

"You? Why you?"

"She asked if I'd taken it."

"She wasn't calling you a thief."

"No. I was seven. Just the same."

"My God. And how she loved you."

"I know." Benny grinned "Remember Uncle Chaim?"

Jacob was puzzled.

"It was a story she told me. That I had an Uncle Chaim in Russia who was a halvah miner. Every morning he put his lamp on his hat and went down on the elevator and dug out great chunks."

"My God, I forgot. And he put them on the little

trains and they came out and somebody wrapped them. Who wrapped them?''

"Tante Gittel. I used to open a box and look for a note.''

"Ah, she was a good woman.''

"I know. I miss her.'' Benny puffed, thoughtful, wondering just what it was that he missed.

"Yes. You'll have your own wife.''

"Ha. Not for a while.''

"Well. You have your girls.''

And you? Benny wanted to ask, but did not. This lonesome father. Who knew? Perhaps a lunch-hour romance. A mistress on Avenue A. "I like girls," he said.

"And the girls like you," Jacob said with satisfaction.

"Some of them.''

"The ones who speak Latin.'' They laughed. "What is that thing anyway?''

Benny named his cigar. "I just pointed at the box and bought a couple.''

"A rope,'' Jacob said. "Don't buy them in drugstores. I'll give you an address on Seventh Avenue, and have your own made up. That much I'll contribute to your college education.''

"Thank you. A little kirsch now?''

"Good,'' Jacob said. "The only doctor who knew what was wrong was an Indian.''

"A redskin?''

"No. From India. He called it right away. The rest were afraid. I remember he looked me in the eye, a little fellow, my own size, and brown eyes like mine and curly hair. He said there was no hope, and it was like he and I had met in the desert and he was talking about the

38

whole human race. I never felt so close to a stranger in my life. Did you have a good doctor in Paris?"

"No. They were all cheerful."

Jacob groaned, and said abruptly, "That's good about the girls," fiercely, "that's good. Be a lover. You can always die later. Do what I tell you, Benny. Be a prince."

Benny grinned at this Franz-Josef and said, "To oblige his father must always be the object of a devoted son."

"Oh boy," Jacob said. The brown eyes glowed. "Is that a talker! Prosit."

"Prosit," Benny said, and so they passed the winter.

3

BENNY'S FINGERS, QUICKER than the eye, stained slides, caressed tumultuous pulses and performed auscultations major and minor, amateur and professional; fiddler's fingers. But the first time he practiced gynecological chores on a female, or once-female, cadaver he gagged severely. Rospos had already vomited several times, the sight of a string of intestine offending his ancient Attic sensibilities. They were merciless: "That's how your ancestors said sooth."

"Never." Rospos was tall, pale, black-haired, intensely handsome. "Chickens at most. My regrets, gentlemen; you behold a vegetarian."

"Strong meat belongeth to them that are full of age," Dr. Asher said. "You'll get over it."

"Never. It's a question of good taste. Aesthetics." Rospos had struggled up from a slum; his father owned an ice-cream parlor "with flyspecks for chocolate sprinkles," a round clumsy man, as he told it, whose efforts to prepare a banana split in a cardboard container had once reduced his son to bitter tears of shame. Even in the fourth year, most of Benny's friends were foreigners, or dubious Americans like himself. Rospos roomed with a Persian named Demavin whose English was, and seemed to remain, rudimentary; they shared a private joke, Demavin saying ''Bore, bore'' (in lectures) or ''bar, bar'' (where have you been?) or ''bare, bare'' (the cadavers) or any of a dozen variations, while Rospos laughed. When they met Benny the little Iranian whooped and shouted, ''Beer! Beer!'' reducing Rospos to giggles. Twenty years later Benny would understand. Demavin was swarthy and short, more Central Asian than Near Eastern, and they all felt that he would bring a needed shamanism to the practice of medicine. Makkar was Tunisian; he owned a prayer mat and used it.

Lin Li-kang was from Fukien via Shanghai and proved annoyingly brilliant; he knew more of English literature, German music, French art, American slang and nuclear physics (what?) than any of them. His father had been a banker with Chiang Kai-shek, and Lin had been shipped to America during the war to study at Reed College. He was horny and cold: ''I intend to go through Barnard College,'' he said, ''like corn through a blue goose.'' He dressed like a film star, and used cologne. Adapting a technique of ancient Chinese navy yards, he had painted an alert dragon's eye to either side of the forward median line, or bowsprit, of his drawers. ''Der Jasager,'' he announced one day, ''is a Nō play,'' and Benny realized a week later that he had made a pun in three languages. To Lin's practical work, slides and sutures and blood samples and injections, he brought the delicacy and dexterity of a worker in ivory. The others envied him and laughed with him when he called them peasants. The women he smuggled into the dormitory were an extraordinary collection. He and

41

Benny roomed together for a time and Benny did most of his studying in the common room, but refused to give up his sleep. Lin rebuked him and called him a stiff-necked Isaiah. Benny ran to the Bible and came back to tell him, "This is the will of God, even your sanctification, that ye should refrain from fornication." "That's Christian," Lin said. "You're a cultural magpie. And what about your own sins?" "Fungoo," Benny said. Lin was shocked. "*Fun goo?* Can you not even curse in Yiddish?"

"I learned in the streets. I'm a New Yorker and not a religious fanatic."

"But fungoo. You don't even know what it means."

Benny told him, but Lin was already thinking of other matters. "Did I ever tell you about the Jews of Kaifeng-fu?"

"You know too much," Benny said. "A Japanese in disguise."

Lin was truly offended. Benny apologized and then, because he cared deeply for Lin, asked him to go on.

"An Englishman," Lin said, "a Victorian traveler—you know the sort, like Burton, they went everywhere—this fellow wound up in Kaifeng-fu, in Honan, and went to the marketplace to look for bargains, like a pot or a hanging he could buy for a pound that was worth half a million. And he saw a vendor standing there holding up a scroll, and he went to look at the scroll and it was in Hebrew. The Englishman went crazy with excitement, and in time he got the whole story. Hundreds of years before, a bunch of Jews had fled from someplace and crossed all of Asia and settled in Kaifeng. After a while they were assimilated and forgot who they were, but there were always those weird scrolls and books that nobody could read anymore. So every market day one of them went out and stood there, holding up the scroll, hoping that some traveler could enlighten him. Funny thing was, they still kept the Sabbath. It was on a Wednesday or some such day because the western calendar had changed and the Chinese never cared too much about the day of the week anyway, but they kept it.''

Benny was silent in pride, wonder, sorrow; they sat for a time, and it was as if they had been friends a thousand years before.

There were also a black American named White, a white American named Black, and a red Yugoslav named Prpl who was possibly randier than Lin: where Lin was rarely seen twice with the same quiff, Prpl was a model of old-fashioned constancy, deriving inordinate mileage from each chassis and leaving it finally at the roadside, bearings burned, pistons jammed, tires bald. He moaned and twittered and brava'd, and his ladies loved it. He wore rogue shirts. ''Bawdy by Fishair!'' he cried, and blew an admiring kiss; a dream from Cos Cob dimpled and yielded. Benny explained that certain of those phrases dated from 1936 or so and were to be eschewed on cultural and not moral grounds; Prpl grinned and asked, ''You get-ting moch?'' At the time Benny was not getting much. Benny was working like a mule in order later to kill as few as possible. He explained this and was ridiculed.

Benny cried truce and worked harder. One night he came back after an Italian dinner with Jacob and found Lin and Prpl in his room sharing a plump, happy girl who even naked seemed to be an usherette. For an instant Benny saw the epaulets, the piping, and he almost reached for his ticket; and then a rage came upon

43

him, and he saw the faces of Parsons and Pistol and Bardolph, and once again 57359. In an irrational fury he swept them to the hall; he flung clothes after them, locked his door and stood trembling. He walked the streets at midnight and wondered what sorrow was a part of him forever. But in the morning he was ashamed. Lin was pensive. "You're a maniac. A puritan."

"No, no," Benny said apologetically. "Not at all. But there was something else. The sadism."

"*Sadism*?" Lin was appalled. "We positively lavished affection on that young lady. She went home in a glow. In raptures. It was one of the crucial experiences of her intellectual life."

"She was a side of beef, that's all."

Lin said stiffly, "You have accused me of bestiality and necrophilia."

"Oh shut up," Benny said. "I guess I can't explain it."

"Then consider that you may be wrong to take on so. The victim of blind prejudice, writhing in your own frustration and striking out in neurotic fury."

"Thanks, doc. What about this gleet here?"

Benny was rewarded; Lin laughed, and the black eyes sparkled, the black hair flopped, straight, over the high forehead.

"I suppose you surgeons have to be without emotion," Benny went on.

"Surgeons," Lin said mournfully. "Thank God for the fourth year. It's all been band-aids so far."

"What'll you do afterward?"

"I'll go back."

"To China."

"Yes."

44

"But the Reds have got it all. Almost."

"I'll go back."

Benny considered this obstinacy. "It makes no sense. They won't have you, with your cuff links and English shoes."

"They'll have me. I'm Chinese."

"But the wine and women, and all that. I don't see you as a Stakhanovite."

"Nonsense." Lin smiled in mockery. "Quality will tell. You'll see. I'll be a commissar."

"My God," Benny said. "You're a patriot, that's what."

"Don't make fun of me," Lin said. "I'd go back tomorrow if I could, and I'll tell you why: not because I'm tired of your cheap jokes about no starch but because if they had a . . . a *Japanese* in charge it would still be the most civilized country in the world."

"I forgot. All those mandarins. Five hundred million mandarins. Who washes the shirts? Wetbacks from India?"

Lin glared, and swore musically in Chinese.

At the end of his third year Benny committed matrimony. Uncoerced and to his own surprise. He married a lovely girl named Carol and quitted the dormitory amid ceremonies and celebrations; he announced that he would henceforth live a life of probity and respectability, and his little league of nations huzzahed and flung rice.

But even Citizen Beer, householder and family man, was no match for a smirking fate; there was no escaping, six months later, the long bony arm, the inexorably beckoning finger. Fate's agent this time was Prpl; her season winter; her purposes obscure. Bonesetter Benny was bustling off to an afternoon of solemn urology ("Take care," Lin warned him; "do not reduce the scrotal total") and the Serb, fleeing work, nabbed him at the door: "Party. Tonight. Stop in. A holiday from family life."

"A party! I am exhausted."

"You're a slave." Prpl spoke the address. "After supper. Any time. All night." Later Benny, detained by a stunning chancre, called home and took supper uptown; returning he saw Miss Subways ("hopes to be a fashion model; is deeply religious") and disembarked betimes, walked two blocks freezing, climbed a flight of stairs and burst into a mob scene. Noise jolted him and he knew he should not have come, but he accepted the obligatory highball, noted the obligatory bullfight poster, greeted the obligatory Negro, the obligatory homosexual, the obligatory poet, and sat on the obligatory pouf for the obligatory ten minutes with his intense, stoatlike hostess, who wore an optional sari. He waved to Prpl, who winked. He wandered, then, among instructors and students and drunks, and was escaping toward more ice, in a dim hallway lit by one red bulb overhead, when he found himself face to face with a woman he should most surely have met a year earlier or not at all. Benny gazed upon her and was shattered. Perhaps, he thought bitterly, God did exist and it was merely that he had a puckish sense of humor. The hallway tilted, and with it his brief lifetime. Friendly sheets of flame broiled him; his knees trembled and the backs of his legs prickled. She stood still. So did he. Speech seemed petty. After some moments the sounds of the party roused them; Benny, impelled by utter, inarguable necessity, stepped to her and kissed her. Only their lips touched. He spoke: "Come on."

46

They walked arm in arm against the cold. He told her all about himself in thirty seconds. "I don't care," she said. "Have you ever," Benny asked, "had the following: chicken pox, measles, mumps, scarlet fever?" "Five foot six," she said, "one hundred and thirty pounds," as Benny contemplated this latter through her duffel coat and groaned aloud; "will you want a sandwich?" "You're insane," he said fervently.

At four Miss Swinburne slept. Benny extricated himself from her, from the sheets, from the blanket, and half dressed. He sat foolishly in a stuffed armchair and watched over her as dawn broke. Well, old God of Abraham and Isaac, he marveled, thou hast vouchsafed unto me a miracle. A piece of cosmic mistiming but I thank thee. Benny is annihilated and has become pure spirit. I am lighter than air. I have given myself, and there is nothing left.

You know how the Orientals name their years—the year of the rat and the year of the tiger and so on, and they pass in cycles, once in every twelve years or twenty. Well, this was the year of Nan and all the rest was foolishness, maintenance, upholstery; it was the year of Nan and it never came again, not in twelve years or twenty or a century. She had thick, wavy blond hair and dark brown eyes and paradoxically a slight, tantalizing, shifting, Oriental look; take her features one by one and she was merely superlative; take her as a whole and she was a half-caste goddess. She was from Arizona, a lapsed Catholic family, and when she entered a room Benny half expected the walls and furnishings to melt away, leave not a rack behind, only Nan in a deep green glade at the foot of a mountain on the rim of a desert, giving birth every hour to another magnifi-

47

cent tawny child while the sun shone and the rain fell and crops grew and cattle multiplied and birds-of-paradise caroled. To make love to her was to walk barefoot through the botanical-zoological gardens, temperature 80° Fahrenheit, humidity 50%, scattered cirrus clouds, a southwest breeze at five knots bearing a hint of spring rain and the sweet smell of pears and pomegranates. Vital signs: 98.6°, pulse 72, respiration 18, blood pressure 110/70, identical to Benny's.

The demigod had found his demigoddess and they yielded cheerfully to every demiurge; when they stood unclothed, gravely gazing, half a room apart, solemnly teasing, it was a sacrament, an act of pure worship, of adoration, each the other's godhead and each merging fully with godhead; where the mystics failed, they succeeded, where the mystics lost, they won. A matter of glands, your friendly neighborhood physician will tell you; but Benny is your friendly neighborhood physician and he will tell you that it was not so. He was twenty-five and she was twenty-two, and they did not have all the time in the world.

Blessed are they who make love on the fly, for they know not ennui. They rarely had more than half a night together, or an afternoon hour. Her breasts were too full and sagged slightly; that excited Benny inordinately, and he thought of her as a true goddess, ancient Greek and not Botticelli, fertile, hot, full of hormones, nectar, ambrosia, ichor. She perverted him: she waited naked and when they had made love he delighted in clothing her, adorning her with doilies, antimacassars, table-cloths, his own sweater, his khaki trousers. They made love historically and pastorally, tragically and comically, on beds, sofas, chairs, the kitchen table, the carpet, the bare floor, standing, seated, prone and supine, looking out her window, washing dishes. Children! She was quickly roused and avaricious, taking a violent revenge on her early years, on her parents, on the Blessed Virgin Mary, and at times it seemed to him that he was living out a ghastly anti-morality play: Everyman Beer, burgher, doctor, alderman, meets the witch Swinburne and they proceed to exhaust the catalog of orgasm while waiting for the birth of God, or the Devil, who is never born; the seasons roll on and so do Benny and Nan and there is no retribution or even remission.

But more often it was simply funny, vulgar, stupendous, a series of one-line jokes from a suppressed (and properly so) magazine. Suitably illustrated. Tawdry. But to lovers? Uproarious. No sense was denied employment. "I can't rank them," he said. "If I could see you but not touch you I'd go mad. If I could touch you but not taste you I'd go mad. I like your smell and I like your voice. I may go mad anyway. I just hope we don't kill ourselves." Children!

His life was saved by aeons without her; in class, on the subway, at the clinic, at home (home, yes, important matters). Benny stared at a stained slide (gonococcus), a poster (Remember now thy Creator in the days of thy youth), a wall of books, a dish of beans or a dead whitefish, and always, between or beyond, hovered the fuzzy, wavering, persistent lineaments of his love, that unforgettable face constantly forgotten, the brows, the nose, the mouth melting and merging with Irene's, Felicia's, Marian's, Frances's: Nan, Nan, return! He thought of Athena, popping up in human guise; he wished a janitor good day, shared the elevator with an eminent obstetrician, ordered a sandwich from an acned soda jerk, and wondered if one or more of them were Nan. He loved everybody.

He was sad, too, sometimes. So was she. "I wish we had another lifetime," he said. "Don't," she said, "don't," and he knew that she was thinking, or trying not to, of Fred. Fred was her fiancé and she loved him. In Arizona. Fred Wilcox. Really Alfred. Exotic, like an early English king. She loved him. They shared ecstasies, an accent, geography, mathematics (she was a graduate student in statistics). But for now it scarcely mattered. But. Therefore. Consequently. Nevertheless. "We all do so much damn explaining," she said. "I suppose it's the Bible, all those stories when I was nine. Now I have a big black Hebrew of my own. Next thing to a beautiful Negro." Benny was shocked but recovered quickly. His experience of master races was not encouraging. He pictured himself with a black girl. She was a housemaid. Conscientiously he gave her other occupations but to his shame his mind pressed her continually back into servitude. He saw her dusting, raised her skirt. Dismayed by this infidelity, he nibbled at Nan. His succulent pink pig, his Arizona ham.

Nan feared the irrevocable word and never said that she loved Benny. She said everything else: want, adore, need, assorted drivel. Benny too refrained from oratory but it broke out: "God! I love!" And their sadness never lingered. Twenty-five; twenty-two; what else mattered? What else should matter? Romp and hurrah and the world their oyster!

And the acrobatics! In the center ring Beniamino sways, twirls, swings from hoop to hoop in loops and twists and gyres and gainers, grinning like a seal, barking and snuffling likewise, peering through blond

canyons, chasms and coppices at a sternum, a collar-
bone, a smile, a row of vertebrae caravanning single
file over a tawny desert toward a tawny nape. And Nan,
scaling the flanks of Ben Beer, blushed. Morals? Mere
exertion? Blushed here, blushed there, checkered and
patched pink and white—"It's your beard," she said,
and he ran to shave. Sometimes he was Benny the
Navigator, dauntlessly ranging the hemispheres, pitch-
ing and rolling and yawing, beating and reaching and
running, pausing in astonishment to check his position
(celestial! stem to stern!) as if he were the first that ever
burst into that silent she; then the laughter died; and
waves rose to meet the black sky. Once he was Benny
Agonized (he: ruined for life! she: the first fine careless
rupture!) but recovered. That frightened him. He had
heard from an earnest colleague that each man had in
him precisely three thousand fucks; should he save one
or two for his old age? Nah! Onward and upward with
der Arzt!

Children. And yet they attempted respectability, as if
desperately needing confirmation of an external, objec-
tive world. They talked. They talked of God and politics and sport, of books and movies. They talked of her
family and his, her body and his, her first piece (Ford)
and his (basement). They ate sandwiches and drank
milk. Once they visited a restaurant. Benny was
charmed and horrified by this outlander who doused
eggs with ketchup, who guzzled coffee and spurned
tea. They tried a movie and found public life unbear-
able. "Movies!" he groaned. "There's no time. I'm
only superhuman, not omnipotent."

"I wonder," she murmured, and that killed another
hour and took a few years off Benny's life. "Painters
would die for you," he said. "Sculptors would kill for

51

you." "Two boys beat each other up for me," she said. "We were sixteen. I loved it." He told her about his scars, about 57359. Fred had served in the Navy and soon she told him about that, and about Fred's brilliance in Boolean algebras and such, and the coming Ph.D.

She moved with a heavy, touching (because one day it would desert her) grace, the breasts he loved swinging gently, the large rosy nipples almost winking as he watched in delight; otherwise she was firm and did not bobble. He loved coming close behind her, taking a breast in either hand, pressing himself to her luxurious buttocks until his heat rose; feeling his strength she twisted, slammed herself against him, sought his mouth. Kissing her was a love affair in itself, no end to the smooch, lick, nibble, chew; he said it was like kissing a basket of eels and she said eels were essential to a good smorgasbord. They drowned in each other's liquids, unguents, nectars. But they parted always with a gentle domestic buss like their first kiss, as if each separation might be the last, as if they shared (they did, they did) a tender ache of foreknowledge.

Spring came, and bruised them. Days fled. The end was upon them and neither knew how it would come. For her a master's degree and Arizona. For him an M.D. and more, much more. In late May he left her for two days to be present at an accouchement of surpassing importance; he paced the waiting room with the others and chewed cigars, read magazines, worked puzzles, ran through the quartets. When it was all over he called her. They sat in a small oasis on upper Broadway, a minuscule park peopled by old men with wens and walking-sticks. The old men sat in the sun all day.

52

They wore neckties and their faces were gray; the sun itself ignored them. Buses roared.

They found a bench to themselves. The sun was bright and a faint smell of sap and leaves softened the air. Small dogs frisked, straining leashes. An aged woman sat across the path from them reading a tabloid.

"What was it?" She sat stiffly on the green bench, her hair almost white in the sunlight.

"A boy."

"Everything all right?"

"Everything's all right." Benny touched her hair.

"No," she said.

"Yes," he said. "No."

"Yes," she said, and turned to face him. They stared hot-eyed while the universe dissolved.

They kissed then, a chaste kiss, long, tender, annihilating; the sky fell; and she rose and walked away. She crossed a street. She turned a corner. She was gone.

It had been a magnificent year, but Benny was married to a lovely girl named Carol, and they called the boy Joseph.

4

HER NAME WAS Carol Untermeyer and she was the daughter of Amos Untermeyer, M.D., F.A.C.P., eminent internist and professor, and of his wife Sylvia; he ruddy and frail, strutting, nervously taking his own pulse in public, wearing eyeglasses and an elegant thin mustache, Sylvia more Egyptian, plump, benign, ordinary save for an occasional ironic lightning in the splendid Fayum eyes.

Benny and Carol had met at a hospital, where Amos taught one morning each week. Benny emerged from a comprehensive lecture on malfunctions of the spleen and almost ran down a little girl in the corridor. "I beg your pardon," he said, and halted, focused, attended, and added, "my sweet." She was indeed sweet, black-haired, with dark blue eyes and full arresting features. He also saw that she was twenty or so, obvious of breast and narrow of waist.

And steady of eye. "Your sweet?"

Benny nodded solemnly. "Will you have dinner with me?" He reconnoitered a possible ring, found none, and spied upon her full lips.

"Daddy," she said, "can I have dinner with this one?"

Benny flinched like a thief, and turned.

"What? Dinner?" Amos Untermeyer blinked behind horn-rims, and glared grumpily. "Dinner? Why not? Which one are you?"

"Benjamin Beer. Third year."

"Ah yes. Anaplastic nuclei. A silly mistake, my boy. You can't tell an adenoma from an adenosarcoma and you want to take my daughter to dinner."

"Damn," Benny said. "You know about that."

"Conklin told me. Said you weren't bad."

"Thank you." God bless Conklin.

"Friend of that Chinese boy."

Benny nodded.

"He'll go far. Well. Sorry to hear you have time to take young ladies to dinner. I haven't."

They all laughed and soon enough the old man scampered off.

"First name," Benny said.

"Carol. Don't be familiar."

"My dear Miss Untermeyer. I'm saving everything for the right girl."

That night Benny squired Carol to dinner at the Auberge des Bergers. "Romantic," he said. "Pastoral. Do I wear leather shorts and suspenders?"

"The boss is named Sid Berger," she said. She drank vermouth and smoked a cigarette; raked the artificial-candle-lit room with desperate, empty glances, as if seeking a celebrity; rearranged her silver; poked at her straight black hair. Her brows too were black, and thick; her frown was emphatic. She wore dark blue wool and sat tense, ungiving; spoke as if acknowledging his presence. Benny, urbane, kept a distance. She was in her last year at Hunter College. She might go on to graduate school. Genetics. Drosophila. Human genetics might someday require engineering. In her spare hours she had worked as a laboratory technician. Not certified. "Nickel and dime pathology. Daddy was pleased. Why do you order chopped liver here?"

"If the pâté maison is good," he said, "you can trust the rest. In an American restaurant chipped beef is the key."

She blew smoke disdainfully. "A connoisseur."

"Horseflesh and women."

"I knew it," she said wearily, and looked about her at other couples; she might have been a jaded heiress on a Mediterranean cruise, in the first-class dining room.

Benny chose silence; he brooded into his whiskey, filched one of her cigarettes and smoked it without pleasure, thought of anaplastic nuclei, of Latin-American songs, of Prpl who would charm even this neurotic. She kept her upper arms close to her flanks, and gestured from the elbow. Recalled to a sense of duty, he groped for small talk. Politics: what could be smaller?

What the hell. Menstruating, doubtless. "Smile," he said.

"Buy me another drink. Comfort me with flagons."

"Oh." His quick concern was real; her gaze softened. "I'm sorry. You're on the rebound."

She showed grief, and nodded.

"I'll be respectful and sympathetic," he said. "And it's stay me with flagons. Comfort me with apples. Shall I order an apple?"

She did smile. "I've spoiled your evening."

"No. Nothing could."

"How gallant."

"It's a stroke of luck," he said. "You might have been engaged, or somebody's mistress. Another medical student?"

"No," she said, and then wailed, "it was a god damn basketball player from New Jersey."

Now her eyes were moist. In pity, but more in embarrassment, Benny stared at the bottom of his glass. Calf-love had passed him by; a boy of the streets, a fornicator at fifteen, he had been denied the more sublime agonies of the youthful heart; blasted incessantly by lightnings of lust, he had suffered for sex and mocked romance. He risked a glance, and caught his breath at the childish vulnerability on the wan face, in the dark blue eyes. And yet how trivial! Or was misery an absolute? For an instant 57359, in a striped prison suit, stood beside Miss Carol Untermeyer, who surely wore furs in winter. Her eyes were wide, her nose straight, a warm, lovely face, the features generous; and she had been hurt. By a sweating, indifferent athlete, crew-cut surely, boisterous, who would kiss his teammates in moments of glory. For the moment that pain defined her. What pains had Benny, all unknowing, inflicted?

He yielded uncertainly to a new and perplexing emotion.

"How's the pâté?" Carol asked him.

"Good. Want some?"

"No. Doesn't go with pike. Or whatever this is. Where'd you learn French?"

Benny was offended: "I am careful not to speak French with waiters."

"You did all right with quenelles. Kennel?"

"Quenelles. I was in France for a while."

"What's that look mean? You had a good time in France. Low life in Paris. I bet the tourists were watching you through a peephole."

"I had a rotten time in France." He told her. As he talked his third eye roamed her, bright, unquenchable, male. Her small teeth were quite white, the skin of her throat was firm; she was high-breasted, rather conical perhaps, and he wondered if the arms pressed close to the body, the slightly rounded shoulder, the capacious bodice were defensive, self-deprecating. It was a figure that might wear well. He wondered what sort of figure her mother maintained; he had yet to meet her mother. He was still talking when the cutlets were set before them, and the claret poured.

"But that's interesting," she said. "Not just that war-movie junk. And you have no idea who he was."

"None." Two and a half years of his life: war-movie junk. He had saved the world for her.

"Or where the dog tags are."

"None."

"You've got to find him."

"We've tried. We'll keep trying. It's like having a twin brother you've never seen. What is he now? The dictator of some small country. A bank robber in Australia. A maniac, hiding in Hamburg and assassinating ex-Nazis. Then in ten years you find out he's a grocer in Israel. Or an undertaker."

"No, no," she said. "A scholar. An authority on enzymes. And the first you hear of him is a Nobel Prize."

Benny laughed uproariously, and she joined him; across the table affection blossomed almost visibly. "You Jewish mama," he said.

"Do you suppose that's what I am?" She meditated briefly.

"Whoa," Benny said. "There's a great big world out there just waiting for genetics engineers. Although . . ."

"Although." She nodded cheerfully. "Well, who knows. We don't have to decide tonight."

Benny's hand checked; he spilled a drop of wine. "We? Decide what?"

"Oh my God," she said. "I didn't mean that."

"The spell I cast." He grinned amiably, spoke lightly. "To know him is to love him."

She sniffed. "I shall never love again." She astonished him with a wink: "But you dried my bitter tears."

"It's a start," Benny said.

Mellowed by wine, Carol laughed joyfully when Benny told her Jacob's explanation, years before, of the white line down the middle of the Holland Tunnel: "For bicycles." Sid Berger heard the laughter and came to say hello, becomingly stout and jovial, balding and veined: "Good evening, Miss Untermeyer." "Hello, Sid. Sid Berger, Benny Beer." They shook hands and Benny saw his face, name, tailoring and appetites filed away. After minor chat—"My best to the doctor and your mother"—Berger moved off, and shortly there arrived free booze (he said), complimentary brandy (she rebuked).

"My father's really a nice guy," she said. "Big success, and all that damn *importance*, but a nice guy.

My mother's strange. She's so ordinary you wonder about her. She reads best-sellers and works for organizations. She's an Abravanel, you know, big-shot Sephardic. Condescends to the Untermeyers.''

"Who condescend to the Beers. Honor thy father and thy mother, kiddo.''

Kiddo. Of course; she was young. A good kid, real flesh and blood, though a bit small for him; he would not so much embrace her as surround her. As she chattered he meditated love with her, and the tinkling hum of the small restaurant was a chorus to his flight of fancy; she would need kindness, delicacy, simple physical care. With surprise he recalled that he had never—barring a few inconclusive adolescent bouts— made love to a Jewish girl. Folklore: they save it.

The murals were abominable, a sickly brown, heliotrope, magenta, deformed sheep; his eyes accepted them dolefully, as his palate had accepted the overseasoned escalope, the famous claret of a bad year. And these others, oddly metallic women with their apparently dyspeptic swains: how many pounds of meat had they all ingested, what acids foamed within, what gases pressed? And Carol. He took pleasure in Carol. A new pleasure; a suspicious glow. A tribal bond? Life in a tent, among cattle speckled and ringstraked.

"You're not listening.''

"No. I was thinking about us. May I smoke a cigar?''

"Oh dear. Go ahead.''

"Hand-rolled. Forty cents.''

"Forty cents, gee. What do you suppose dinner cost?''

He savored rich smoke. "You chose the place.''

"It smells good," she said. "I'm sorry if I sound bitchy. Last week I wanted to die."

"Basketball. Are you pregnant?"

"Am I—" She sat back and assumed defiance. "What kind of girl do you think I am?"

He laughed. "A stylist. You learned to talk at the movies."

"Well, all right." She smiled in rue. "But I am most certainly not pregnant. That was insulting. I'm a good girl."

"If you weren't sleeping with him," Benny said, "it isn't a tragedy."

"A man of the world," she said. "And a virgin let you kiss her hand."

He kissed her goodnight too, a cool kiss and gentle, and left it at that. On the subway platform he saved a drunk from plunging to the rails. The drunk muttered, surly, burly, white-haired. Patiently Benny saw him aboard. A young couple dozed, in their teens, the boy in black tie and stinking of lotions, the girl in a yellow ball-gown, boasting a gardenia. Benny remembered his fierce desire to be twenty-two. Music filled his mind, to the clack of the wheels. Themes converged: age, school, now this woman. Marriage, warmth, soup. An end and a beginning: Benny that was, Benny the boy, fading fast; Benny that will be, Benny the man, doctor, father, rising from a sea of relatives, classmates, hopes, and striking forth into the uncharted fetches of an alien land. Citizen Beer. The implacable grime of subways. Shifting, he experienced minor lust; his lips roamed Carol; he dreamed. Well, it was a life; perhaps the life that luck had laid out for him. Odd: as if a decision had been made. By whom? By what? Omens: he looked for

61

a sign. The dozing children nestled together. There's your sign: that's what life is. Wild oats followed by . . . crab grass. He grinned. By God, I like that girl. A nice mind and no bore. Well. Easy does it. Dr. and Mrs. Amos Untermeyer announce. Maybe it's time. Then move out, the west, someplace like Phoenix or Salt Lake. Cattle. Speckled and ringstraked. Clean snow. A lodge in the mountains. Old Doc Beer.

Good God. After one date.

Dinner with Amos and Sylvia, too, some weeks after that first date, and Jacob cordially invited, and high-class conversation. Benny had hoped for Pinsky's: would Amos fidget, rattled by that exotic ambiance, or would he jig and shout rowdy Yiddish? Would Sylvia wear a mantilla to make her position clear? But no; it was the Copenhagen, or Maxl's Rathskeller, or the Romanoff, or Mandarin House. Benny saw them as a family of Phoenician traders, roving from port to port. "Nothing like eel," Amos announced, and Jacob paled. "The Swedes drink too much. I read about it. For centuries every family made its own aquavit. Suicide," Amos said. "Welfare."

"This is fine whitefish," Jacob said heartily.

"Nothing like smorgasbord," Amos said. "All protein. During the war they had no meat and no heart attacks. No butter, no cheese."

"I think I'd like a little aquavit," Benny petitioned humbly. "Good for the heart action."

"Absolutely," Amos said. He was utterly groomed; his fingernails flashed, his hair lay flat. Sylvia's scent flavored the fish; her jersey clung. Amos wore blue cheviot, a white-on-white shirt, a shiny monogrammed necktie; beside him Jacob, in rumpled sharkskin, was a clown from the Yiddish theater. Carol wore a gray suit that mantled her figure. "Your ribbon," Sylvia murmured; Carol's hands flew to her hair.

The acquavit was poured, the talk continued: skoal, skoal. Sylvia glanced from Carol to Benny, from Benny to Carol. "Flukes," Amos said, and later, "bilharziasis." With a second course they had leprosy and gingivitis; Amos approached Pap smears and retreated.

Carol spoke suddenly. "Benny. Tell them about that little man."

They waited. Benny hesitated, reluctant to offer up 57359 on this sumptuous altar. Finally he told them. Tears rose to Sylvia's eyes. Amos meditated before pronouncing, and Benny felt that he had worked a miracle. "God in heaven," Amos said softly; they stared at him and Benny understood, with relief, that Amos too was flesh and blood. "I'm not sure the human race is worth it," Amos said. He set down his fork. "The dark places of the earth are full of the habitations of cruelty." He gazed beyond them, groped for his glass. "You've heard nothing?"

"Nothing," Benny said. "We wrote to the people at UNRRA, and the Jewish groups, and the Israeli government. There's no record of him anywhere."

"He may have been killed."

"Yes. But I have a hunch he's alive. Maybe it's just a wish."

"Such a nothingness," Amos said quietly. "An infinity. He could be dead. He could be crippled, a beggar. He could have gone mad. He could have amnesia."

"He could be in South America," Benny said. "Anywhere. I couldn't even tell how old he was."

"God damn them," Amos said. "Excuse me."

In the car Amos said, "Benny. When you were talking about that little man I had an insight." Amos paused, chose his words: "For two thousand years the only good Christians have been the Jews."

So in August of 1949 Jacob stood by Benny among the crimson curtains bound with silver braid and looked out the french windows at the fair noonday; in the park were lovers, and children shouted. "I'm not losing a son," he said, "I'm gaining a trust. I was introduced to a millionaire. You can tell. They dress from department stores."

"My relatives," Benny grinned.

Jacob too smiled. "A beautiful, beautiful girl. So what if she has money. Love conquers all. Oh Benny. Will you be happy!"

Among Untermeyers Benny murmured and was courtly: many uncles, many aunts. By his side he held his mother-in-law, who said, "Don't be nervous. In a hundred years you'll forget it."

"You're a help." But Benny looked kindly upon Sylvia; she patted his cheek. There were diamonds at her bosom. Between rubies, Benny thought, and was appalled by his baseness, and fixed his eyes on hers; her scent rose, and pleased him, she was plump and sleek and deep, and her eyes were dark and Moorish. "I'm supposed to be weepy," she said.

"Not you."

Jacob and Pinsky were inspecting the tables like scouts for some starving village. Pinsky sniffed, pointed.

"No. Just take care of her."

"Of course I will," Benny said gently.

"Don't just keep her safe," Sylvia said. "Keep her happy. Don't be too . . . busy."

Her eyes flashed, widened, drew him in; an instant of naked intimacy left him aghast. "I plan to try," he managed, as Amos came up to them.

"Well. What are you two plotting?"

"Our daughter's future," she said. "The musicians are here," and she left them.

Amos gazed after her and admired. "Look at that articulation! I hope you'll do better than I did," he added privily. "That damn woman's been eating an apple a day since we married." He shivered himself into laughing fragments. Benny considered prayer.

Uncle Arthur Untermeyer heaped a plate with meats and said, "Winter weddings are better. You can always tell how classy a winter wedding is by the amount of out-of-season fruit." Benny laughed inordinately. From the head of the table Amos waved. Across from Benny, Jacob beamed, eyes moist, a noggin of whiskey beside his empty wineglass. "Amos is a good fellow," Arthur said. "Pleased with himself, but a good fellow. A generous man." Carol's cousin Deborah glided through the conversation piece, craning like a hen to sip at her champagne; a plain girl but stoutly made, and Benny's third eye observed. Behind him the band cater-wauled savagely, and made a joyful noise unto the Lord.

"Irv is also all right," Arthur said, stuffing himself merrily. "He had to be a druggist because there was only money for one medical school. I was luckiest. With me they gave up and let me go into the fur business, so I'm rolling in it. By the way, if you need help don't hesitate. But Gordon is a bastard, the baby brother and spoiled rotten. Don't trust him. Notice how the names go. From Amos to Gordon in regular steps. That's called assimilation. Little Deborah's not so little any more."

Benny understood that replies were not required. Arthur ate; Arthur talked. Good. He turned to his own Aunt Rose. "How goes it, Rosey?"

"It goes all right. Nobody starves here. Your girl's beautiful, Benny. I mean really beautiful. It made my heart ache, so young and beautiful. You'll be happy."

"I'm happy now. But getting married is murder."

"Murder, no. Suicide, maybe."

Besotted by ceremony, brutalized by gluttony, aching for the road, Benny clutched his wineglass and contemplated this new world. Prpl and Lin debated across a whiskey bottle. Stout burghers shook fingers, declaimed; others fox-trotted. Miss Carol Abravanel Untermeyer and Mr. Benjamin Beer. Joined today in matrimony by the learned rabbi—what was his name? Issachar. Zebulun. It would be on the certificate, doubtless illegible. Uncle Gordon breathed at a pince-nez, polished it on a serge sleeve. Mrs. Beer is the daughter of Dr. Amos Untermeyer, a notorious bungler, and Mrs. Untermeyer, a sexy bit, could be brighter but after all. Of Central Park West, the downtown end with palms in the lobby.

Miriam Karp came up to kiss him, and with her Ruth Pinsky, weeping. Benny patted, soothed, joked.

The groom is the son of Mr. Jacob Beer of Union Square, a widower specializing in hand-stitched single-breasted, waistcoat optional; ranking member of local klaberjass and pinochle clubs. A black waiter poured champagne, inscrutable, imperial. The bride was attended by Miss Deborah Abravanel, a saftig bundle who reported unsolicited attentions from Uncle Arthur Untermeyer, known among the desert tribes as Hands-in-Motion. Brief honeymoon. Groom will return to College of Leeching and Cupping, where he is concentrating in astrology. At home. Please send money.

Benny rose from the table and strode forth. He reclaimed his bride, kissed her soundly in the presence of witnesses, and danced before the Lord with all his might.

While Carol changed, the exhausted few wallowed among wedding presents. "Tiffany's," Sylvia said. Stuporous, Benny admired a tablecloth. Jacob appraised. Amos collapsed into a leather chair: "Too much champagne. Too early in the day." Jacob had given them five hundred dollars: "Nothing," he confided. "What Amos tips the doorman. All the same, a little pin money." Amos had lavished his all upon them: fifty shares of General Motors, fifty of Jersey Standard, a year's lease of a small flat on Riverside Drive, a view of the Hudson, elevators, beige corridors, incinerators. "Dunhill's," Sylvia said. "Don't touch those stocks," Amos ordered. "Solid gold. Put the profits back in." Benny agreed. Romance, romance, where is romance? Am I burned out at twenty-five? No. Full of aunts and uncles and funeral baked meats. Christ Almighty. Weddings. A barbarism. A rotten full belly now and doubtless his breath stank. "Gimbel's?" Sylvia said. Jacob stood forlorn, and Benny's cup, his stirrup cup, a cup of sudden grief, ran over: man's lot was loneliness. He threw an arm across Jacob's shoulders. Jacob blinked through tears; one trickled down the sharp nose. "I'm leaving you again," Benny said quietly, and Jacob nodded. Benny hugged him: "I'll give you grandchildren." Jacob brightened. "I'll be a baby-sitter," Jacob said. "You can teach them pinochle," Benny said.

Carol emerged, a vision, bright, frightened, the Aztec maiden breathless beneath the obsidian knife. Benny went to her and kissed her gently. Sylvia wept at last. Amos cleared his throat. Jacob hung back, diffident, and Carol went to him and embraced him, with a glance at Benny; she knew, and in that moment Benny gave her all the heart. Jacob patted her shoulder. "A lovely couple," he said. "Never a prettier couple. L'chayim. A thousand years." "Ten thousand years," Amos trumped. "Banzai."

The newlyweds left them, Benny with a last easy wink for Jacob, and rode downstairs to a rented Ford, and drove north in quiet silence. At a red light Benny kissed Carol again, and she seized him. "Thank God," she almost sobbed. "Let's never get married again. Let's never go back."

"You too?" Benny laughed in giddy joy. "I thought you'd love it. All that silly fuss. All those people. Monsters. Here comes the bride."

"I love you truly," she gasped. "Tell you one thing about relatives."

"Tell me."

"They make the groom look good." She snuggled. "Let's go to Australia."

Happiness ebbed and flowed, ebbed and flowed. Benny drove and dreamed, squeezed her thigh, blessed his luck, subdued his lust. Late summer, and the thickets beside the highway gleamed rich green, lush and heavy, dales and glens, love nests; crows picked at a dead cat, glared balefully, flapped and glided; the sun rode westward. Benny mused upon the night to come, the adventure, the unknown; upon many nights to come; his breath quickened. My God, what a chance to take! One woman forever! He resolved to be tender. She knew so little. She was his to teach. Doctor Professor Beer. Never a cold bed, he thought fiercely. Never! He angled into a service station, stalled, set the brake and embraced her; frantically they kissed, lovingly he cupped her breasts. "Let's get arrested," he said. She giggled and broke free. As a gangling attendant emerged they roared off, laughing wildly. Never a cold bed, he thought. One hundred and seven ways to make love. You lecher. This pure bride, and you plot her ruin. Doctor Professor Beer will lecture on the Kamasutra, with slides. Eminent practitioner of Jewish acupuncture. A dirty, dirty man! He groaned at his depravity.

"What was that? Regret?"

"Impatience."

"Why sir, what have you in mind? I little thought, when I accepted this ride—"

"All in good time, my child." She was silent, and he went on, "It's fun, you know. It's the most fun there is."

"Better than mah-jongg?"

"I may beat you," he said.

And so they voyaged to a honeymoon in the mountains, registering with appropriate aplomb and disappearing from human ken for some days. That night they learned what strangers they were, and for the first and only time Benny's pride and joy failed him. They soon cured this mysterious ailment, and joked about it, and Carol was breathless and acquiescent and curious and obedient. But there was plenty of the ancient Roman in

69

Benny and not all the eagles in the world flying on his right hand would cancel out the omen. He lay awake in the middle watch straining to see through the fog of the future, but he was human, blind, doomed, and the fates were mute.

Weary, languid, they returned to Riverside Drive, and Carol set about cataloging, ranging, repairing, storing, stitching and baking; she proved severe with tradesmen, and Benny admired. She resolved to work for a year and think later about genetics, but changed her mind almost immediately; adventurous one night, Benny was put off gently, and Carol said softly, "The honeymoon is over." Benny froze, but she hugged him and went on, "There's three of us now. Don't knock him around."

Benny sat up and pressed a switch; Carol was grinning as if in guilt. Popeyed, stupefied, he could not speak. "Now everybody'll know what we've been doing," she said.

"Jesus," Benny managed. He kissed her. "Little mother. So soon!"

"I didn't know it was loaded," she said, and he wheezed at the ancient joke. To his acute shame thoughts of other women crossed his mind, and he wondered briefly if unknown Beer by-blows might exist. He recalled himself to order. "Carol! A child. A baby Beer! A crown prince!"

"Yup. How's that for service?"

"Oh best of women," he said, and kissed her again, slowly, warmly; he kissed her eyes, her throat, her breasts; lovingly, firmly, he kissed her downy mound, and said, "Thank you, little mother."

"You pig," she said. "Come back here."

They rubbed noses. "Do you want to work anyway?"

"No. I think I'll do everything right. Quit smoking and get fat and eat chalk and truffles."

"Damn right," Benny said. "As a medical man, madam, I must inform you that frequent intercourse eases childbirth."

"I married a maniac," she said. "Well, get on with it." And Benny, suffused with love, with awe, with the pride of a hundred generations, got on with it; and Carol, sparkling, pummeled him and laughed. In the morning he called Jacob, and she called Amos, who mentioned a trust fund.

And yet the event diminished Benny; beneath the natural joy an unnatural alteration worked, a confusion, an ambiguous and agonizing demand for new strengths and new dignities. Some of it he understood: a portion of his prodigious, transcendent sexual frenzy was being distilled to compassion; his bawdy Doppelgänger, his ruttish twin, a splendidly psychotic Deutero-Benny, a fiendish gonad in human form, had fallen afoul of a mysterious constabulary. At the obscure command of that enigmatic force he must consciously—if regretfully—subdue his infantile fantasies, deliberately—if regretfully—expurgate and abridge his Kamasutra. He must concede (not without sighs) that the companion of his joys and sorrows deserved a more human lord, and should be spared the scurvy monstrosities of a deranged incubus. She was not a succubus; she was Carol, who might some day be a geneticist, who was now a bachelor of science and a laboratory technician, whose mind and heart he had also married, who bore his child; a certain decorum seemed meet, classical and correct.

Where she demurred (and she had) he would not insist; hating slavery, he renounced mastery.

It was not easy. He was, had been, hoped always to be, frank with himself, freely admitting to the deer park of his mind the most incendiary extremes of fanaticism, blasphemy, salacity—staunchly certain that his tender respect for all living things would happily, ungrudgingly police his behavior. But now he was acknowledging new hegemonies; colonized by a morality once scorned (which unchecked, established, dominant, became death-in-life), he grappled with the intruder. To Deutero-Benny marriage meant license, orgy; in theological disputation he defined heavenly bliss as eternal orgasm. In mortal combat now, Deutero-Benny fought back satanically: would Citizen Beer, by exorcising his gorgeously debauched shadow, work a secret and fatal violence upon himself? The old fiend, the mad doctor, was at any rate a lunatic lover; the reformed libertine might be an agent of doom and destruction. The angel of death was, after all, an angel and not a cheerful pornographer.

Some evenings Benny sat looking out at barges and sailboats, tankers and scows, as darkness gathered and the last sunlight faded over the western bank, and with mingled sorrow, righteousness and wry laughter bade farewell to his carnival youth. This was, he supposed tentatively, the onset of maturity: a necessary girding against reality's assaults, a stern replacement of polymorphous calisthenics by more useful exercises of power. Carol was sweet, loving, grateful, now an exquisite little girl playing house, now a grave matron sorting silver and napery. Another kind of fairy tale, grimmer and more worldly, had come true: place,

72

family, work, future were his; nothing now lacked, and he would one day be king.

These ruminations were intense but infrequent; he was amply occupied by his fourth year among the phagocytes, purpuras and quaternary agues, by visits to Jacob, by the crown prince's progress, by plans for internship and a glance at the market, by spaghetti dinners and snow and sleet, by Van Gogh on the walls, bookcases of brick and plank, Beethoven by candlelight, Amos and Sylvia bustling in to bestow upon them roasts, a quilt, advice, twenty-dollar bills. It was an obstetrician's year, Carol's year, a year of blooming and rounding, of light exercises and manuals of childbirth, of lists of names, boys' names, girls' names, family names, Biblical names. They debated natural childbirth. Benny was properly chaffed by his classmates, and received in the mail tables of Jukes and Kallikaks. In bed Carol cried, "Quick! Quick!" and he was dismayed, heartsore: she wanted him not to start quickly but to finish quickly. He made allowances for a pregnant woman. Soon she drew apart from him to sit, to muse, to dream in an inviolable glow of privacy; he made further allowances, and was lonely. He was kind and flattering and utterly confused. She caressed her own belly, spoke to the child, smiled at nothing. She cooked interminably, and he was sated with planked fish, meat soups, roasts; "Protein," she explained. The obstetrician guessed at a date: nine months and three days from the wedding! Amos jested: "If it's premature you'll answer to me, young man." Sylvia hovered; soon her figure was better than Carol's and when she showed it off Benny fell silent and sardonic.

He kept busy, rushing from class to clinic; he waded

through glaucoma, cancer, cirrhosis, diabetes; he inhaled mists of pus, of blood, of urine; he cultivated—desperately he cultivated!—a cold unconcern, a professional indifference to raw wounds, shiny organs, pathetic senility, dead babies. Ah no, no, not an indifference, not an unconcern, but he coined a new definition of "doctor": the one man in the room who is forbidden to weep. Rarely he found a moment for Pinsky's with Karp and Jacob. He was joshed; if it was a boy Karp would cut him a caftan, and Pinsky would supply the first year's sturgeon. Naturally it would be a boy. They took to calling Jacob grandpa. Jacob beamed. Benny too beamed, and drank tea like an old-timer, slurping and nodding. "I'll do the bar mitzvah free," Pinsky said, and jiggled. Benny aged, and remembered his early loves, and tried to be scornful of young lust, and berated his licentious colleagues at work.

That was the year that became the year of Nan, that never came again, not in twelve years or twenty or a century, that reduced Benny to despair, treason, death in the soul, that magnified him to impossible exaltations. And yet he lived, roared, worked, howled through days and nights like a hurricane; survived, defied, swore great oaths and repulsed inexorable seas. His failings engendered energies: sleepless, he grew in strength; heartless, he grew in love; mindless, he grew in skill; hopeless he hoped, deathless he died; ignorant of all that was to come, he waited, bided, nerved himself, roused ancient forces to meet man's fate.

When a man hath taken a new wife, he shall not go out to war, neither shall he be charged with any business; but he shall be free at home one year, and shall cheer up his wife which he hath taken. Benny was granted that much. In September of 1950, when Joseph was four months old and Carol had someone else to love, the government of the United States, which had paid for much of Doctor Beer's medical education, sent him the bill. He was impressed into service—an emergency, they assured him—and was sent to Korea, where a war had been agreed upon.

Pee-joe Die-foo

5

THE BRONCHIAL TRUCK ran a fever and died, Beer's luck, at the lip of a long downhill sweep, died with a clank and a rattle and a last obscene poop. Swede let her run down the hill, there was a building, shelter and maybe water. Closer we saw how big it was, how solid, and I worried about the enemy. By now no one knew for sure who the enemy was. Ewald steered our dead dinosaur into a courtyard; we tumbled out and inspected the building, an inn it was or a roadhouse, disused and silent, cavernous. Outside again we poked at the radio with cold fingers. Squeals. A voice, officious, crackled through static. I was staring at brown mountains, a bloated gray sky, skeletons of endless forest; my breath steamed and I was sure there would be snow and I felt like a damn fool saying "Blue two, Beer on."

Blue two did not know who Beer was.

"Your doctor," I said. "Your friendly neighborhood gynecologist. I need another truck."

Blue two complained. *He* complained. So I apologized. Blue two meditated that. Blue two asked where

I was, and I gave coordinates. I heard no gunfire. I described the building.

Blue two said that all of them might be falling back, and perhaps I should set up where I was. That was agreeable. "There's another doctor on the way," I told him. "On the main drag there. Noonan. No. N for Nan. Send him here if you fall back. Also transport. Trucks, for the wounded. Could they cut us off to the south?"

Blue two said, "Yes." Blue two went on at length, as if it was important to explain this defeat to Lieutenant Beer. I truly expected to live only a short while, and was bored by these details.

"Blue two out," Blue two said finally.

"Bye bye," I said.

"How bad is it?" Ewald wanted to know.

"Very bad. Even the good parts are bad. Lots of Chinese, they think. Anyway, this is home. Let's unload."

"Home," Ewald repeated, and moved to the tailgate. Ewald was short, fat, yellow-haired, a buttery boy of twenty-one, and it is my fault as much as any man's that he is dead. I remembered being twenty-one and wanting desperately to be twenty-two. Now I was twenty-six and wanted desperately to be twenty-two. The afternoon air was crisp and still; no aircraft streaked the opal silence, no gunfire. I looked about me, great distances, far across the barren mountains. I saw patches of snow. I stared to the north, suddenly breathless, alien. I was fifty miles from Manchuria.

Two fireplaces. A well out behind, bucket and windlass, and the water tasted good, cold and sweet. We opened the ponderous drafts and built fires, and Ewald made coffee. I lay on a blanket and smoked a cigarette. This was not a war for cigar smokers.

Ewald brought me coffee and said, "What's so funny?"

"Nothing. Thinking of my little boy. Soldiers in far-off places always supposed to think of their little boy. No way to fight a war."

"Not much war right now."

"Don't knock it. You realize if I was a banker or a broker or some god damn yachtsman I wouldn't even be here?"

"You talk like a three-year man." Ewald had a slow, bright, round smile as on some blue-eyed boy doll, eyelids flipping open, fat arms.

"I am a three-year man. Almost. I got ribbons. I'm five years older and nothing's changed."

"You'll be too old for the next one," Ewald said.

"I'm too old for this one," I said.

"Quiet out there," Ewald said.

"That plane scared hell out of me."

"It was ours anyway.

"They're all ours."

"Not all," Ewald said. "We knocked one of theirs down a while ago. Jet against jet. First time in history. It was on the bulletin board."

"Another milestone for the human race. I wish I knew what it was all about. I get the feeling we're not even in Korea. Chile, or Siberia. And we sit here with a dandy little clinic, and a dead truck, and several dollars' worth of equipment, snake oil and rectal sandpaper and such, and the god damn phone doesn't even ring." I must have smiled about then, sourly.

81

"You missed the worst," Ewald said. "They shot prisoners."

"We will too."

"I don't believe that."

"Believe it." I felt harsh, remote, old. The first surprise in that war: everybody was so young. "I've seen red-blooded American boys shoot down German prisoners, white men, blue eyes, blond hair. Gooks are nothing. Cockroaches."

"They started it," Ewald said sullenly.

"Right," I said.

Ewald made peace: "I hear there's tigers in this country."

"I heard that too. And snow leopards. We got a weapon in here?"

Ewald shook his head. "Against the rules."

"Right," I said.

Ewald's father had farmed until the big war and then opened a liquor store in Minneapolis. Ewald's mother was a good cook and missed the farm. She hated the city. Nothing tasted right. Ewald's father was a rural agnostic but Ewald himself was inclined to believe. Ewald's mother had had her gall bladder removed. Ewald's father suffered a recurrent stricture; he required the old man's operation but kept putting it off. Ewald had two sisters, both younger, one of them engaged to a water-softening expert who was also a qualified surveyor, and a Catholic, which distressed the parents on both sides. Ewald hoped to marry soon. It must be great to sleep with a woman every night.

"Right," I said.

● ● ●

The radiophone crackled. "Beer on."

"We're falling back all right," Blue two said. "Noonan's dead. Mortars."

"We're ready," I said.

"See you soon," Blue two said. We were both wrong.

We began badly but soon had no time for omens and auguries. A jeep skidded into the courtyard, the driver shouting, and Ewald was there with a stretcher and an unconscious soldier was on the table in seconds and I was cutting his uniform away. It was a single shot in the abdomen. "Aaach," I said, knowing, and felt the faint, fluttery pulse, washed the belly with one quick motion, a little excited now, a real patient, echoes and memories of a hundred classrooms and clinics, but the man was dead before the dressing touched him. The driver pushed in with another case, this one walking, or stumbling, bandages caked brown on an arm that had to come off. They toted the corpse into a corner and shot number two full of morphine and I went to work; trimmed the wound, pumped a little plasma into him. Ewald tagged him, and he was ready: "Take him," I said. "Where?" the driver asked, another boy—God Almighty, how young they were! "Anju," I said. "Just run south. Take that body too."

"Body." The boy shook his head.

"You've got room. We haven't. Or leave him for the crows," and there was hubbub outside, and Ewald ran to the door. "Jesus," he said. There was plenty of noise now, jets, and farther off crumps and rattles. "Jesus," Ewald said. I was afraid, cold, but again there was no time. Men staggered in; men were carried in. "Christ, he's all gray." A raw red hole in him,

hipbone to kidney, blood vessels; more plasma, while I
swabbed and packed. "Transport. What've we got out
there?" "Two trucks." "Plenty of room." "For
now." "Any officers?" "Not conscious." "Call
home," I said. "Tell them we're busy and need
wheels. Or choppers. Tag this man."

Next on the table a Negro. That was another difference, Negro soldiers, a surprise. Otherwise the world
seemed much the same. The language was as foul, and
before long I would regain my former virtuosity.
Perhaps not. I felt forty. Perhaps as we aged we spoke
less, reserving grand obscenities for true crises. The
choppers were a difference too, but there were not
many, not enough. "And find out what's happened to
the chain of evacuation. Are we number one or what?"
I remembered a phrase: "quickly to restore to duty
those suffering from minor ailments." No minor ailments today. Chest. Good Christ, what can I do about a
chest? I staunched, cleaned, packed, a mechanic. My
God, I'm all alone. Ewald with the syrette. Oh Christ,
the femoral artery too. Hunter's canal wide open.
Barges, tugboats. My gloves slipped through blood,
tripped and groped through small masses of jelly.
"He's dead," Ewald said. "God yes," I said. Men
lugged it away. It was replaced. "Good," I said. "Broken femur." "He's conscious." "Knock him out."
"They'll send trucks," Ewald said. "A bunch coming
down. Choppers if they can. The mobile hospitals are
on the run too, so we're just about number one."

"Call back," I said. "Tell them we're it and we need
everything. Doctors, medics, plasma, dressings, the
works. Lamps, even. All right, that splint now. Keep
these men warm." No one listened; no matter. I
worked, I muttered; iron-headed generals killing their

84

own men, too good to think about a retreat. Chinese won't dare! There. You're all right, mister. You'll live to fight again. Move him. Next. A corporal would have done better. Corporals *always* think about a retreat. I heard motors, horns, shouts. Corporal Beer wondered if we would all be overrun, dead by dawn; Doctor Beer worked. Men crowded into the room, and icy breezes froze my sweat and I hollered, "Shut the door." The line was longer. "Ewald: Get some of these live ones to work. Keep the bad ones warm and comfortable. No water. The others can clean up some of this shit. Find me a live officer." Holy Jesus Christ, a nose and an eye. The room tilted and I took hold of the table. After some blinking and deep breathing I was well again. "Easy, fella, you'll live." Time. An hour perhaps, seemed like seconds.

"Sir."

"What do you want?"

"Lieutenant Hovey. What can I do?"

"Take charge," I told him. "Everything not medical is yours. Organize evacuation. Steal all the rations you can, and medical supplies, sulfa, syrettes, stuff we'll need here, before you send men out. Don't let anybody run off with an empty vehicle. Nothing goes south without a wounded man. That's orders. Anybody argues, shoot him. Get somebody to supervise loading, somebody else unloading. Clear the dead bodies outside."

"Yessir," Hovey said, greenish.

"How many healthy men out there?"

"About thirty."

"Thirty!" I straightened up, stretched. "A real retreat?"

"Looks like it."

85

"Damn. Get on the radio. Find out how bad it is."

"Yessir. Sounds like a chopper coming in."

"Good. Next! Next, for God's sake! Get out there and have them clear a pad. Ewald! Ewald, where the hell are you?"

He pushed through the crowd. "Yessir."

"Tag the worst ones for the chopper. Make up a detail and move them carefully."

"Lieutenant," Ewald said.

His eyes were hard, ice-blue and mock-old in the round young face. He was acting. He had seen many exciting war movies.

"Some of these bad ones," he said. "Some of them —well, some of them going to die pretty quick. Should we maybe—"

"No," I said. "Tag the worst ones for the chopper."

"Yessir."

"Hovey," I said. But Hovey was gone. "You. Sergeant."

"Yessir." Black, frozen.

"Anybody not hurt or working stays outside. They can build a fire, eat, anything, but outside."

"It's snowing."

"Tough. Damn. Can they use choppers in snow?"

"I don't know. Never saw snow before."

The innocence of it. "Clear this room anyway. It's a hospital, not a hotel."

"Yessir."

I stared down at a liver, and experienced the beginnings of a vast arctic horror. Don't cry.

By nightfall my arms were weary. I worked. I made and lost acquaintances. Hovey was gone, replaced by a captain named Wyatt. Sergeants assumed responsibilities and shortly moved out, omitting farewells and leaving confusion behind. With darkness the firing diminished. Trade remained brisk. I had not understood how truly random nature could be. Bullets flew about like atoms and hit anybody anywhere. I had idiotically imagined a war in which soldiers were politely shot in the shoulder or the fleshy part of the leg. Or cleanly, painlessly, expired from a single clean and painless wound won in a noble action. The triumph of myth over experience. I knew better but my mind had balked. It was still balking but without conviction, mainly because I was repairing arms, legs, bellies, necks, heads, hands and feet, white bone, red meat, slippery veins and slippery arteries, some of the meat nicely marbled. I must remember to tell Pinsky; I was carving a brisket, well marbled. I neatened up: removed a pair of mashed testicles and looked for further damage; none, it was a clean shot, the coup du roi, a hundred points and a teddy bear, nothing touched but the scrotum and that gone forever. Perhaps it had been a double. Over and under or left and right? Into a bucket. Future Einsteins, Kallikaks. Better off dead. That was wrong, they would say that was wrong but I could oppose a vigorous argument. It would bear thinking about. Instead, or also, I thought of Carol, and was immobilized by a flaming, inexplicable burst of pure rage; then for an instant stupefied. That too would bear thinking about. "That fire outside," Wyatt said. "It's a target."

"Any planes up?"

"No."

"Artillery?"

"Damn little. But if they take a big enough hill. Or come close enough for mortars."

87

"You watch," I told him. "Some general's going to get a big fat gold medal. Good news, they'll say. An exemplary retreat. Christ, Wyatt, I just got here. I haven't even talked to a Korean yet."

"What about that fire?"

"You're in charge out there. I don't need it, if that's what you're asking."

"Okay. No fire. Can they come back in?"

My back ached. Occupational hazard. Compensation, partial disability. "How many now?"

"Too many. Forty. Fifty. But maybe in shifts."

"All right. You do it. Keep them out of my way."

Wyatt looked like a wispy blond poet and wore a West Point ring.

"Doc. Something wrong? Is he dead?"

"I'm tired. I need a clamp."

"I don't know what that is."

It was not Ewald but a stranger. "Where's Ewald?"

"Here, Lieutenant. Coming. Sorry."

"A clamp. Tag him. Morphine and plasma."

At dawn I stripped off another pair of gloves and stumbled outside. The courtyard was full. Men slept in pairs like lovers, un-American, treason, hugging and groaning, livid in the pearly light, powdered white by snow. Motors droned and thumped. I counted eight trucks, two jeeps. Snow fell in sparse, minute flakes; to the east the sky was clearer. I breathed. I trudged into the brush and relieved myself, stiff, tired; yes, made Korea my own. My breath steamed and my head was laden. I buttoned up, found a match, smoked. I walked on back. "How you doing, Swede?"

Ewald nodded. "I slept a little. This is bad, isn't it."

"Bad as can be. Any word from anybody about anything?"

"Big retreat. Anju and maybe farther. In the east too, right down to the ocean."

"We're in trouble."

"They're still coming in," Ewald said.

"As long as they come, we stay."

"Okay. I wasn't asking."

"You sound like you want a transfer."

"Soon as possible," Ewald said.

A light booming commenced in the north. "The Chinese," Ewald said. "Millions of Chinese."

"Five years ago they were all heroes." Lin was at Bellevue. Another year and Lin might come down from the north with a red star on his cap.

No. Hazily, puzzled, I received an illumination: such meetings were not life. I would not find Lin in an exotic Oriental compound. I would never see 57359 again. Or . . . or her. Paths crossed, diverged; the past was always prologue. And the future was never a tidy epilogue; the future was opaque until it became the present, and then it was the past, and more prologue, and possibly I had already made my greatest and most irrevocable decisions and mistakes. But I would never know. I might never see Jacob again, or Carol, or Joseph. "Take some chocolate and coffee to the table, will you? I'll come in."

"All right. You need sleep."

"Soon. No word about another doctor?"

"No word."

I would never talk to Blue two again. Or to Wyatt, or the Negro sergeant, or after a while to Ewald. I was a dead fish floating on life's tide, a tide neither friendly nor hostile but inexorable. I was a chip, a bubble, a nothing; only a function. Here or there, then or now, I was a doctor. That was something. I saw myself driven by a silent destiny to a tent in Central Asia, an igloo in the Arctic, a hut in Samoa, each day new faces, new wounds, new ills, and Benny nameless, homeless, friendless, repairing men, women, children, whose language he could not speak.

The sweet German dance I love came to me, and I shouted aloud in pain.

Business slacked off in midmorning. By then I was accustomed once more to the noise of war, and could distinguish a variety of instruments: mortars, machine guns, distant single rounds like firecrackers; perhaps a carbine. In a corner of my clinic stood several rifles. 'Tis expressly against the law of arms. Bits and pieces of equipment—and, I supposed, of men—littered the room: cartridge belts, a mess kit, packs, ration boxes. Outside were many corpses; within, a skinny sergeant with a broken arm and probably a bad concussion; he was conscious and smoking but with the empty, incandescent eyes of a parrot. On the table was a young man who had lost a one-inch ribbon of his left side from armpit to hip; bits of rib flashed white as I swabbed and trimmed. "Ewald, my boy, we may have missed the last bus. How long since a vehicle went past?"

"Half an hour anyway."

"And no foot soldiers either."

"I hear some now," Ewald said.

"Raise him up a little," I said. "I hear them too. It's been lovely, Ewald."

"God damn it," he said. "You were supposed to get me out of this."

"I was supposed to treat the wounded," I said. "So were you. Let him down now, easy." I was as good as drunk (no, not quite as good; I would have given a deal to be rowdy drunk), wallowing in bloody bits, waving red hands, exhausted, blinking gritty eyes, hungry.

It was not over. All day long they trickled in.

Dark again, and brutish silence, like a cheap saloon at dawn; along one wall, six patients in a row, one whimpering, others asleep, unconscious, one smoking in the half-light. In the courtyard another vehicle, slamming to a stop; boots on stone, the door flung open: "Bring him in! Bring him in!"

"What are you driving?" I forced my eyes wide, stretched my mouth, went to a basin of cold water and washed my face, and left the drops to dry: to make me wakeful and brave and talented.

"Little old ten-tonner."

"Load those men onto it."

"We can't—"

"You can."

Behind the man two others bore a sagging burden. "Here," I told them. "What is it?"

"Head," someone said.

"Lay him down. Load up those others and take off."

"Take off!" Murmurs, breathy exclamations. "We can't leave this man, doc. We been together a long time. This is old Jack. We'll just stick by him."

"Bullshit. Load up those men and move out."

Consultations. "No sir. We just can't do that."

I set down my scalpel. "I guess old Jack's had it," I said cheerfully.

Scruffy, cadaverous, their leader gaped. "You mean you won't fix him up?"

"All or none. You take care of my six, I take care of Jack. It don't make me no never mind. I could use some sleep, and a smoke."

The leader turned. "Pile those men in the truck."

"With great care," I said. "Two of them can walk. The one with the bandages on his head, sit him up if you can wedge him tight and keep him wedged. The others flat on their backs. Then take off."

"We'll take off when Jack can go."

"You'll take off now," I said. "That's an order. I'll stay with Jack. That's a promise."

I set to work on Jack while the others hefted and complained and scuffed and made cold breezes. "Some small clamps, Ewald. Look at this, down the neck like a razor. Just missed the artery," I was whispering, crooning, to myself as much as to Ewald, working and explaining and keeping awake, lecturing, a patter of applause from the balcony, triumphantly Benny brandishes a string of sausages, "and just missed the jugular, and sliced right through the trapezius." I sucked in air, swayed, steadied. Dizzy; light danced. "More swabs. Now sir, this is a problem. Yessir. This went deep. Deep, deep, deep, deep and clean." Not speech, incantation. The room was clear. We were alone. A motor burped, roared. Ewald seemed gray and drawn. "You could have gone." I know," he said. "Thanks," I said. "Plasma's done." Ewald coiled tubing. I nipped and tucked. "Throw another log on the fire," I said. "We may have a chance to sleep. Open a ration. Happy Thanksgiving, or Christmas, we're in there somewhere. I'm drunk now or I'd love a drink. A glass of whiskey and a cigarette, and the dartboard and all the auld gang down to the pub—"

The door swung open. I paused in mid-stitch to complain about the breeze and thought at first that I was addressing a Korean, a soldier, perhaps a servant, a chauffeur come for me and Ewald; until I saw a red star, implacably hostile eyes and the vast, round muzzle of an automatic weapon, and I understood that I was face to face with a Chinese soldier. Shock paralyzed me, not fear but simple primitive shock; across thousands of miles and thousands of years, across seas and straits, languages and scripts, epicanthic folds and circumcisions, chopsticks and forks, famine and Pinsky's, this Mongolian warrior menaced this Jewish doctor. "Diefoo," I said, the Mandarin for doctor, and added a phrase Lin had taught me: literally, have you finished eating, but it was a very classy idiom for hello, how are you. The Chinese eyes widened briefly; the man gestured and two others entered, bearing a third. Ewald was flattened against the wall beside the fireplace, face a rictus, as if he would hiss, a saffron cat among rattlers. "Ewald, come over here," I said firmly. "Stand at the table here and be a medic." I pointed to Ewald and said again, "Die-foo."

"Die-foo," the Chinese said, and a further string of syllables. I shook my head. More syllables. I shook my head again and went on stitching. "Die-foo," the Chinese said more urgently. He pointed to his fallen comrade, still slung between the two soldiers; an officer, I sensed. Ewald moved quickly to the table and stood across from me, rigid. I nodded to the Chinese. "You're next," I said, or gasped, and realized that I had hardly breathed since the irruption. I indicated Jack, half-stitched. The Chinese spoke curtly. I waved a hand: "Let me finish, you're next." The Chinese placed the muzzle of his automatic weapon at Jack's head and fired a short, thunderous burst. Jack's head blew open, some of it staining me but most of it spattering the wall. The Chinese shoved Jack off the table and issued orders. His men brought their patient to me. "Die-foo," the Chinese said, and urged me to work, prodding politely. I opened the patient's padded jacket. The Chinese spoke and his soldiers stepped forward to assist. Ewald's face was a mask, elemental; hate, terror; a mask for snakes, lightning, unexpected foul gods. I signed to the soldiers, roll him over a bit. One shot, maybe two, entry anterior just below the sixth rib, maybe nicked the spleen maybe not, seems to have missed the lung, how do you know?—"Ewald. Plasma"—tore through the diaphragm, blew a big hole on the way out—"Plasma, Ewald"—exit posterior just below the eighth rib. Doctor Beer will pull this one through by the force of personality. "Ewald, we have a badly wounded man on the table."

"A badly—" Ewald's mad eyes rolled.

"Ewald. Plasma. That's an order. Move."

He leaned forward and spoke in a rush, spattering me with a fine spray of saliva. "For these sons of bitches? That shot our guys in the back of the head? I'll kill you. I'll kill you first."

"You're spitting on the patient," I said. "Now listen."

"There's some guns in the corner," he muttered quickly. "I'll drift over there and cover them. When I do, you get that burp gun." He was out there west of the Pecos.

"Plasma," I said. "We need it *now*." I too leaned forward; as hard as I could I slapped Ewald, catching his cheek and temple. He hopped sideways and almost fell; recovering, he drew an outraged breath, glared, raised both hands like claws. The muzzle of the burp gun twitched. "You're attracting attention," I said. "Plasma. Right now."

The Chinese—officer? noncom, I guessed—nodded, expressionless yet approving, impassive yet attentive. Ewald prepared the plasma. I cleaned and trimmed. I glanced again at my supervisor and met a flat stare, the hint of a nod. I concentrated: as well that this man not die; no, he would not die this time. "Ewald," I said, "you don't like this at all. You don't understand it."

"I understand it. You're yellow."

"Yes, that would be it. Don't let this gent hear you use that word that way." My patient stirred. "Somewhere in Washington is the man who decided that I had to come to Korea. It was a mistake. Some clerk. I hadn't interned and they took no such. Only me. And we couldn't fight the god damn machine. Now if that clerk was on the table here, I'd do exactly the same for him. Understand?"

"No. Shut up. If we get out alive—"

"If we get out alive you threatened an officer. Furthermore you permitted weapons in an aid station against my strict orders. You—"

"Me?" His fists clenched. "I had nothing to do with that. You cut that out, Lieutenant."

"Watch it. This man's coming to."

I finished stitching. How did they say "temporary" in Chinese? They'd figure it out. "Okay," I said.

"Okay," the noncom said. He spoke to his two men, who covered the patient, and then he walked about the room taking inventory. He slung his burp gun and spoke, obviously warning us not to be foolish. "Don't fool," I told Ewald.

"Some day," Ewald said, "and I hope I'm there."

"Can't please 'em all," I said.

The noncom offered me a cigarette. I accepted. He

95

joined me, and lit a wooden match for us both. Contemptuously Ewald drew a package of American cigarettes from his shirt pocket; ostentatiously he lit one. I almost giggled. "Good," he said.

I nodded strenuously. "Yessirree bob. Sure beats these damn communist weeds." I waved the cigarette and smiled—grimaced—thanks at the noncom. He pointed to Ewald, tapped the burp gun and looked the question. "Good God no," I said, and shook my head and frowned like an officer. "No. No. No." He smiled. He was amused and sympathetic.

He went to the radio and to Ewald's astonishment operated it. That seemed inconceivable to me too: how could an American radio speak Chinese? I remembered first meeting a Negro who spoke only French: how wrong! My own uncles: the shvartzers are *Americans*, don't forget, as good as anybody! How long without sleep now—forty hours? "Hey," I said. The noncom hushed me. His call completed, he turned to me. I pointed to my pack and made eating motions. Pointed to my wristwatch and fingered a series of circles. He nodded but unslung the burp gun as I rummaged. His men were removing the American arms and some of the plasma. As I ate I wandered among the supplies, extracting what two packs might accommodate, gesturing and saying, "Die-foo, die-foo, die-foo. Ewald, wherever we wind up we'll need this stuff. Help me now and have your tantrum later." The patient moaned and stirred; I checked him and reassured the noncom.

When a vehicle pulled into the courtyard voices rose, and the sounds of loading; four men entered, scavenged thoroughly, chatted with the noncom, removed the wounded officer. The noncom committed Ewald and his bulging pack to the care of a soldier, and walked beside me to the door. He seemed thoughtful and not inscrutable. At the door he halted me and brought the muzzle of the burp gun to my throat. I tried to read his eyes and could not, and the imminence of death ripped through me like an electric shock; my knees dissolved. The Chinese reached inside my shirt and ripped away my dog tags. I felt old aches, magic hangovers, universal déjà vu, everything, always.

Outside in the dark I stumbled and sagged. I made signs for beddy-bye and they let me lie on the floor of the truck, where I was cold. I found a stack of my own blankets and wrapped myself in one and said, "Die-foo," and the Chinese all laughed.

6

"Parsons." Benny spoke the name slowly. This was a dream, or a trick. The ship rolled, and Benny seemed to glide.

"You remember me." Parsons rose to shake hands. "How do you feel?"

"Seasick," Benny said. "But I'd . . ." He gestured, open hands. "I'd rather be seasick than . . ."

"I imagine so. Sit down."

Benny examined the metal chair. "It's bolted to the floor."

"Yes."

Benny sat. "You? How come . . . ?"

"I asked for you." Parsons smiled. "Old friends, and all that." The table between them was round and covered in green baize. "Just took your name off one list and put it on another." Parsons too sat down, and they squirmed and settled like card players. Parsons poked at a file folder. "You're all right physically. I'm glad of that."

It was a sizable room, perhaps a wardroom or a saloon. They were alone in it.

"It's nice on deck," Benny said. "The sunshine, and the ocean."

"Quite a change. So you got into medical school all right."

"I almost wish I hadn't." Portholes. Wodden trim here and there, dark. Bright screws. Tables and shelves hinged to the wall. Bulkhead.

"You know," Parsons said, "this is a tremendous problem we have on our hands."

A phrase-maker. He did not mean Ewald, Benny knew. All problems were tremendous. "I suppose so." No rats. No lice. So antiseptic!

"We have nine of these transports, all doing the same job. We're just collecting facts, you know."

Earnest. Earnest Parsons, as in an old play. What was his Christian name?

"Glad to help," Benny said. He belched gently. "Sorry. Still adjusting to food. You have no idea what tropical storms a little soda pop can generate." The ship rolled tamely, languidly; he blinked and breathed deeply.

"Are you all right?" The remote tones: Parsons. Parsons wore silver oak-leaves.

"I'm all right. All tanned. Gaining weight."

"You were down to one fifty."

"From two oh five. I'll get it back."

"Yes. A nice slow trip and all you can eat."

"And whiskey in the officers' quarters."

"Go easy," Parsons said. "You've got to get used to things all over again. You've come out of an absolutely regulated life, every decision made for you, no choices, no options."

"Decisions?" Benny said. "Choices? Ah, Colonel: every minute of every day."

99

Parsons considered, pursed his lips, clucked. "Maybe so."

"You're older," Benny said. "You've lost some hair."

Parsons smiled sadly. "I'm forty."

"And a light colonel. You'll be a general in the next one."

"You're older too," Parsons said.

"Several decades older," Benny said. Outside the porthole blue sky, an endless tilting sea.

"Why don't you call me Alex," Parsons said. "We're old friends."

"Alex." Benny approved. "Good. Companions in arms."

"That's what we are," Parsons said. "Benny, nobody here is your enemy, but I have to remind you of article thirty-one of the uniform code of military justice. You may decline to answer any question if you feel that the answer will tend to incriminate or degrade you. But anything you do say may be held against you."

7

IN A SEARING white dawn they prodded us off the truck and into a temple. Ewald's face was yellow wax, frozen, set hard. We had no fire and now no blankets. We: a dozen or so. Ewald moved away from me and curled up on the floor. I went after him: "Stay close, Corporal. I'll need that pack." He made no answer. Men stirred. I defined myself and asked who needed help. "He does," they said, and waved at a bulky Negro.

"Unconscious or asleep?"

"Unconscious. Maybe dead."

"Give me a hand. Turn him over. Gently."

Aiee. Bad. Projectile in the back, beside the first lumbar vertebra, slashed in angling to the outside, still in there. Nerves, maybe; kidney, maybe. A mess. Little blood. The dog tags: Howard, Charles Arthur, Protestant, type O. Fever minimal. Respiration too. A lump. "Turn him back." Bladder full. I pressed lightly. Hell. I unslung the pack. Catheter, grease, needle, clamp. I drew a cc. of water into the syringe. I had to be calm and not shaky and not blasphemous and not suicidal; but a tiny black void blossomed at my precise

101

center. I took his penis in my hand and inserted the catheter, slid it all the way up. (Taking this in? A day in the field with our boys. Penology, you might call it.) This long tube went right up into his bladder, and at the inner end was a small balloon (whee!), with a separate channel of access, and that was what the cc. of water was for: I shot it into the smaller channel and it filled the balloon which then sat in the neck of the bladder so that the catheter could not slip out. Meanwhile the poor bastard was draining into my canteen cup. Seven hundred cc.'s, I estimated. Old Doc Beer, hewer of bone and drawer of pee. The drugstore joke: Do you do urinalysis? Yes. Then wash your hands and make me a ham sandwich. I think by now there were tears in my eyes. But no blood in the urine. Thank God for the least of his blessings. Naturally not responsible for sordors and agonies. When the flow ceased I clamped the tube. Shock. He needed plasma. "Has he been conscious at all?" "He groans." "Watch him. If he wakes, give him all the water he can hold."

"Not supposed to give a wounded man water."

"Thanks," I said. "Make him drink." I had a considerable audience, some gagging. Always something new out of Asia. Join the army. Enlist now. I held forth the cup: "Get rid of this." A hand took it. "Who's in charge?"

"I am." A sergeant, southern voice. "Trezevant. First regiment, twenty-fourth." Big and black.

"Forget that. Name, rank, serial number, date of birth. If they march us we'll need a litter for this man. I want you to detail four men to carry him, two on, two off. I'll tag him. Anybody else?"

"Cuts and bruises. A smashed shoulder."

102

"I'll look at them. Pool the food? Share and share alike?"

"Later," the sergeant said. "Let 'em sleep."

"Any hot water?"

"Nothin."

"Here's your cup," someone said.

I rinsed it and scrubbed it with dirty snow. "Ewald. Let's get some plasma into this man."

"God's sake," he said. "Here and now?"

"Here and now. This fellow may not have any there and then."

Afterward we froze in silence. I ate a chocolate bar, sipped from my canteen, smoked. Then I sat back against the stone wall of that house of worship and dozed. Attend the church of your choice. It occurred to me that I might soon die. Or was already dead. The Tibetan hell was a vast lake of ice and the damned stood entombed to the neck crying "ha-ha." The spark of life: a good phrase and you never knew how good until the fire burned low. I wound my watch.

Later there were thirty-odd in the temple and I had performed minor embroidery. One of the newcomers was a major. "Kinsella," the major announced. "You keep these men in shape." He was a short, hard, dark-haired man, energetic, would rise early, and he reminded me of plains colleges, fields of rimed stubble, a good wing shot. He made a speech. "You take your orders from me. You refer all problems to me. You maintain discipline and respect for rank." No one cheered. He stood taut, angry. "You just do what I tell you," he said, and came to sit beside me. "We need a litter," I said. "Right," he said, and bounced up and went to the door to holler for a guard. This small tyrant;

103

I almost smiled. Kinsella instructed, made signs; the guard stared blankly and went away. He returned with an officer and Kinsella resumed. The officer spoke English and I joined them. In a pause I spoke my one Chinese idiom and the officer grunted. "We have one man badly hurt and unconscious," I said. "If you can give me a litter we'll carry him.'

"We have no stretcher."

"Two poles and a blanket."

"Who are you?"

"Die-foo."

"You come."

"The stretcher."

"Yes. The stretcher. You come."

Kinsella nodded okay. I took up my pack and followed the officer. The temple was surrounded by guards. We crunched up a frosted slope to a wooden building—monks' quarters?—and inside. I treated four Chinese, minor lacerations, a crushed hand; I set new dressings, enjoyed the warmth, and accepted a cigarette. Also a bowl of warm grain. I did not recognize it but supposed it was millet. A small cup—a cup? a little porcelain cup!—of tea. The officer escorted me back to the temple. Above us the sky was dead, pallid.

Shortly two men arrived with the improvised litter. The officer followed and told us to prepare to march. "Three minutes," he said. Kinsella strode forward and made another speech. "We march in three minutes," he finished up. "Carry all you've got and stay together. Any man who drops out may be left behind."

"The hell he will," I said. "If a man drops out you'll pick him up and carry him."

Kinsella said furiously, "Lieutenant! It's my job to save as many men as possible."

"Major," I said, "it's my job to save them all."

We marched north on an open road and I drifted up and down the line. The men were tired and hungry. Now they feared our own aircraft. Some had lost blood but there was no sense of doom until the snow fell. It began in midafternoon, heavy, wet, lazy flakes, great soggy feathers of snow; in half an hour the land was white and from the rear I could not see the point. I was stiff and still ached but the walking warmed me. Trezevant trudged along beside Howard's litter. I inspected my patient every quarter-hour. The man would doubtless die but there was plenty of time for that. Kinsella too moved among them, striding briskly on short legs, provoking, pleading, swearing; at the head of the column he shouted at the guards, "Rest! Rest! We need rest!" No one answered.

The litter-bearers swapped off. "I wish the son of a bitch would hurry up and die." Our boys. I took Trezevant's place and wiped snow from Howard. He needed nourishment. He needed a hospital and a surgeon, and radiators, and intravenous feeding. We marched. Twilight gathered, but we marched. The guards marched, iron men. Jeep-like vehicles approached, stopped, passed on. A line of four came out of the north, lights pricking through the snow, and faded to the south. Kinsella loomed out of the gray dusk. "Two men down," he bawled. "Come along." I dropped back. At the end of the column two men supported two others. "Cramp," one called. "Legs all seized up."

"Lay them down and rub."

"Guards won't let us. They stuck me once."

"Then keep going." In the wind and whirling snow our voices were soft and spooky.

"I'll send relief," Kinsella called. "Just drag 'em along. These bastards got to stop soon." To me he said, "All right, all right, we'll do all we can. God damn snow."

We turned to move forward together and barely glimpsed the litter at the roadside.

"God damn!" Kinsella yelled. "Give me a hand. I'll bust their asses for that!"

We knelt over Howard. His pulse was thin. "He's alive," I said, and then a blow in the side drove the breath out of me, whoosh, and I skidded through the snow on my face. I rolled over and spat and rose to a crouch. I stared through the gloom. A guard spat too, on me. "Die-foo!" I shouted. "Die-foo!" The guard hesitated. I stood up and took the rear of the litter; Kinsella and I hoisted, and shambled forward. "Son of a bitch *kicked* me," I panted. I started to cry. Kinsella trotted; I gulped air and kept up. We found Trezevant. "I need bearers," I told him. "The good ones. Not those other two." Men took the litter. I wiped snow from my face and breathed hard.

Kinsella and I slogged along together. Many times his hand rose, and his thumb sought the sling of a vanished carbine. Later he groaned and said, "It's no use. I got to check the rear. If they want to kill us, why don't they just shoot us?"

"Beats me. Send word if you need me."

Kinsella squinted. "You look like hell."

I tried to smile, and failed. "No sleep. Overwork. I need a doctor."

106

*   *   *

Two hours later we were herded into a dark, snowy courtyard at the center of a dark, snowy village. The men dropped in place and a vast groan arose, a common cry for peace and rest, and then there was silence except for the sobs. Kinsella called out, "Massage those men. There's still tomorrow. Move that litter out of the snow. Somewhere. Against the wall."

"Lay the blanket over him," I said.

"Where's that officer?" Kinsella stormed off.

"Trezevant," I said, "bring those two men over here."

He hesitated. "We're all in bad shape."

"Bring them."

He found them and brought them to me. We could all hear Kinsella raging and sputtering. I inspected the two men. They were boys. They stood sullen and snow fell on them, gliding out of the black night into the faint light of torches. "We thought he was dead," one mumbled. I swayed but gathered myself up, stood with my feet set apart and was briefly, nastily, almost happily, a corporal again. "Take off your helmets." They stared. "Take off your helmets." Slowly they fumbled their helmets off. Snow whitened their crew cuts. They were not as big as me but I slapped them both, hard. "That's all." I felt foolish.

One of them said, "That's a court-martial."

"You remember that," I said. "Write it down."

They went off. Trezevant said, "He's going to die anyway."

"We all are. But the toughest last. I didn't do that for Howard. I did it for them."

Kinsella joined us and said, "They'll give us a kettle of hot water and that's all. No fire. There's thirty-three

107

of us. Trezevant, the hot water's for drinking, or tea or coffee if anybody has it. Any man without food, find him some, must be a few with something in their pocket."

"We ought to pool the food," I said.

"Who'd carry it, Lieutenant? No. Let 'em keep their own, and share it out at each stop."

We made a meal that night, and slept in the snow, men embracing again; in the morning two were dead, each with a live and horrified lover. "Not frozen," I said. "Cold and exhausted."

"They'll blame it on me," Kinsella said.

"And me." I relieved myself and Howard. The march resumed, without benefit of hot water. I saw men weeping. Still it snowed. At noon we were allowed to rest at the roadside, and to eat; men strung out along the ditch and sat like cadavers. They chewed slowly, with heartbreaking effort. At six we did the same, and the food was almost gone. I dragged myself up and down the line of limp soldiers; none had strength enough to complain. My canteen was empty; I stuffed it with snow, an interminable labor. Ewald was a ghost but still bore his pack; it was lighter now, and so was mine. Howard was dying. I sat beside him and was helpless. Kinsella sat with me. There was nothing to say.

When we heard the motor and the ponderous clanking we stood up. "Off the road," Kinsella shouted, "get well off the road." We waited in darkness until a hugh, squat shape shook the earth and rumbled by. "That's a Pershing," Kinsella said in outrage. "M-six," I said, "captured." "From us or from Chiang Kai-shek," Kinsella said, "or maybe bought from

108

some Nationalist general." "That's treason," I said. Talking was no longer simple. "Treason hell," Kinsella said. "I heard there was a brisk trade. Why do we have to fight everybody's wars for them? Why can't they do anything right? They never do any god damn fighting until they're on the other side. Then they turn into soldiers. How'd you know what it was? Were you in the last one?" "Yes, Germany," I said. "Medic?" "No. Infantry. Corporal." "I was a lieutenant," Kinsella said. "New Guinea and the Philippines." "Trezevant?" "Too young," Kinsella said. "This guy dead here?" "No," I said, "but it won't be long." The guards were shouting and prodding. "Up and at 'em." Kinsella said. "We're going to lose a few." "Maybe," I said. I ordered two men to carry Howard and the column started off. I marched half-asleep, kept a bleary eye on stragglers. Dim, almost invisible, the column stretched before me. A guard peered, another, breathing white plumes.

I was foundering and had begun to feel vulnerable. I had begun to feel several thousand years old and was no longer an American soldier but a Scythian captive. This column was as old as these hills, had always existed, had marched with stone axes and later with spears, through ice ages. This road had been worn flat by the feet of slaves. I had been taken by a Mongol horde, banner after banner riding league upon league over the frozen plains of Central Asia, the horizon a thousand miles off; stopping to slit a vein in their mounts' necks and drink a meal, plastering the gash with mud and riding on; their shadows cantered beside me, their bloodthirsty yip-yip-yip floated through the frigid air. Mountains, the endless bare steppe, frozen rivers to cross. I shivered. I was a prisoner in a cruel land, a land of tigers and snow leopards and Mongoleyes, a prisoner perhaps for life. Slavery. Would they blind me? Castrate me? There were no police to call, no statesmen to protest to. No heralds in tabards, no ambassadors in silken knee-breeches. Nothing. In the beginning was the void. Only the iron cold and the swirling snow, the hard, indifferent guards and the marching column and the endless night. Tears started again. I ground my teeth.

I moved quickly when a man forward staggered and fell to the side. I wondered how I could have seen that in the night and the snow. Another prisoner had moved faster and was crouching over the body. I ran to help him. The crouching man looked up, spun away, disappeared into the column. The fallen man was crying out; his jacket lay open. "My ration," he cried. "He got my ration." I went breathless with anger but tugged at the man. I shouted. Kinsella was there. "Let's get him up," he said. "I can't," the man said. "You can," Kinsella said. A guard spoke sharply. We heaved the man to his feet. "Walk!" Kinsella ordered. "Just walk!" The man was sobbing but walked. The whitened column moved again.

"Some son of a bitch stole a ration from him," I said, "like that, like a cat." "You'll see more of it," Kinsella said. "Right," I said. "We'll lose some more," Kinsella said, "unless we stop soon." We were moving up the line side by side. A face swiveled, bloomed, white-eyed: "We're supposed to have trucks," the man said. "They were supposed to pull us out."

"Shut up," Kinsella said. "Keep moving."

An owl hooted through the snowy night.

Half an hour later I had understood life, the secret: glazed, frozen and dopey I trudged, one straight line from birth to death, from nothing to nothing, and I knew now that the first men had done it right and nobody since: thirty, forty years, kill a few mastodons, eat when hungry, sleep when tired, fuck when lusty, worship the sun and the moon, die gratefully. I did not reminisce. I shut my eyes against the relentless snow and shuffled toward my final resting place, a lonely ditch, a heap of leaves, pine needles. The snow leopards would have me and welcome.

Dimly shouts billowed. I woke when Kinsella shook me. "Quick." The column had halted; they stood like statues, a seamy modern sculpture, a group in dead wood and white stone, heroes, a snow machine, and the world passing on to the next exhibit. I stumbled after Kinsella to the abandoned litter. Howard was well off the line of march this time, and he was dead, I knew that. We knelt. I confirmed the diagnosis. Kinsella took the dog tags. "The shoes," I said. "What else?" "Nothing," Kinsella said. "He's been stripped. No watch, no food, no butts, no nothing. His buddies." "May he rest in peace." "Amen."

We rejoined the column. "God damn," he said. "They ought to be flogged."

"They're dead men," I said.

"No they're not," he said fiercely, and I saw him on another day, the sun winking off gold leaves, buttons, medals, the eyes bright, white gloves, a band playing, the major at ecstatic attention, taut, flat eyes, perfect reflexes, iron cross, S.S. lightnings, steel teeth; this man like all men, born of woman, forged by the sun, tempered by the rain, polished smooth by the army and

111

painted by legend, blue eyes, red cheeks, gold balls, and the crowd kneeling. "They're babies," he said. "They're just not soldiers."

"They don't want to be."

"They will be," he said, "god damn them."

They fell with bleats and groans, dropped to the earth floor, pressed to the iron stove, shivered and scrabbled in the orange half-light. "Sick and wounded to the fire!" Kinsella's parade-ground tenor shamed them all. "It's a schoolhouse," I said to Ewald. He had nothing to say but did not flee, or even glare. In a warm room, out of the cold, the snow, the wind, I was drowsy. I leaned against the wooden wall, and soon I slid to the floor. In the morning I said, "It wasn't a faint. I just fell asleep like a horse."

"Well rub your eyes and think fast," Kinsella said. "They want to talk to us. We have thirty-two men now and two officers. One doctor, one medic. Name, rank, serial number and date of birth. You men!" They fell silent; muzzily I contemplated them, scarecrows, our turn now, Americans, barbed wire and scrapping for scraps. "You men! The Chinese want to see your officers. We may not come back here. Trezevant's in charge. Maintain discipline, maintain the chain of command, take your orders from Trezevant and Trezevant will do the talking with the Chinese. Take care of each other. Keep clean. Name, rank, serial number and date of birth. That's all. Good luck." We marched out, escorted, a cold clear morning, football, ice-skating, and then we were at attention before a Chinese officer, who nodded and led us away. Two guards marched behind us, port arms, bayonets fixed; when I turned to look, one of them growled.

We were in a village, and the villagers had turned out to see the freaks. I envied them their padded gowns, fur hats. Cloth shoes: warm? Canvas boots. Dark eyes, like mine; the faces were surely expressionless but I read reproach into them. Pain flickered through my shoulders, back, thighs; my calves twitched. Three nights and two days, and before that the aid station, aeons ago. We marched down the middle of the road, between rows of silent spectators, no fuss. I wanted to say hello, to nod, to raise a hand. At the town hall— brick, yellowed brick, electricity, a WPA post office, 1937—we were halted and searched roughly, and the crowd murmured, pleased. Kinsella bore himself stiffly and coldly. I tried to do the same but kept absorbing details: a hat of fox, another of otter; these civilians were Korean (or were they? where was I?) but all the soldiers seemed Chinese, or was it only the uniform, and how could you tell? Within the building I saw sacks, gunny sacks against the wall, and on the floor coal balls. Coal balls. I had never seen coal balls before. I was a big-city boy, and heat came from drunken janitors.

For a time now there would be nothing that I could do about anything. I was standing in the lobby of a town hall in North Korea, and I was a free man for the first time in my life.

We were led to an office, and met the boss. He seemed to be Chinese, surprisingly large and bearish, a bit like me but smoother and sleeker. "Good morning," he said. "I am Ou-yang. The equivalent of your lieutenant-colonel. I am a graduate of the Whangpoa military academy and have been in America in 1944. Who are you?"

"Kinsella, John Peter, Major," and he gave his

number and age, "June twenty-eighth, nineteen fifteen."

The dark eyes shifted to me; I sought purchase in
them, found none. I spoke the essentials and added,
"I'm a doctor, a die-foo."

"You don't have to tell him that," Kinsella said.

"Don't be an ass," I said. It was disrespectful but I
was a free man. To the Chinese I said, Have you
finished eating, and quickly added, "because we
haven't. We're collapsing of hunger and cold and simple exhaustion."

Ou-yang spoke and a guard went away. "How much
Chinese have you?"

"That's all," I said.

Kinsella said, "If you start this way you'll end up in
his pocket."

"Childish," Ou-yang said. "I have many *hundred*
prisoners and no place to lodge them. And no doctors,
so you will be needed."

I told him I had sick and wounded and dying, and
needed antiseptics, dressings, instruments.

He stood up, and I was shocked, almost angry; he
was taller than I. Big sleek head, big round shoulders. I
saw him in America, grappling with words, burly and
friendless, armored, a quick empty smile, a bob of the
head, no girl. He said, "Yes, yes, anesthesia and
penicillin, and *afterward* beef broth and ice cream and
handicrafts. Use what you have."

"It's about gone."

"My own men come first."

"The Geneva—" Kinsella began, and Ou-yang
pounced; he had waited for that: "You never signed it.
If you had, it would mean *nothing*. You sign anything
and then kill children."

114

"We don't kill children," Kinsella said angrily.

"I have sick and wounded," I said.

The guard came back with a tray and Ou-yang said, "Have some boiled millet, and even tea. Tea is a *luxury* in parts of China, you never knew that; but after all, *officers*."

"We're entitled to food," Kinsella said swiftly. "It's all right, Beer."

I said, "Right."

For now we would command our own men. There would be millet and boiling water morning and night; a detail, under guard, might fetch and carry. Only the one iron stove could be spared, but there was a *superfluity* of firewood. The men would emerge on command in groups of six or less, from time to time, for exercise in place. The latrine was in the open air, altogether public; Ou-yang was wearily contemptuous of Kinsella's complaint. We must survive without further help until transfer to a permanent camp. When would that be? No one knows. Would it be in Korea or in Manchuria? No one knows. "But I imagine it will be Korea. China is not at war."

Kinsella snorted. I was dizzy and sipped hard at the tea. Ou-yang went on about their borders and their airspace and their hydroelectric power. Kinsella argued and Ou-yang silenced him. He told me I would examine his men too in emergencies. I said all right. I was gliding somewhat, side to side. "You will not," Kinsella said.

"I have no choice."

"You are not required—"

"A prior oath," I said dreamily, floating, swaying. "Just take my word for it. I have no choice."

"It's working for the enemy."

"Doctors have no enemies unless they sue," I said, and was giddy, this vaudeville, this Irishman and this Chinese and this Jew, you see, they were walking down a street in Korea and one of them says—I am still alive. I am still alive. The room whirled, and I with it, serenely, grandly, regally, and Ou-yang caught the small teacup as Kinsella caught me. Shame. A grown man. He told me I lay there smiling.

8

THIS TIME ANOTHER officer sat with Parsons. It was another day. Benny said to himself, another day, another dolor. He had slept well but had dreamed of Howard rising from the dead, walking. "You look better every day," Parsons said. Alex.

"Thank you," Benny said. "It's a healthy life. The help are courteous and efficient."

Parsons smiled, not politely but in real pleasure, as one might say, I like jokes. "Sit down. This is Captain Gabol."

"How do you do."

"How do you do." Captain Gabol was handsome and red-haired with a wide nose and wide nostrils. He was Benny's notion of a farm agent in Indiana. "I'm a psychiatrist," he said.

"Freudian?"

Gabol grinned. "Eclectic."

"I'm somewhat eclectic myself," Benny said.

"That's all right then," Gabol welcomed him.

"How goes the questionnaire?" Alex asked.

Benny said, "It's long. You'll have a problem with

some of these comic-book fans." He was no longer seasick and rather enjoyed the comfort and conversation of the wardroom, the elegant saloon. "I'm not really answering the way you want me to. I'm just writing it all down. Everything."

Gabol offered a cigarette and Benny declined politely: "I quit some time ago."

"So we heard."

"Should you be telling me what you've heard?"

"Some of it. Why not?"

"Some of it," Benny said.

"You were a cigar smoker," Parsons said.

"You're in the right job," Benny said. "You remember things. That's how you got to be a spelling champ."

Parsons laughed happily. "You too, you remember."

"Everything," Benny said. "Every bloody thing that ever happened to me. Every time I hurt anybody or did wrong. Every time I was too smart for my own good. Every wrong guess."

"The right ones too," Gabol said.

"No. You forget those."

Gabol asked, "Why did they hurt each other?"

"I can't tell you," Benny said. "Or I can give you ten reasons, which amounts to no reason at all. Mainly because they'd never had to worry about survival before, hardly knew what the word meant, and all of a sudden they were right up against it. Don't ask me to judge them."

"No," Parsons said. "It's not our job to judge. Only to gather information."

"That's a judgment right there," Benny said.

"Some of them killed. Their own comrades. That is, buddies."

Now Benny laughed. It was a moderately painful experience. "Comrades is all right," he said. "An ancient and honorable word."

"You're thinking better," Parsons said. "Quicker."

"Good food," Benny said, "fresh air. Shuffleboard."

"You got the cable?"

"Yes."

"You knew about the little girl."

"Yes. I had three letters in all."

"Home soon," Parsons said, and sighed.

"Are you married?"

"No," Parsons said. "Almost, once. Better without. I move around too much."

"I move around too much too," Benny said.

"You've never seen your son?" Gabol asked.

"Oh yes. He was three or four months old when I left. The usual pound of hamburger."

"It'll all be so new," Parsons said.

"Well yes," Benny explained. "I've been away for some time."

Gabol said, "If you were a tough professional officer, what sort of thing would you report? What sort of bad conduct? In general. Never mind about Ewald."

Dying, Benny thought. The worst sin. Maybe the only sin, the ones who simply sat there and died. "You're asking me to judge." The hopeless. But hope was the last sham. Man's whatness; nature's so-whatness.

"Use military standards," Gabol said. "We won't

hold you to them or ask for names. We just want an idea."

"All right," Benny said. "Stealing food and cigarettes, even from the wounded. Also clothes. Informing. Assault on an officer. And at least one officer struck enlisted men and beat one up. Murder. Refusal to obey orders. Refusal to accept, abide by, acknowledge rank. Refusal to escape. Refusal to live."

A silence followed. Benny gazed first at Parsons and then at Gabol and then at his own hands folded in his lap. He felt prim and wanted to laugh.

"Well, you've left out at least one," Parsons said finally. "Collaboration."

"Let's talk about that one," Gabol said.

"All men are second cousins," Benny said.

9

FROM THE COMPOUND we could see the Yalu River, gray and sluggish, jostling sullen floes westward; unnamed black birds swept low, beat lazy wings, planed into the white woods. The camp had been a village, and I wondered where the villagers were. We had been shipped north by truck, some of the trucks open and the men freezing again, hunched and huddled again, too cold for tears. Again we had arrived by night, so that I never knew through what gate, beneath what sign of doom or welcome, I had entered upon a new life; and we were herded into huts, again regaled with millet and boiling water. In the morning we saw that our huts were houses, homes once, thatched, mud walls, two or three rooms. After more millet and hot water I took a turn about the grounds, checking my men in three of the huts and repulsed by guards here and there until I knew my perimeter. I could see the river and dozens of huts and decided that this would be home for some time. Back in my own hut I attempted cheer. "They going to give us food?" Bewley asked. Bewley was a slim black Pfc. and a Christian.

"I hope so. Happy Valentine's Day."

Trezevant said, "No stoves, Lieutenant. But there's a crazy kind of basement, a hole in the ground and some kind of tunnel."

"I'll ask. I saw smoke."

"Yuscavage's shoulder's bleeding again."

"We need food."

"We need clothes too. Socks worn out and all."

"Paper panes," I said. "They have glass in one of the huts."

"Some of the men shitting their clothes a lot."

"I know. Let's put them together."

There were eleven of us in the three rooms. Thronging the largest, we sat against dusty walls. In the dim morning light we were phantoms, the remnant of a plague. "We can't change clothes," Scafa said weakly. "No clothes." He picked at a scabby pimple. Pale: they were paper-pale.

"It's all right," I lied. "We all smell rotten. I'll see the commander today. Or somebody. It can't get worse. Now listen, you've got to take care of each other. You've got to take care of the sick ones. The rest of you have got to have work, something to do, some purpose. You understand?"

No one spoke.

"They're going to starve us," Trezevant said.

"I doubt it."

"They'll just let us die," Yuscavage said. "I got blood all over."

"No. They could have shot us. They don't give a damn about us, but we're hostages and we've got some of theirs too."

"They don't give a shit about theirs," Mulberg said.

122

"There's millions of them. They don't care if they lose half."

"They're men and they care," I said, not sure. "And then"—the foolish things a man could say—"there's public opinion. World opinion. Propaganda. We have to hang on, live till spring. We start with today." Hit that line. "We live one day at a time. Settle in all you can, and try to keep clean. How many dysenteries?"

Three.

"You three in one room. Trezevant, detail orderlies. Two hours each healthy man, for two hours he's responsible for the sick. Feeds them and cleans them up."

"With what?"

"Rags, anything. I'll scrounge. Keep moving all you can. Walk around."

"I can't walk ten steps," Scafa said.

"Not you three."

Mulberg asked, "Where's the toilet?"

We gaped at him. "Somewhere outside," I said. "Another thing: decide among yourselves whether you want to share and share alike. There may be a cigarette now and then, or a piece of bread."

"Bread." Collins clowned, panting like a dog. "Jesus Christ, bread."

"Try not to think about food," I said. "It won't be easy, but try not to think about it." I sought the right words, why was I not Kinsella. "This is the worst you'll ever have it. In your whole lives. Whatever you have in you, God or politics or gung ho, you need it now. You can die like pigs or live like pigs and it doesn't seem much of a choice but it is. The one big

123

choice and nobody can make it for you. You can starve and freeze and live up to your nose in shit and blood and pus and vomit and still make it. If it's any help, the officers are no better off."

"No officers here," Mulberg said.

"I said officers. You'll do what Trezevant says and Trezevant will do what I say."

"Bullshit," Mulberg said.

Collins said, "Haw."

"Shut up," Trezevant said.

"We're dying," Mulberg snarled. "What the hell good is officers?"

"You're not dying," I said. "And if your officers are no good, you'll know about it soon enough. For now, do as you're told. Start with a dressing for Yuscavage. He'll tell you how. I'll go make trouble, and see what happens. Settle in, now."

Scafa said, "Will we get mail?"

So I made a sortie to my perimeter, and was menaced by a guard, a rifle, a bayonet, and pronounced the magic words. "Die-foo." The guard paused. I pointed with authority to a tendril of gray smoke rising from the center of the village. "Die-foo. I want to talk to an officer." I prodded imaginary epaulets. The guard inspected me like a motorcycle cop; he grounded the weapon and cocked his head instead. He wore a quilted coat and a fur hat and canvas boots. Our steaming breath mingled. Right. All men are brothers. "Die-foo," he said. I nodded. I wondered what I looked like. Helmet, lined jacket bloody now, wool trousers also bloody, even the boots, encrustations and gobbets. Long hair, dirty beard: a god damn guerrilla, that's what I was. I took heart. Partisan Beer. And then, a moment I would always remember, the end of the war, the end of all war, bizarre and durable mankind vanquishing the poxy fates, this guard dug into a pocket, extracted a cardboard box, drew from it one cigarette, and offered the cigarette to me. I stood paralyzed: old movies again, a trap. Nonsense. Slowly my hand rose; I accepted the cigarette, and nodded. "Hsieh-hsieh," I said, Benny of a thousand tongues, knowing "thank you" by now, the rootless cosmopolite, and the guard grinned, erupting in a long string of nonsense syllables, his eyes laughing. I smiled weakly, a forced smile but the first in some time; I felt the unaccustomed tug at socially atrophied muscles. Therapy required. I slipped the cigarette into a shirt pocket. I gestured again at the rising smoke and gabbled, making the sign for speech with my frozen fingers. White man speak with forked thumb. The guard seemed dubious, and waved me back to the hut.

Inside, I handed the cigarette to Trezevant delicately, cautiously, ceremoniously, and said, "Sergeant, distribute this."

Before noon Ou-yang came to us with a squad of armed soldiers. "Doctor Beer," he said. "I trust I find you *well*."

"We need everything," I said. We were standing in the doorway, Trezevant a little way off; the others sprawled or came to sit against the walls; they watched like orphans. "This is inhuman."

"We too need everything," Ou-yang said harshly. "Unlike you, we are not *prepared* to make war all over the world."

I stood mute.

After an angry moment he went on. "How many are you?"

"Eleven."

"And how many able-bodied?"

"Seven, counting myself."

"Have four men go with these two. They will carry wood. Who is your second in command?"

"Sergeant Trezevant," I said, and Trez stepped forward.

"A Negro," Ou-yang said. "How do you do, Sergeant." He extended a hand. Trezevant hesitated.

"It's all right," I said.

They shook hands. Ou-yang spoke in Chinese and then said to Trezevant, "Go with this man. He will *demonstrate* the stove."

My men murmured and sighed. "Go along," I said. "Mulberg. Collins. Bewley. Sunderman. Go with these soldiers and fetch wood. Don't fool around. Just do it."

To Ou-yang I said, "We need blankets badly and some cloth for dressings and cleaning. Warm clothes. I see wires and a socket. Is there power? Can we have a bulb?"

Ou-yang smiled, suddenly and broadly. Why? I was taken by surprise, almost by warmth. "Yes," he said. "You may have a *bulb*. You will not need blankets."

"We're not supermen," I said. "We freeze to death like anybody else."

"I must remember that," he said, and laughed. "You will not need blankets because the *heat* of the fires will circulate beneath the *floor*."

"Thank God. We can strip the sick."

"I can give you rags. There will be a *distribution* of clothing this afternoon. There are no medicines. But in

126

honor of your arrival there will be an extra ration
tonight.''

Again the men murmured and sighed. Ou-yang took
them all in with an orator's glance. "We are, whatever
you think, civilized people, far more so than you. We
have not invaded California. We have no prisoners
abandoned to their fate in camps along the Canadian
border." He chuckled, jolly and pleased, and fell cold
again. "You are prisoners, and not guests. We will not
let you die but we will not . . . *baby* you either."
Another linguist. What was this odd habit, this affecta-
tion, where had he learned it, emphasizing a word here
and there, shouting it almost, as if he were transposing
Chinese tones into English. At *random*. "You will
fetch your own wood, every day, under guard, or every
second day. You may wash clothes when there is water
left from meals. You may dig a latrine under guard.
Later on you will perhaps write *letters* and be given
reading material. An officer will come later with *more*
regulations. And in summer," he paused and nodded
amiably, dreamily, the emperor, the great Khan, a
boon, a boon, "in summer you may *swim* in the Yalu
River."

The frozen earth refused spades. Bewley was
marched off and returned with two picks. He and Ewald
assaulted the adamant ground, alternating blows, mar-
rying into an angry, explosive rhythm; we others
watched, breathed at the same angry pace so that each
stroke seemed to raise a puff of frosty mist. Bewley and
Ewald set their teeth; their eyes glittered, their chests
heaved, the picks rose and fell, rose and fell; they
grunted and we grunted with them; stroke, grunt, puff,
stroke, grunt, puff. They halted, we all halted; Collins

127

and Mulberg stepped in. Bewley slumped. Ewald stood grim, triumphant. We—they—worked for a full hour. We admired our creation. Ewald urinated before us all and a cheer went up with the hiss, the hovering white steam. Bewley and Sunderman were marched off with the tools. "Good arch," Trezevant said to Ewald, "great range." We returned to the hut. Scafa had fouled himself. We sprawled. We waited.

The extra ration proved to be one cup of cracked corn for each man. The black kettle squatted neutral over the fire; into the boiling water we chuted our millet, our cracked corn; Trezevant stirred, like an alchemist. The men sat sullen, cradling cups like blind beggars. Collins and Mulberg swore steadily. Those two were brown-haired, large-nosed, might have been brothers; Mulberg was taller and heavier. I fed Scafa, Trezevant fed Cuttis, then I fed Oldridge. It was more than dysentery; it was exhaustion, despair, hunger, loss of blood, of juices. Sunderman said, "How long till real chow, I wonder," and I had not the heart to tell him, but Trezevant did: "This is real chow. You eat it all, soldier. Remember there's children starving in China."

"I mean, when the kitchens get set up."

"The kitchens are all set up," Trezevant said, hulking, calm. "Shit. I grew up on meals like this." The men were warm; in places the floor was hot, and they shifted.

"Plenty of wood, anyway," I said. "We'll keep a fire watch at night."

Mulberg said, "We?"

"You," I said. For a moment, after the grainy slush, the belly was full, but soon the hunger returned, like a boy's lust, a miser's greed. In the first camp shock had protected us; in the storm of rage, hate, guilt and fear there had been little passion to spare for hunger. And then days of dull indifference; reprieved from death by fire, we clotted slowly into death by ice, and the spirit glimmered low; even Kinsella congealed. Then we had been moved, and it was as if the simple conquest of physical space revived us; first onto the trucks, then into the sharp wind; men complained of hunger again, and I rejoiced that they were so alive. In the hour before our arrival, and for the rest of that night, I had known hunger as a cancer, an intruder, a hostile foreign body sucking my substance; I had contracted, quivered, clenched my teeth against it; I was popeyed and brittle with hunger, and visions of sugarplums danced in my head, also brisket, Yankee bean soup, charlotte russe, fried eggs and even beef testicles, which I had eaten only once and which were prodigiously listed as frivolités du chef ("The turnover in the kitchen," my then inamorata had remarked, "must be considerable").

All this running through my cretin's noggin, my gut pleading. In thine image. At the point of death man is obliged to fart and giggle. Retching and yakking. Well enough to warn the men against culinary fantasies, but a man brought up on Hannah's and Pinsky's notions of the necessary tended toward gustatory masturbation in the best of times. Trezevant scoffed but had not achieved a couple of hundred pounds on collard greens alone, whatever they were; I would ask him. Chitlins I knew, and hominy. And Ewald, silent vengeful Ewald, buttery Ewald: on what Scandinavian glories had he waxed fat? I guessed at eight or nine hundred calories a day, so far; and our army liked thirty-five hundred. The Chinese army? Less. Far less, and it would not be easy

129

now to explain that Americans were different. Different. How, different?

Trezevant disinterred the cigarette, lit it, held it to Oldridge's lips. "A cigarette!" Sunderman said. Trezevant held it to Cuttis's lips, to Scafa's, took a drag himself and passed it on. I opened my mouth to decline the gift, but an obscure echo of some militant uncle checked the impulse: if Trez should think it was color? I drew in smoke, passed the cigarette: "No more for me. I quit." "I don't smoke," Mulberg said, and Ewald declined with a shake of the head.

There had been no distribution of clothing, but three wadded yards of cheap cotton had been flung into the hut. I had sponged Yuscavage's shoulder with hot water and bound him up, no infection; the wound would heal slowly but it would heal. There were other wounds to come, some perhaps that would not heal.

They rested, limp in the light of the puny bulb.

"Sons of bitches never brought clothes," Collins said.

"That corn was enough excitement for one day," I said. "Hell, we're warm."

Collins scoffed. "Corn. And those slant bastards eating chop suey. With meat. And then fucking each other."

"Shut up," I said.

"That's what I heard," Collins said. "They fuck each other."

"Shut up," I said.

"Go to hell," Collins said.

"Democracy," I said. "No more officers."

"That's it," he said.

"Step outside?"

Trezevant laughed and I caught, or thought I caught, a gleam of approval. Trezevant was no child. Ewald might be. I looked at my little platoon, each in turn, and wondered who would live and who would die.

Next day we were marched, those who could walk, to a long wooden shed where each man was issued a pair of cotton socks and a padded blue cotton uniform; and then marched home again. A flying squad arrived shortly with an identical issue for the prostrate, though we did not dress the dysenteries. The uniforms were all the same size, 38 short, I judged, single-breasted, good needlework, nothing fancy in the cut. Chinese quartermasters seemed, like all quartermasters, grudging malcontents. As in any advanced society we were listed: name, rank, serial number, date of birth. Under guard, Kinsella visited and delivered a brief but pungent patriotic oration. He left amid silence. I wondered if our little world was improving or degenerating: we had heat now, and clothing, and what might pass for food, but in the new uniforms the men seemed more, well, uniform: more silent, passive, acquiescent, as if made brutish, almost content by the ordeal and its end. At the noonday meal they were complacent, considerate, benevolent. I too accepted: perhaps now I would not die. I thought of Carol, and of Jacob, and was too empty for tears.

"Ou-yang," I said to the guard, and was escorted to Ou-yang. I was offered a chair and a cup of tea. I accepted a cigarette. I had decided that I would decline nothing. Mark that down. I stuck the cigarette behind my ear and was startled by the soundless echo of a Frenchman who had once taken two from me: "pour

131

mon frère qui n'a pas de travail." "How many doctors have you?"

"One," Ou-yang said. "Pee-joe. Do you know that word?" I shook my head.

"Pee-joe," Ou-yang said. "It means *beer* in Chinese."

"Die-foo pee-joe," I said.

"No. Pee-joe die-foo. Name first, title second. We Chinese, you know. Backward. *Upside* down. Look here." He opened a desk drawer, rummaged, unfolded a map. "The world." He passed it to me, and I examined it with a bewildering sense of error and dislocation: a huge central land-mass, bracketed by oceans in turn bracketed by small strips of the good old U.S. of A.; the edges of the map ran through Grand Forks, Oklahoma City, Fort Worth. "A new perspective," I said.

"Travel is broadening," he said.

I returned the map. "I want permission to move freely. Let me have bandages and a simple antiseptic."

"House calls," Ou-yang said, and I could not help laughing. Treason. Sorry. The laughter seized me and I struggled to control it. We would all go mad and die laughing. Perhaps the Chinese would win quickly. For the first time I contemplated the war's end, and was sobered. Perhaps the Americans would drop the bomb. Perhaps we would kill everybody and occupy Asia. Homesteaders. Frontiers. Free land for all, no more unemployment.

Deliberately I calmed myself. On a shelf behind Ou-yang stood a small white porcelain bowl inlaid with a translucent pattern of rice grains. I concentrated on the bowl. I counted the grains. Sanity returned. I craned: in the bowl were three gnarled tubers, yellow-brown.

Ou-yang was pensive, and sipped tea. This was so civilized. I recalled movies, the British and German officers discussing Shakespeare. Von Waldstein with his year at Oxford. You must understand, my dear Cavendish, that the sun has set on the British empire. "Naturally," I said, additional dialogue by B. Beer, "you have my word for my good conduct."

"But is it not," von Ou-yang asked politely, "every officer's duty to escape?"

"Not this time," I said. "Where? Manchuria? Siberia?"

"Not this time," he said. He appeared to be meditating vaster concepts. "Yes. It's a good idea. You must let me *think* about it."

"Is there a clinic here? For your own men?"

"We have an infirmary," he said. "Two beds, a thermometer, two medicines, one for loose *bowels* and one for constipation. We have *herbs*, for fever. We have not much of anything. Our medical people are in the lines. And the villages," he added sourly. "All war is total war now."

I agreed wearily. "Forget that. We have other problems, terrible problems. This is a real mess, the end of the world. There are men who need amputations. Transfusions. There'll be pneumonia. There's dysentery, there's internal bleeding, there's starvation. We need a whole hospital. Do you see? If I can't treat them, a lot of these men will die."

"Then they will die," Ou-yang said equably. "Many have died already."

"It's inhuman." I remember my fists were balled in my lap and I was no longer full of insane laughter. "Let me use your infirmary."

"No."

"Two hours a day. An hour."

"No."

No. Redress, petition. My congressman. The Red
Cross. I bowed my head and emitted a sobbing growl,
pure defeat, pain.

"You are not a permanent soldier," Ou-yang said.

"Sometimes I wonder," I said. "No. I was drafted.
I think of myself as a permanent doctor. And now a
permanent prisoner."

"No. Some day you will go *home*." He smiled.
"The sooner the better."

"Amen." We were back in the cinema but the senti-
ment was acceptable.

"Return to your hut," he said. "I will send for
you."

"What are those?" Those tubers.

He turned to see, and frowned. "Wait. I forget the
name in English. Like carrots."

"Turnips."

"Turnips. Pickled."

"Give them to me."

"To you?"

Glumly I sorted phrases. Oh for a world of yes and
no, I live I die I love I hate. "The day may come," I
said, "when we fight for a blade of grass. When we
drink the wind and eat the dead. We can't count on a
damn thing."

"Take them," he shrugged, and dismissed me.

10

"WHAT DOES IT matter who?" Benny asked, starchy, peeved at these gnats. Though Major Cornelius was no mite: tall, thin, white-blond, azure-eyed. A watercolor, slightly run, highlights of intelligence and secret depravity in the eyes. "You want to know why."

"We want to know all we can," Cornelius said. "And now this." He tapped the questionnaire. "Not as straightforward as we would have liked."

"I don't imagine anything is." To Parsons Benny said, "May I have a cup of that coffee?"

"Sugar? Vap?"

"Both, thanks. You're spoiled rotten."

Alex smiled, sympathetic and priestly.

Gabol asked, "How's your weight?"

"What do you care? You're a shrink."

"Hah. You're an intern."

Without budging, Cornelius seemed to rap for order. "One man in three collaborated," he said.

"One man in three died," Benny said.

"Then start there. Of what?"

"Wounds, dysentery, pneumonia, one heart attack that I know of; inanition."

"And at the hands of the Chinese?"

"None that I know of. Sorry to disappoint. Several beatings, and sustained psychological pressure, but no physical torture and no killings. Not on my turf, anyway."

"On your what?"

"Never mind," Benny said.

"How many could have been saved by good medical care?"

"Two-thirds," Benny said. "Maybe all. And good food. Or no war."

"How did the survivors react?"

"React?" This albino. "Same way civilians do, down deep. Indifference. Relief that it was the other guy, or that there was more to go around."

"Benny," Gabol said reproachfully.

"Socks particularly," Benny said. "Socks wore out fast. In winter an extra pair was useful."

Cornelius sighed.

"Oh listen," Benny said, "we were all half-dead. There were bunches that hung together, took care of each other. But death was a fact of life. At first, anyway. Hardly anybody died after the first six months, but we never knew. It wasn't a special occasion. No flowers, no music. Just haul him out and bury him. We had one man used to say a prayer when he heard about a death, but he was a crazy."

"Did progressives and reactionaries respond the same way?" Alex spoke softly, genuinely curious. "To the deaths, I mean."

"There weren't any progressives and reactionaries while we were dying. That came later."

"Your own feelings?"

"Frustration."

136

"Anger?"

"Professional."

"Sympathy?"

Benny took refuge in coffee. Soon he said, "Yes."

They waited. "Go on," Cornelius said.

"I can't," Benny said. "Any man who dies, it might have been you. So you're sorry for him. Millions of people die every day."

"You're a help," Gabol said.

"You haven't really asked me anything," Benny said. "It's like the third grade here. We must all be happy that they went to heaven."

"We'll change the subject," Cornelius said. "Tell us about the quarrels, the fights. Race, politics, whatever."

"There wasn't much, considering how long we were there. A few fights about thieving, a few raids, a little gang war, a little racial stuff, but that was unimportant."

"Religion?"

Benny shook his head.

"Politics?"

"Some." Ewald: rest in peace. "Not so much between progs and reactionaries either. They were segregated."

"Then what was it?"

Benny indulged impish longings. "One: whether we should have gone in there or not. Two: whether it was better to give them what they wanted and take the food, the privileges, the amenities, or tell them to go to hell. Later on, three: whether our own government was selling us out. Four: whether Eisenhower was or was not less, as much, or more of a horse's ass than Truman."

"You take this lightly," Cornelius said, icy.

"Yessir. But it's the truth."

"If he starts talking polite talk," Gabol said, "it won't help us. Some of these other fellows are lying all the time."

"Well, I understand that," Cornelius said. "I can understand that normal standards of respect would suffer erosion."

"Hear hear," Benny said easily. Respect! Erosion! A plague on all their houses, on every plump, prating, pious Pecksniff . . . paranoia. "It was the only entertainment we had."

"Tell us more about your second point," Alex said. "The collaborating."

"Nothing you can't guess. Once in a while a man would disappear suddenly, transferred or whatever, and we used to wonder if he'd gone over, or what. So somebody would say he damn well should have, and a fight would start. But anybody who said he damn well should have, could have done it himself, and didn't, so he was only making noise. More entertainment."

"You're speaking now of your own squad. Platoon."

"Yes. There were others. The broadcasts. The defectors. You know more about that than I do."

"Yuscavage? Bewley?"

"Yuscavage just disappeared. Bewley was a Christian. And a Negro. Maybe that mattered." He asked Gabol, "Any correlations?"

"Correlations? We haven't even got the facts yet."

"Oh," Benny said. "Facts."

Cornelius tacked: "Were there women in the camp?"

"A few. Clerks. Not for us. Couldn't tell them from

the men, hardly. Baggy pants, baggy jackets.''

"Were they used?''

"Used?''

"Bait?''

"Not that I know of.'' Benny smiled wistfully but at the notion he glowed, prickled and throbbed. "They missed a trick, didn't they. Puritan revolutionaries. Listen,'' he said earnestly, "the Chinese are not savages. You understand? They are highly civilized and very angry and contemptuous of barbarians. They don't use women that way. Women were slaves for centuries, but now some of their heroes are women.'' And mine, he thought, perturbed and ashamed, a lecherous mutt, a man of the past. No room for him now with his antique gallantries and peremptory prick.

Gabol asked, "Would it have worked?''

Benny shrugged.

"You're full of news,'' Cornelius said.

"Hell,'' Benny said, "this is just gossip. All I really know about is myself.''

"Then talk about yourself,'' Alex said.

"Just a moment,'' Cornelius said, and made a great play of leaning back and assuming magisterial airs. "You're being deliberately evasive, we know that, and you're doing your men a disservice. You had some freedom of motion. You saw a lot, including misconduct. You saw a friend killed. You've got to help now. You've got to level.''

"Oh I know some things that happened,'' Benny said, "but not their consequences. Not whether they were right or wrong. I won't judge. Nobody has the right. And I didn't see him killed. I saw him dead.''

"The right?'' Cornelius was almost lofty. "Some of these men betrayed themselves, their army, their country. You may not want to believe it, but this is for their own good. For everybody's.''

"Maybe their army and their country betrayed them. Where were you when we needed you?''

Cornelius scowled. "If we'd known how to prepare them, they'd have done better. Not died, turned on their own, defected. We're not out to hang anybody.''

"Ah, come on,'' Benny said.

"Benny,'' Alex said gently, and Benny remembered that Cornelius was a major but Alex a lieutenant-colonel, the chain of command, remembered who was boss here, shadowy regions of cop and dossier. "Benny, some of these men made propaganda for the enemy. Somewhere there may be a line between that and firing on your own troops; if there is such a line we want to find it. A lot of what happened was shameful. Some of it was treason.''

Benny groaned. "Propaganda. What a big word. And was it all lies? Do we incinerate white kids? You're worried about good and bad,'' he burst out bitterly, a spasm of twisted pride, "well, I'm worried about good and evil.''

"Do you think there was truth in it?''

"Yes,'' Benny said more quietly. "A little. Possibility, if not truth. Hang me.''

"Nonsense,'' Alex murmured. "We're old friends. But the major's right: you're not much help.''

"All I know is me.''

"Then talk about you.''

"Peccavi.'' Benny sighed. In this chrome-and-teak confessional. The lulling throb of engines. Portholes, blue circles. This morning bacon and eggs. Last night chicken. Salt, pepper, soft bread, hot coffee. Sheets, magazines, soap, pinups. "I never killed,'' he began correctly. "I never informed. I cut no records, wrote no speeches, transmitted no Christmas greetings. Never stole from my own men," he was in his stride now, "and not that I recall from the Chinese—though I would have. I assaulted no officers, but in moments of severe and understandable stress I walloped a couple of enlisted men. I practiced medicine on any human being in need, and once accepted food for myself that I could not distribute among the men." He had his second wind now. "I cursed a lot, and indiscriminately. I quit once, but was restored to active duty by a few well-chosen words. I was falsely accused by my own men of high crimes and misdemeanors. I was flagrantly lacking in reverence, optimism and moral tone. I made no effort to escape. I declined to pray."

"That'll do," Cornelius said.

"I begged," Benny recited. "I humbled myself in the face of the enemy and begged turnips and aspirin. Pickled turnips."

Wearily Cornelius said, "We're only trying to avoid a repetition of this sort of collapse."

"The Chinese told me," Benny said, "that they were only trying to avoid a repetition of this sort of war."

Cornelius snorted. "And you believed them."

Benny laughed aloud.

"You never believed in this war." Alex was matter-of-fact.

"Not for me. Wasn't even supposed to be there." After brief consideration he went on: "I'll give you the same answer I once gave Ou-yang. I do not believe in killing anyone today for the sake of some maybe-if-we're-lucky better world tomorrow. Because that automatically makes it a worse world tomorrow, right

141

there. I can conceive of dying today for a better tomorrow. But not killing."

Gabol asked if he would kill one man to save ten.

"Sure," Benny said, "but not on some politician's say-so. Hell, I've killed. You forget I was a corporal once, down there where life is real and earnest."

"What about World War Two?" Cornelius pounced, real and earnest. "If you had it to do again, would you fight?"

They eyed him hard, like wary guards. He saw prison camps, kapos, saw himself in a striped suit, 57359; the blood hummed in him. Hitler! "I might not," he said tightly, prickling and flushing as vengeful ranks of uncles and aunts surged in hieratic wrath; "I might not," he said again, breathless (God! leave me alone! all I want is to be left alone!); and sat panting in the warm Pacific air. "Oh hell," he said, "of course I'd fight." Hunched and stiff, he rocked briefly. "But there's another answer somewhere. Something I don't know yet."

"You killed for your country," Cornelius said.

"Moy nayshun," Benny grieved. "What ish moy nayshun?"

Agog, they dithered and scowled.

Alex shook his head ruefully. "Benny, you can't lick us; better join us. Let me ask you something. Suppose I said I thought being Jewish had something to do with this."

Hello again. Benny started to say, "I am that I am," but refrained, not wishing to be offensive. Cornelius spoke for him. "That's out of order, Alex. There are dead Jewish soldiers buried in Korea."

As opposed, Benny thought, to live Jewish soldiers buried in Korea.

"Amen," Gabol said.

Benny rather thought that Alex was right. Alex twinkled. He and Benny understood.

"And plenty of good white Christians collaborated," Cornelius said.

Any second now, Benny thought, he will tell us that there are good and bad in all races.

"I didn't say worse," Alex said mildly. "I only said different. Maybe even better."

"There's good and bad in all races," Cornelius said.

"Amen," Gabol said.

Benny decided that it was not his quarrel.

"Let's drop this," Alex said. "Come back to it later. Why did the Turks behave so well?"

"Okay," Benny said. "Let me think a minute." He glanced out the porthole; he rose, and went to stare at the calm sea, the deep, serene blue, everlasting. Some day he would learn to sail, and would sit alone in a small white boat, sleepy under the blazing sun, alone and untroubled. "The Turks," he said, still gazing out at the sea, "were a real army. Superiors had the power of life and death over subordinates. Perfect fascism to do a fascists' job. They were trained to kill and they signed on to kill, and the big fellows threw the fear of death into the little fellows. Hell, their officers gave *orders*. Their enlisted men refused absolutely to obey the Chinese, and took orders only from their own officers, and the Chinese respected that. The Turks were *soldiers*."

Cornelius said impatiently, "What's all this got to do with our boys?"

11

OUT OF A white sky, sweeping across the gray Yalu, an incessant, merciless wind beat down from Manchuria. "I'm a Mediterranean type," I mourned.

At the fence Kinsella said, "They don't want us to die." We stared emptily at an impassive guard, an armed bundle of quilted garments. Somewhere tailors, stitching, Chinese Jacobs. Kinsella's eyes roved, sunken, black hollows. "We have to believe that. What did he tell you?"

"Haircuts. Soon."

"Photographers," he said. "Remember in the war they took pictures, both sides, showing off? Barbershops, volleyball."

I shivered. "Let's go back." My knees wobbled. The earth was iron-hard.

Kinsella puffed, "Maybe they'll give us a banana for the pictures, or a tennis racket."

"Better a banana."

"Refuse it," he said. "Tell your men. They're smart bastards and they'll use us. I don't know how but they'll use us."

"I asked him if we could farm in spring. He said no."

"God damn. An ear of corn."

"Butter. Salt." My stomach contracted, fluttered.

"I figured something out," Kinsella said. "Their turbines are all along here, the Yalu, their dams and power plants. I bet this village was workers' housing once, and they put us here so we wouldn't bomb the plants and all. It stands to reason."

"Sounds right. Small comfort."

"You're working for them."

I was too tired to make speeches.

"The men don't like it."

"Where you from?" I asked him.

"Oklahoma."

"How long you been in?"

"Since forty-one."

"I heal the sick," I said. "Most of the time not even that. We're losing dozens, Major."

"You're working for them too."

"For us too. You rather they lock me up?"

"No skin off my ass," Kinsella said. "Just remember you're an American soldier."

"Right," I said.

"You've got an obligation to escape."

Less weary, I might have been startled. I scuffed along, skinny and scant of breath.

"You've got an obligation to help others escape. We've been talking it over. You're in a privileged position." For a dozen paces he meditated. "Beer," he said, "I want you to bring me every scrap of information that might help."

A lunatic.

"About the guards, the fences, lights, arms, gates—

145

ánything. You have a great responsibility and a great opportunity.''

"Yessir," I said.

"Has he said anything about the other camps?"

"No."

"God damn. Spring and summer's the best shot, maybe early fall, lots of cover and growing things. For food.''

"Right.''

"If we could get to the river.''

"If you could get to the river," I said, "you'd drift down into the bay. Then what? Port Arthur?''

"Our navy," he said. "These bastards have no navy. I bet our ships are patroling right now."

I was silent. Such a mind exacted admiration.

"Find out all you can. Report to me every day.''

"Yessir," I said.

I woke in boneless terror, out of breath, freezing; a hand covered my mouth. By the dawn's milky light I saw that it was Trezevant's; I breathed, my pulse stuttered alive. Trez's eyes directed my own; without budging I scouted the doorway, and sighted two lean brown rats, alert, one sitting up on his hindquarters and peering about. I observed. Even in the half-light they were bright-eyed, tiny glass beads, and they were whiskered, and had small ears that twitched and pricked, and long tails. The tails were gray and naked; otherwise these might be pets, wee wild creatures, short-haired, clean, nervous.

Trezevant sat up. The rats slid out of sight.

Two dawns later Scafa screamed. I stumbled into the sickroom and found him keening in horror, hands over his ears, fingers stiff, on the edge of madness. "A rat, a rat on my chest." He heaved and gasped.

"Just a wood rat," I said, soothing, crooning; a wood rat, yes, the fields and forests, nature's creatures, like bunnies and squirrels, "just a wood rat. They eat roots and berries. They won't hurt you."

"Oh, oh," Scafa said. "You sure, Lieutenant?"

"I'm sure," I lied, and after that we saw rats often, at dawn, or in the dugout basement; and heard them, skitter skitter, rejoiced in them, named them, and argued whether this one was MacArthur or Mao. I would have had the men cook and eat them, at least in a stew, but their horror was primordial; they glared, pointed, unclean, unclean; I feared mutiny, anarchy, the chaos of despair, and shut up.

"Yo, it hurts," Trez moaned. "Shooting pains in the legs here, at night mostly."

I contemplated this big black man. Travel was broadening, no question. Cela change les idées. We were sipping hot water, two military gentlemen at tea, a brief chat, morale, faction and pother amongst the other ranks. "Me too. Keep it quiet. If we quit they'll all quit."

"Be pleased to quit," Trezevant said. "Purely love to quit."

"Not you."

"Well no." He summoned a grin. "First time in years though, I wouldn't mind going home."

"Where's that?"

"Lee County, Arkansas, about ten mile from Marianna. Real shitkicker country."

"What did you do before?"

"Ate shit," he said comfortably, "and joined the army as soon as I could." The grin again. "Lied about my age."

"Sharecropper?"

"My papa. Still is when he ain't sick. Mama died from too many children and too little else. I suppose you had it real good."

"I did."

"I heard you were in the war."

"That's right," I said. "Corporal."

"Then you know a little."

"A little."

"Fight much?"

"Germany. Purple Heart, even." Braggart, hero. All men are little brothers.

"I wonder do you get a Purple Heart for prisoner."

"No. Back pay."

"Better yet. What about these pains, now?"

"It's scurvy," I said.

"Scurvy? I thought that was sailors."

"It's diet. No greens, no fruit. They'll all have it."

"Mm. Oldridge going to make it?"

"No," I said, "but keep quiet about it."

"Funny fellow," Trezevant said. "Little old Florida cracker, old and fat. They call him Pinky, you know that?"

"Pinky. I could save him with spinach, oranges."

"Oranges. Oranges from Florida. Maybe we ought to eat those rats."

"We will," I said. "Bet a dollar."

"That's a bet," the big man said. "You first. Officers first." He laughed softly.

●　　●　　●

148

I treated Turks from the Turkish Brigade, Britons from the 27th Commonwealth Brigade. "Just forget those designations," Kinsella said crisply. "You know nothing about the units."

"They know it all," I said. "How many Turkish brigades are there? Or British?"

"Just the same," Kinsella said. "How many you figure we are all of us? You move around."

"Seven, eight hundred." Filipinos, Koreans.

"I don't suppose we could bust out."

"We couldn't bust out of a used condom," I said. "There's a hundred men dying and nobody else can even pee straight." Thus myself, concertmaster and friend of Beethoven. Gourmets may rhapsodize. Those who eat shit talk shit. In the house of the hanged man everybody mentions rope. Soon we would be speculating on the afterlife. Some would go mad: Beer first. No. I was a species of captain and would leave the ship last.

Oldridge died that night. In the morning we found him dead and I bore his dog tags to Kinsella. He was a collector of dog tags, a numismatist, a heap in a sack like a hoard of strange shillings. "It's bad," he said.

"It'll be worse," I said. "He's sent for me again."

"Tell him we're dying. We absolutely must have more food. Remind him about Nuremberg."

"Nuremberg." I made a serious effort to comprehend.

"War crimes," Kinsella said briskly.

"Right," I said.

Ou-yang's very bulk lent him authority; I felt scrawny, obsequious, a flunky. "Come with me," Ou-yang

said, and I nodded dumbly. We walked beneath un-
shaded light bulbs, passed offices, a storeroom, a toilet—a toilet! I gaped: an Oriental toilet, one hunkered,
footrests of stone, a chain. I hurried along. The infirmary: a small room, an overhead lamp, a table, cots.
Three patients. "These two," Ou-yang announced,
"have a *rash*. This one has a *wet* ear."

I examined, grunted, emitted the imposing sonorities
of expertise. I must consult with Untermeyer, the mak-
ings of a tragedy, an epidemic of underwear fungus,
evacuate the women, children and bladder. Untermeyer. Ah, to see the Untermeyers here! An unworthy
thought. "These two should wash more often. Bathe it
twice a day with potassium permanganate. All right
then, alcohol. All right then, *soap*, for God's sake.
This one has an infection. Keep it clean and if there's
penicillin, use it."

"Ah, penicillin." Ou-yang spoke; a soldier un-
locked a small cabinet. "Go ahead," Ou-yang said.

Dreamily I inspected the vial, the syringe, the needle. "You took these from me."

Ou-yang said, "Yes."

"My men are dying," I said. "They need food.
They've all got pneumonia. They need medicine."

"We have no medicine. Keep them warm."

I set down the syringe. "I can't do this. I can't come
here and . . . I can't . . ." What was I trying to say? I
prepared the dose, administered the injection. Skin,
blood, all skin was skin, all blood, blood. "Have the
needle sterilized," I said. "Is this aspirin?"

"Yes."

I unscrewed the lid and took six tablets. I wrapped
them in a scrap of newspaper and defied Ou-yang
sullenly, an animal, a dog with a bare bone.

"Keep them," Ou-yang said. "Come with me." He spoke to a soldier. We went back to his office. Already jaded, I ignored the toilet. Ou-yang told me to be *seated*. "We have no food," he said. "It goes to the front lines. All over China people are *hungry*. Some are starving. We have had the country only one year, and there is so much to do. Did you think we *wanted* this war?" He brooded, stocky and sad. "When there is food it will be *distributed*. We are not torturers."

"That may be too late," I said. "We have scurvy now, lots of it."

Ou-yang shrugged. He gestured and a stately plump bald corporal came from the doorway bearing a bowl of rice on which lay two crossed leeks. I gobbled, shoveling the food into a parched mouth. "Tea? Is there tea?" Ou-yang himself poured. I guzzled, and was abruptly and savagely overcome by shame; my throat closed. I pondered that. Then I summoned up all my moral corruption, and ate. In joyous iniquity I cleaned my plate; there are children starving in China. I grew calm, and sucked a tooth. "A mirror," I said. "Is there a mirror?"

"Yes, yes." Ou-yang rummaged. On his desk, a magazine: eagerly I scanned the mysterious characters. Ou-yang handed me a small mirror, and was amused.

My dark stringy hair hung like a wild girl's. My beard—a rabbi! at last!—curled, dry, wiry. My eyes peered from the brush like field mice. My lips were cracked, baked mud. This face. That haunched a thousand hips. "I look like a convict," I said.

"You *are* a convict," Ou-yang said.

"You have no right," Kinsella said flatly.
"Here," I said. "Take three."

151

"What is it?"

"Aspirin."

"Aspirin! God damn, man, that's no help."

"He said there was no food. When it comes we'll have it. I told him it might be too late."

"You're *fraternizing*!" Kinsella said. "Damn you, Beer, you're in trouble!"

"You're kidding," I said.

"You're a soldier," he said. To myself I acknowledged now, hardly hearing him as he rattled on, that I had never known what it was to be a real soldier: to wake with energy, to love plans and tactics and camouflage and the heart-stopping glimpse of an enemy in your sights, the lilting recoil; the satisfying, how satisfying it must be if you love it at all, contortions of flopping dolls that had intended your death and met their own. The coffee and the cigarettes and the tall stories about other battles, women, legendary sergeants, enfilades.

"I had a sergeant once," I said, "who used to take us out for grenade practice and tell us to watch out for flyin derbis."

"You what?"

"Flyin derbis," I said.

"God damn," Kinsella said. "What's that all about?"

"Right," I said.

So I roved my little hell, stumbled over corpses, made my rounds without instruments, without medicine, without hope. I offered vain advice, instructed men in nursing care. I excised dead flesh with a long fingernail, with a contraband metal spoon. I displayed the aspirin to my men, who crowded around me and exclaimed. Trezevant was appointed its keeper. A cold rain persisted, and dark earth swelled through the snow like mange on a polar bear. There was no news of the war. What war? I had a vision: the war was over, the others had all gone home, and these here were penitents, this was their infernal landscape, their limbo, each had killed or betrayed, committed undefined sacrilege, inexpiable. Cuttis went on living, freckled and friendly. Scafa declined. Bewley conversed with Jesus. I stood gaping at the Yalu like a village idiot, and adjured myself to survive.

We were much beset, and business picked up. In every hut a miser's hoard of dog tags. My own still lost. I could steal a pair and be anyone ever after. Never. I am that I am. One morning Collins, sleeping like a fetus, was unable to straighten his legs. "Jesus Christ," he shouted, "I'm paralyzed!" I examined him, stringy Collins, never fat and now all sticks and stones. Wearily but gently, gratefully, it was an occupation, mon métier, I massaged him. Trezevant brought him hot water to sip. The left leg relaxed, millimeter by millimeter slacked and stretched. Ewald worked at the right leg. In half an hour Collins was walking. Ewald went so far as to smile.

I conferred with Trezevant, and he made the announcement: "Only one way to stay alive and this is it, so you men listen. From now on you get up in the morning when we tell you. Never mind seven o'clock and never mind the Chinese. We get you up. Then you wash. And you wash Cuttis and Scafa and anybody else real sick. After chow you police the hut and the grounds. After that you sit down and hunt lice. You dig 'em out and you pop 'em. From now on we fetch wood every day and not every second day. Also, in that room by Cuttis, we make a checkerboard on the floor. We use stones for checkers and every man gets to play two games every day, and you keep track. A tournament, you hear? Prizes to be announced later. And every day before lunch, calisthenics.''

The bitching groan was the first truly human noise out of them in weeks.

But next morning they balked, jeered, cursed. Collins refused to rise at all, and took his ease. Sunderman and Ewald, the firewood detail, shrugged: ''Plenty time tomorrow.'' I looked to Trez for iron, for bone; Trez too shrugged. Trez, Bewley and I turned out for calisthenics. We stood in the wind, hopeless and aimless. ''Well, let's do a few,'' Trez said. We did a few, and returned to the warm hut.

Then Mulberg guttered. For some days he sat mute, staring into his past. The others shied. It was his business. Yuscavage complained of the shoulder. Bewley prayed in a tenor drone and said, ''Jesus the best healer.'' Mulberg ate mechanically or not at all. Then he spent most of several days lying down. ''There's some like that in every hut,'' Kinsella said.

''It's not sickness,'' I said. ''Not like scurvy.'' My own legs were agony at night. Murderous.

''What do you think?''

''I don't know.''

Mulberg asked for ice water. He asked for sherbet. During the third week he refused to eat unless he could have soda water.

''Ice water.'' Kinsella was astounded. ''There's about a dozen asking for different drinks. Root beer. God damn. What is it, anyway?''

''I don't know,'' I said. ''Maybe he's going crazy. I'll do something.''

154

With Trez I went in to Mulberg, who had removed his jacket and covered his head with it. "Mulberg," I called; there was no answer. Trez shook him and nothing happened. "Chow time," I said. Nothing. Together we raised him to a sitting position and I unwrapped his head, then slapped him twice. Modern medicine. He blinked and growled. "Ewald," I called, "bring a bowl of soup." Dull of eye, Ewald would not stir; Trez fetched the millet. He pried Mulberg's mouth open and I poured soup into it. Mulberg gagged, flopped, spat and twisted away. We tried again. He roared and spewed. I slapped him again: "Don't waste food." It was all so useless. But he swallowed the next mouthful; we made him finish, and left him. Next morning we did it again. After chow Mulberg urinated on the floor, lying brutish on his side, his hose limp, spraying; Trez and I were not so much disgusted by bad manners as revolted by gross ignobility. We dragged him outside, stood him up, and played medicine ball with him; shoved him back and forth until he fell, dragged him erect and shoved him some more. We stripped him and threw pebbles at him. He protected his jewels. We tore his hands away; he fought. He rose and howled. He lunged for his pants. We let him dress. "No more shit," Trezevant said. Mulberg stood there panting. "Jumping jacks," Trezevant ordered, and counted. Mulberg executed ten jumping jacks and glowered.

"Three of them just died," Kinsella said. "They just lay down and died."

"Force them," I said. "Humiliate them. Go for the balls."

We kept a few more alive. What for?

● ● ●

155

In early March a social event, a dizzying week. First haircuts, the men sheared, suddenly children, gangling, morons. Then Ou-yang sent for me. He trembled with courteous effort but finally gaffawed. "I must parade you all. You will look like a, a, a field of *melons*."

I smiled sheepishly. Samson, shorn, hot with embarrassment, uneasy, squirming and not tragic at all. Disproportion, chagrin. Vast ears. Dying bums with lice.

"I have some extremely *good* news," Ou-yang said.

I believed nothing and only waited.

Ou-yang's hand rose, a magician's swoop, and a necklace glittered and dangled.

"My dog tags." I was full of wonder.

"And," Ou-yang declaimed, "a box of cigarettes, and a bag of dried peas. And very soon there will be soybeans for your men. Protein."

Dried peas. Soybeans. I tamed a rush of tears.

"So," I told Kinsella, "I patched him up. No idea who he was," and I added awkwardly, perturbed, unquiet, "under duress."

Kinsella was silent and severe.

"It seems he was a political officer, young, rising, God knows, important, brilliant. So I got a reward. And my dog tags back."

Kinsella's hand waited. I dropped the necklace into it. He read, nodded returned it; I looped it into place, a debutante, pearls. "My bunch come first," I said, "but there's these left over." Kinsella took the box, sniffed at it, offered; I declined. He fished at his waistband and produced matches; he lit a cigarette pensively, inhaled, blew smoke, a reverie, jets from his nose. He smiled. "God damn."

"You're trading with the enemy."

"The hell I am. They owe us a damn sight more than this."

"That's something else. He says there's soybeans coming."

"Soybeans." He inhaled again, smiled again. I thought again of newsreels.

"Soybeans are full of good stuff," I said. "Protein."

"Soybeans are for cattle."

"That's us," I said. "Also, this weather's good. Maybe we've hit bottom. Maybe it gets better now."

"Maybe," Kinsella said. "Maybe it's time to crack out of here."

"Right," I said.

We mashed the dried peas in boiling water for Scafa and Cuttis, and I fed them, more useful now, a man with a purpose. I slept with the cloth bag—the peas might last a week—and awoke the first night when Sunderman's hand brushed my face. I didn't know it was Sunderman until I jumped for the bulb, shouting, and scared them all. They scurried and panicked and we lined them up and Trez found the bag in Sunderman's pants. We all stood around quietly, no one moving much or offering suggestions. They were waiting for me to be an officer, but I did not feel at all like an officer. I felt feverish and I tried, made an honest effort (man of the world, doctor, Jew) to do something about the prickles and surges of pure rage, of lunacy almost, that rose and fell; I was trembling inside, and I looked miserably from man to man and probably I would have left Sunderman to them. But Sunderman was also insane and bolted for the door. I grabbed him, a mad dog now, the old corporal; I pushed him off and hit him on the mouth. He caught me on the temple with a right hand and I drove inside it, both arms pumping, to the ribs, the belly, and when he crouched I drew off and hit him where the jaw meets the neck, under the ear, and he went down sideways and slid to the dirt floor. "Pig," I panted, "pig," and the word meant everything. He was conscious and lay there sobbing. The men observed him almost without interest. Trezevant poked at him, big toe to his butt, and said, "All right now. It's over." Sunderman sat up crying, snuffling, four years old, and much—of manhood, passion, hope, resolution—drained out of me. I felt it go. I was very tired. I retrieved my bag of peas and went back to my patch of floor, and lay on my back, and knew that there would be no escape, and that this was the war we had all feared always, the war that would never end. Soon I was crying too. In the morning Scafa was dead.

Kinsella accepted the dog tags and said, "I hear you struck an enlisted man."

"Several times." The warm spell persisted, and the snow was almost gone; bits of green seemed to shout from the earth, and I no longer cared.

"Why?"

"He stole food. Food for the sick."

"You can't maintain discipline by striking enlisted men."

"There is no discipline."

"Yes there is," Kinsella said, "and it's the only hope."

That was unanswerable.

"Don't do it again," he said.

"Yessir."

"How many dead now?"

"Two in my hut. About one in four, all around, maybe one in three."

"God damn," he said. "But it's warmer. Dysentery?"

"My two were. Plenty of that, and pneumonia and scurvy and wounds still open."

"It's inhuman," he said. "And no soybeans yet."

"I quit," I said, and left him. On my way back to the hut I saw a weed, a plain ordinary green weed, the kind with flat leaves and many veins, and I pulled it up and gave it to Trezevant by way of valedictory. "Put it in the pot," I said. "Tell them to find weeds, any kind, and put them in the pot." Then I lay down and did not rise. Trez tried to force-feed me and I pulled rank. "Don't lay a hand on me." On the fourth day, sure enough, I yearned for ice water. Or soda water, what Jacob called Vichy. I saw bottles of it, glistening ranks of bottles on beds of ice, sweating bottles, billions of bubbles. I rolled over and lay face down. I thought of Carol, but her face was misty. "Enough," I said.

I dreamed. I dreamed of a school of fish, a bed of oysters: I was under water with a sack, hovering, slithering, drifting, one floating foot set uncertainly after another in the swirling blue murk; I was harvesting sea cucumbers, greens, greens; and sea slugs, protein, protein. I swept a dozen oysters into my sack, and fish followed, silvery fish with blue and yellow stripes and long fragile trailing fins, and then I saw a hole in the sack and all was lost, no air now. I thrashed, and woke.

Later Kinsella came and said, "Benny, we got sick people. Get up out of there." I made no answer. He stormed and hollered; I heard him, miles away, but I was tired, and tugged the jacket over my head and closed my eyes.

Kinsella ripped the jacket away, pulled me up, and slapped me hard. I smiled faintly and fell back. I knew what he was doing and I approved; he was a good man, a fine fellow, but no. I was at the bottom of the sea and would not rise. I sank into the mud, and my heartbeat slowed. "Oh get up," he said, snarled, "get up." Soon I would die. We were all dying. I would die in three or four weeks. I wished Kinsella would shut up and go away.

His face was close to mine, and I could feel his breath. "Get up," he whispered. "You god damn yellow kike, get up."

Dimly, deeply, I knew his purpose; dimly, deeply, I knew him for my friend, my rock, my major; but I shot up from the floor of the sea, broached with a shriek, and struck for the throat. He slammed me against the wall and agony boiled through me, he had broken me, no air, I tried to shout; my lungs filled, sweet, sweet, salvation! and I wept, and wept, and Kinsella was cradling me and saying it's all right Benny, it's all right Benny, god damn them, it's all right Benny, the soybeans are here. And then he said, this Cuchulainn, a most astonishing thing, and most fiercely he said it. "Man," he said, "remember you weren't born a Jew for nothing."

12

GABOL SAT ROUND-SHOULDERED on a mess table, feet
swinging, countenance engaging, red hair wholesome:
painted silos, Sunday school. "How does it feel, in a
bunch like this?"

Behind a desk Cornelius scowled: progressive education, group therapy, communism. Parsons observed.
Captain Fontaine, stocky, caracul-haired, chewed a
cigar. He had been introduced as a legal officer and
Benny had thought, Good, I'll sue. "We've been living
in a bunch for some time," a Negro lieutenant said.
Grown men tittered.

Gabol said, "None of you knows any of the others.
Or did before. That right?"

Murmurs. That was right.

"No notes," Gabol said. "Feel free."

A lanky man asked, "What's that feel like?" A
corporal.

Another voice: "How about some beer?"

"No beer." Gabol smiled. "Not till you get your
weight back."

Ex-prisoners, they shrugged, wry. More interrogations. They would reach home and their wives would interrogate them.

"Nobody with anything to say? I assume you're glad to be here."

"Food's better," someone said.

"Just talk about whatever you like," Gabol said.

A man yawned. Another blew smoke audibly, whoosh.

Gabol's smile faded. Sour Cornelius puckered.

At the third meeting Cornelius said, "What the hell is the matter with you people? You act like we were the Chinese."

"Haw," someone said.

Benny grinned.

"What's funny?" Cornelius asked.

"Nothing," Benny said.

Cornelius said to Gabol, "This is silly."

"Doctor Beer," Gabol said, "what was the worst time?"

Benny studied his classmates. Gently cynical, experts, jungle-fighters interviewed by a girl from a magazine.

"For me it was the first April," Benny said, "when I stopped being busy and had time to cave in. And then about the first October when we knew there'd be no peace."

"That's the truth," the lanky man said. "That's when I turned in my card and went back to sleep."

"That's when a good many made trouble," Cornelius said. "Those Christmas broadcasts."

"What did you think we were doing?" Gabol asked.

No one spoke. Gabol turned to Benny.

Benny shrugged.

"What did the Chinese say?"

They all looked at Benny.

"Why are you looking at me?"

"We heard," someone said.

"What'd you hear?"

"No hard feelings," the man said. "We all took what we could."

"The hell we did," Benny said. "I could have had chicken every Sunday."

"But you didn't," Cornelius said.

"No."

"Why not?"

Benny shrugged.

"Is that right?" The Negro lieutenant asked. "You didn't?"

"That's right," Benny said.

"Must have done something," the lieutenant said. "Heard your name here and there."

"I doctored."

"Well then."

"I'd do it again."

"You would, hey," the lieutenant said.

"Damn right," the lanky man said. "Long as you ain't an animal you can hold out. Long as you know who you are."

"I'll think about that," the lieutenant said.

"You knew what you were," the lanky man said. "Didn't you now."

"That's a real good point," the lieutenant said. "My apologies, doc."

"Forget it," Benny said.

The lieutenant said, "No, I think I'll try to remember it."

Benny smiled briefly.

"Thing to do," the lanky corporal drawled at Cornelius, "is put us in a little room for three days and wake us at two in the morning and not give us food, and like that."

The men laughed.

Cornelius sighed. Parsons and Fontaine were impassive.

The ship shuddered; engines labored faintly.

Gabol said, "Ve haff vays to make you talk."

An explosion of laughter, murmurs, show biz. Gabol beamed and jiggled his red brows.

A small man spoke, a little dark man with a Roman nose.

"Tell you why I didn't," he said. "I was a cook. I didn't even belong there."

"Nobody belonged there," the lieutenant said.

"I didn't because my captain told me not to," another said. "That man was a real son of a bitch."

"You were all told not to," Cornelius said. "But a third of you did. Not you men, but in general."

"Nobody was getting us out of there," someone said.

"No *news*," someone said. "Far as we knew it was for life."

Murmurs, approval, nods, grunts.

The lanky corporal said, "Hell, the Chinese told us there was lieutenant-colonels cutting records. And on movies."

"That was a long time, dad," someone said. "Two years. And two years by the Yalu is not like two years in the officers' club with beer and pussy."

"Yay ho," someone said.

The corporal again: "The Chinese said you used gas and germs. Did you?"

164

"Of course not," Cornelius said.

Again the breath, the gentle wash, of disbelief.

"Wish you had," the lanky man said. "Got us out of there quicker."

Fontaine spoke for the first time, in a deep rumble. "Suppose we pointed to a man, right now, and said he'd collaborated. How would you feel about him?"

They chewed on it. The lanky corporal spoke. He was blond and slow, a cowboy's face, handsome, wide jaw. "Might not want him to marry my daughter, but I'd pass him a cup of coffee."

"How about me?" the lieutenant asked him.

The corporal grinned. "Got no daughter." The prisoners laughed. Gabol smiled.

"Tell you what you're up against," Benny said. Cornelius squinted, heeding. "What they used to call solidarity. Spend a couple of years in prison. Then ask us."

Approval again, grunts, a council of braves.

"Oh for God's sake," Gabol said. "Help us so this doesn't happen again."

The lieutenant asked politely, "Already planning the next war?"

After a silence a man said, "Solidarity hell. I wouldn't pass him a cup of coffee." He too was a corporal, older, in his thirties, and there were deep lines on his face, sad pouches. "They came for me in the middle of the night. Lots of times. And they put me in a little room for a couple of days. No can, even, a bare floor. And a hundred times they sent for me right before chow, and let me go right after chow. And I never got no mail. And I watched them tear up what letters they let me write. And not only me."

165

"Hell," the lieutenant said, "every man in this room. They ever hit you?"

"No."

"They hit me," the lieutenant said. "That was early on. They hit me twice, drew a little blood even, on the mouth here. And the midnight call. And the no food. And the no mail. And the no exercise. And then they just gave up."

"Okay," the older man said. "And you don't hold it against them damn progs?"

"Ah, maybe a little. But I hold it against these guys too," and he jabbed a thumb at the officers.

"Why?" Gabol asked. "What do you hold against us?"

"Come on," the lieutenant said. "We told you. What the hell were you doing for two years?"

"Making peace," Cornelius said. "It was long and complicated, and we had to fight for every inch. We'd have made peace in a day if they'd been reasonable."

"And they'd have made peace in a day if you'd been reasonable," the lieutenant said reasonably. "And they stalled because they were indoctrinating us, and you stalled because you were indoctrinating their guys."

"That had nothing to do with it," Cornelius said.

"What I'd like to know," Gabol said, "is why you keep calling us 'you.' As if we weren't on your side."

The lieutenant only gazed at him, amiable, almost sunny.

"Oh," Gabol said.

"I once knew a cripple," Benny said, and they all rose to this diversion, a humorous anecdote! a cripple! "And he got drunk one night and told me he wasn't a Democrat or a Republican, capitalist or communist,

Jew or Christian or rich or poor or black or white or even an American, and they could all go to hell; he was a cripple, and nobody who wasn't would ever, ever understand; not just the things you couldn't do at all, but how even reaching for a handkerchief was a job of work, and how the girls looked at you, or didn't, and what a god damn expedition it was to be a hundred yards from a toilet when you had to go, and how everything in the world was upstairs. That was the ultimate wisdom, he said: everything in the world is upstairs.''

Fontaine asked, ''What does all that mean?''

''We're still crippled,'' Benny said. ''What you have here is a bunch of go-to-hell downstairs cripples.''

Gabol said brightly, ''Then maybe you ought to lead this discussion.''

''Not for all the tea in China,'' Benny said, and someone said, ''Yay ho. Yankee go home.''

13

I WAS TEMPTED to meditate upon Jesus. Not because of Bewley; he was merely a pest, lithe, earnest always and lugubrious on Sundays; he hectored us for the day of the week, and made marks on the wall, as if he might miss the big game, the election, whorehouse night. No, not because of Bewley, but because of minor triumphs over the cruelest month—ah, nonsense. Not cruel at all. Little sprigs of green, resurrection: weeds beat scurvy. Ordinary green weeds, two or three varieties unnamable by the asphalt gardener of Union Square, but green: I had the men out like street cleaners, scavenging tares. They shuffled, slaves in blue, and fetched home handfuls of hairy leaf; all through the camp those handfuls went into the pot, and in ten days the pains had vanished, the men's color had risen, the sun approved. Buds fattened. Apollo; why should Jesus have the glory? Hills greened, birds chattered. Weeds beat scurvy.

And a good thing too; with pluck came sass, and the men rejected soybeans. God almighty. They were still reckoning on the old chuck wagon. At first they gobbled the beans. Then they moaned and groaned. Ou-yang sent for me and introduced me to two subordinates, Wei something and Chang something. Wei was to be our political officer and Chang the military commandant. Ou-yang would stay on as chairman of the board. He praised me to the others. They smiled thin, polite acknowledgment. Ou-yang spoke in Chinese and Wei warmed a bit, cocked a friendlier brow. I never learned what had been said. Ou-yang went on, "Your MacArthur has been sent home in disgrace." "Ma ka ta," Wei said, and laughed.

I goggled. A woman? Peculations? What disgrace? Who in the world could send him anywhere, our own Heliogabalus? "A *matter* of policy, I think," Ou-yang said. "Too many planes over there," he pointed to Manchuria, "and a couple, it seems, *all* the way to Vladivostok. Apparently the United States is not yet ready to *liberate* China and Russia," He laughed heartily, a luncheon-club laugh, jolly good fellow.

In an hour the whole camp knew. Mulberg rejoiced. "They'll end the god damn war. They can shove these god damn soybeans." Applause, cheers, boiled soybeans on the floor.

Even Kinsella persuaded himself. "God damn," he said. "That means they quit. They won't come north again. God damn. Why didn't they drop the bomb? What's it *for?*" He paced, the military mind clicking along. "All right. A shift in policy. Stabilization, maybe a truce, prisoner exchange. It stands to reason. All right. Could be worse." Pacing, muttering. "What the hell. Just as well. We'd have had to tunnel a quarter-mile. Unless they let us swim." He peered at the river. "Long swim. Christ, maybe it's good news."

"They won't eat the soybeans."

"God damn babies," he said. "Make them."

"Nobody can make them. Look, Major, we'll have new generals and new generals will have new plans, win the war, and they won't be as good as MacArthur's. We can't win a polite war and you know it. So they're going to fool around for a long time with their games. Bang bang. Strategy."

I thought he might dress me down, but he laughed. "Corporal Beer."

"I'd have been a sergeant by now, and sergeants know everything."

"Okay," he said, "let's ask Trezevant."

So we did. Trezevant said, "Shit, how do I know what those damn fools want to do?" Kinsella laughed like hell. I diagnosed a deep release working within him; he'd yielded to the most treacherous temptation: hope. "A chap which I talked to," Bewley said, "thinks we going home." I began to enjoy Bewley. "Lieutenant," he said, "I hear you a Hebrew."

"No such luck," I said, "just a Jew." "Now you fooling with me," he said. "Lieutenant, you got to come to Jesus Christ. That's how we get out of this, when all come to Jesus Christ." The spirit of Easter lay upon him. I told him I'd think about it.

They let us each write a letter. We were Americans and assumed that the letters would be delivered. They asked us to write out a personal history. Kinsella spread the word: bare vital statistics, nothing military. They announced that a library would be made available. They began to interview the men one at a time. They announced study and discussion groups, some compulsory. A new grain was added to the soup; I never knew what it was, but it was bulkier and mealier than the millet. Days were longer and the sun held steady.

Yuscavage disappeared. He was simply no longer with us. Ou-yang said only that he was safe and well. Then he ordered me to live with the officers. I could make my rounds but must live with Kinsella's bunch. This was a time of confusion. No one was friendly or unfriendly and we all assumed that doom had passed us by, the old angel of death was just plain wore out, but some of us sensed that the future was shifty. "You know what," Kinsella said, "it's like we were here for good. Have they interviewed you yet?" They had not. "Me neither. They're up to something."

Bewley told us what. Dear old Bewley. "Jesus," he announced, "was the first communist." He had been interviewed twice and given a New Testament. He had asked about regular "services of divine worship" and had been fobbed off. "Christ almighty," Kinsella said. "No more interviews. Pass the word." No one listened. Ewald went to meetings from nine to twelve and two to four. "I had an uncle was a Wobbly," he said. At night he went to the library. I asked him what books they had. He said he was reading John Steinbeck. Kinsella was collating gossip; a commander without a command, he talked to himself, cogitated fiercely, speculated, demanded silence and frowned intently.

They sent for him and he was away for four days. They had asked him to cut a recording; as senior officer he was to confirm the good treatment, food for all, medical care. Medical care. That was me. He refused. They stuck him in a dark cell with a waste bucket and hauled him out at odd hours for further discussion. He refused. They released him in honor of May Day. May Day! Union Square! I realized with sudden excitement, a great gasp at this astrological conjunction, that New York was on the same parallel of latitude as this prison camp, give or take a couple of blocks. And I saw the speakers, heard the protests: Bring Benny Home! The fan beards, the skinny Catholic vegetarian, the famous optometrist who put on a blue denim shirt and overalls and had a season; he opened on May Day and closed on Labor Day. And Jacob! Ten thousand miles due east Jacob worried, Jacob wept, Jacob badgered the government and signed petitions. He would see the Untermeyers once a week, and play with Joseph, and Carol would sit grieving, hot, ripe, twenty-three years old and unloved.

I closed my mind to all that and listened to Kinsella. "They want propaganda. We say no. If they need propaganda they can't afford to brutalize us. I figured it out. We stand fast."

When they sent for me he said it again: "Stand fast, Benny."

"Right," I said.

Ou-yang and Wei merely wanted me to see the class-rooms—so Ou-yang called them—and the library. Prisoners sat conversing in low tones, like school kids ordered silent. In one corner a Chinese officer chatted with three of them. The first book I saw was a pamphlet—Lenin it was, *Women and Society*. Women and Society! I needed both. It would be well-thumbed. *The Right of Nations to Self-Determination. A Letter to American Workers.* Stalin. Engels. Magazines, brochures. Imperialism. Union Square! Michelet. Victor Hugo: *Les Misérables*. I had never read it. I had seen the film. George Bernard Shaw, Erskine Caldwell—that too would be thumbed, breast and thigh among the real folk—*Oliver Twist, War and Peace, The Jungle, The Merchant of Venice*.

I was abruptly dizzy. In the stacks, as a young man, I had always experienced a primitive visceral urge, an odd loosening of the bowels, humility in the presence of the unknown, eternity, so much still to read, so much that I would never read. Or perhaps I was slack, greedy, perhaps it was a symptom of intellectual lust; perhaps its opposite, an inadmissible desire to be thence. Now I was merely dizzy, shuttled at the speed of light to another planet, words, letters, the smell of paper and bindings. I turned away. "You are impressed," Ou-yang said.

"Yes," I said, but I was much more impressed and almost fainted when we stepped outside again and I bumped into a woman.

She wore a tan uniform, lightly padded, and she had black hair, shoulder-length, and the reddest cheeks I have ever seen, and her black eyes sparkled and she smelled like a woman. I gulped and ogled and grew hot. Ou-yang introduced us. He called me Pee-joe Die-foo and her name was Ho Wen-chen. I think. I saw her every day and soon we were making love behind the library and it was all so marvelous. No. I never saw her again. She was the first woman I had seen in five months. I have no serious idea now what she looked like, but she was unutterably beautiful and for several seconds I suffered agonies to shame the damned, the mind suddenly ignited so wanting a woman that the body rebelled, exploded; the heart pressed out between the ribs, bones ruptured the hot flesh. She moved on. I watched her walk, watched the silky black hair float. "She assists our political instructors," Ou-yang said. "She keeps records."

They interrogated me once, and I said no, no, no,

and they accepted the decision. Others had been tempted: mail privileges, better food. Most stalled and bluffed, and it became a contest, chess or go, get without giving. But Bewley was serious; "Give up all thou hast," he said. Ewald too; he withdrew even further and we scarcely saw him. I asked Kinsella if Cuttis might play along; he was recovering, but slowly, and the food, the quarters, the company would help. "Absolutely not," Kinsella said. "If you give them *anything* they have you."

"So what?" I was not sure why I had said no, no, no.

"So what?" Kinsella despaired of me, groaned. "They're *soldiers*," he said. "They're still *soldiers*."

"Yessir," I said. "Any news of the war?"

"No news of the war." He glared. "Where the hell would I hear news? You're the collaborator."

"Easy," I said, but neither of us was angry.

So it went for some weeks, and we divided, and the words "progressive" and "reactionary" became common nouns. I wondered: was it for the rewards? did they believe? were they poor farmhands struck for the first time by the lightning of learning? was it simple intellectual ecstasy, the mechanic from Provo who finds that he can speak, read and write Sanskrit? And the others, the reactionaries, what were they defending? flag, home, mother? our shores? their own core? a good service record? Collins was defending Collins: "Fuck 'em all. I been to these lectures. In the states. *Civics*." Mulberg hawhawhawed. I almost joined him, because there was a little of that rat in me too: fuck 'em all. None of this shit about equality and mankind, not while you got me chained to this here wall. It was not the matter; what they were teaching was irrelevant.

(Collins was right. Civics!) For the moment I did not care to be like everybody else. I did not care to be like *anybody* else. Who held out, who said no? (Ah, that monosyllable! Easiest little word in the world, and the hardest one to say, and keep saying, whether they cosset you or clip you.) Those who said no were the guttersnipes and the snobs. I was both. Nothing else mattered—race, religion or lack of it, money, none of that pushed a man one way or the other. I knew men who *were* progressive, one of them might have been a genuine communist, and they said no, maybe because they'd been saying no all their lives; and I knew a ritzy officer from Boston, wealth, banking, Episcopal for Christ's sake, and he said yes, maybe because he'd been saying yes all his life. I still don't know what it is that makes a man inviolable, but I still hope to find out.

I went back to the old hut one day to examine Cuttis and found four strangers at the door. One I recognized, a scarred street Negro named Fennimer, from Philadelphia I think. The other three were white but all four were angry, and they all shared an aspect, an attitude: tough city kids. You could tell right away. Trezevant was holding them off, trying to soothe them. Fennimer rounded on me. "You give us that Ewald."

"What's he done?"

"Stole food. Stole two mon-toes."

Trezevant said, "What's mon-toes?"

"Steamed dough," I told him. "Back home you'd spit it out. How do you know Ewald took them?"

"We know," Fennimer said. "He was there, talking sweet shit about those slants, and them he was gone and they were gone."

"If he's so sweet with the Chinese how come he has

175

to steal food? And where'd you get the mon-toes?''

"Up yours, officer. You give us Ewald. Now.''

Ah, a touch of home and youth! "Yeah, well just hold it,'' I said. "How would that look, we just give you our guy like that. Ewald! You in there?''

"He's in there,'' one of the white guys said.

"Who're you?''

"What do you care, officer?''

"Just curious. Where you from, then?''

"Scranton.''

"You guys?''

"Atlanta.''

"Seattle.''

"New York,'' I said, between tears and laughter, and they heard, the big town, pops, don't mess with Benny the blade; and it sickened me, disgusted and nauseated me, this brutish street scene, quiet talk, don't draw cops, treaties broken, tribal laws, jagged broken milk bottles. Blood must answer blood. God help us.

"We ought to hang together against these people,'' I said. "Got plenty of fights without making more.''

"Never mind these people,'' Fennimer said. "We're in here for *good*. For a good long time. Got to figure that way. Got no more fight with them. Got a fight with Ewald.''

"Sergeant,'' I said, "tell Ewald I want the mon-toes.''

Trezevant stepped inside, and left me alone.

"Sergeant,'' Scranton repeated. "Lieutenants and corporals and all. Got any eagle scouts?''

"Ordinarily I'd let you solve your own problem,'' I said. "But we've got plenty of sick and dying, and we're trying to save all we can.''

"Nobody dying no more,'' Fennimer said.

That was true. I was astonished. No one had died for a couple of weeks.

"Can't save Ewald anyway," Fennimer went on. "Unless you get him a transfer. I mean, Lieutenant, after all, sooner or later, you know."

I nodded. Truth was truth. Sooner or later, you know. "Buy him off, maybe," I said. "He's a medic. We need him. What would you want?"

They conferred in silence. Note well: four grown men, two lumps of steamed dough. The other three left it to Fennimer. He hesitated, so I made the move. "Double the mon-toes, and I'll punish him myself."

"Where you going to get mon-toes?"

"Up yours. I can get you aspirin too."

"Aspirin? What the fuck we going to do with aspirin? That's right, though: you solid with these cats."

"Shut up about that," I said.

"Cigarettes, maybe," Fennimer said.

"Maybe."

Trezevant lazed out and leaned against the jamb, as if he would say, "Gentlemen." Instead he held forth a round white lump and said, "I got one. He ate the other one. Don't seem like much to fight about."

"Two more," Fennimer said, "and the other stuff."

"A deal," I said.

"Solid," he said. "How you going to fix Ewald?"

"There's ways," I said. "It won't happen again. But you lay off, all right? I can make trouble too."

"Last thing we want is trouble," Fennimer said, and they all grinned.

"All right then. You're in eighteen."

"That's right," Fennimer said.

"Where Sumner was."

"That's right," Fennimer said.

"By tomorrow noon," I said. "And you lay off."

"That's right, we lay off," Fennimer said. "I guess we better make it four cigarettes and four aspirins. I mean there's four of us. And you with your connections."

When they were gone Trezevant said, "Sumner?"

"Dysentery," I said. "He smelled bad. So they put him out overnight and he froze to death and they brought him back in before dawn."

"How do you know that?"

"Doctors know everything."

Life was not all crime reporting; there was also the society page, and shortly I was caught up in the mad, bubbling whirl of the international set: I was invited to dinner. Blue suit. Among the notables were Ou-yang, Wei, Chang, a few interrogators and Doctor Li. Li Diefoo. The invitation arrived in the form of a guard who jabbed a stubby finger at me and pointed the way with a mean thumb, like a homicidal hitch-hiker; Kinsella shouted after me, "Stand fast, Beer."

I was ushered into a large room where seven or eight people stood sipping tea and snapping pumpkin seeds; Ou-yang greeted me with a roar of hospitality and a clap on the shoulder, and I stood blinking and ducking like a barbarian at the court in Peking. Introductions. Li Diefoo. I shook hands, stunned. Where had he been when I needed him. Then the interrogators: colloquial English, my confusion compounded. Gossip. News of the war; my new commanding general was someone called Ridgway. Never heard of him. The Chinese were driving south, below the thirty-eighth parallel. My mind raced, slowed, dug in like harassed infantry: they were dissembling, deceiving me. I said little, nibbled pumpkin seeds, slurped tea.

"We will have surgical supplies," Doctor Li informed me, "and antibiotics."

"My men are better now or dead," I said. "What they need is good food."

"That too will improve," Li said. "We plan to conform to the highest international standards. Our goal is twenty-five hundred calories per day for each man." He nodded many times, proudly, smugly.

An interrogator said, "The baseball season has begun."

Li said, "I attended the Peking Union Medical School."

"Northwestern," the interrogator said. "Psychology."

I murmured something polite. This was scarcely credible. After dinner I would be executed, straws beneath the fingernails, the water torture. Or they would turn the conversation to book reviews and the latest vernissage and I would go mad on the spot, gangling, adrool. I groped for civilization, wit. What do you hear from Mao Tse-tung. Lin. "I had a friend in medical school," I said, "named Lin Li-kang. From Fukien."

"In Mandarin, Fu-*djen*," the interrogator said primly. "Lin is a common name there, like Johnson in Minnesota."

"It is a good name for a doctor," Li said, "because—"

"Because the five lin, on the same tone, are the diseases of the bladder," I said. "He told me that."

Joyful cries, extravagant delight. "A scholar!" Li

179

announced. "You must apply yourself, and improve your hours learning Chinese."

Almost anything would improve my hours. Li rambled on about the modern applications of certain ancient simples and nostrums. Acupuncture, he said; my heart contracted, a wrench, some old joke, confusing.

We sat on wooden chairs about a wooden table. We ate rice from bowls, with chopsticks, and in the center of the table, on a wooden platter, lay a huge baked fish in sauce. There were no portions; we all attacked the fish, nipped up flakes of flesh and dropped them, saucy, into the rice; Li spooned more sauce onto mine. There were vegetables, white vegetables Li called them, and lotus root. We had little cups too, and a man came in with earthen jugs and they poured wine into my cup, yellow wine, hot. Ou-yang rose to propose a toast in Chinese; it was to Mao so I did not participate, nothing personal you understand, and waited to be ejected; the bouncer would pad in, a wrestler, grab me by the nape and seat, and fling. They ignored me. A toast of my own, I should offer a toast, but to whom? Harry Truman? George Washington? Benedict Arnold. I knew I should not be there. Photographs. Benny Beer in the fleshpots, among the heathen. Disgrace, loss of citizenship, automobile insurance canceled. After a suitable interval, establishing moral defiance, I sipped. "No, no," Li said. "Dry cup, dry cup." The cups were tiny, three thimblefuls; I quaffed. The cup was filled instantly, magically. The fish diminished, vanished; no bones? Many cups were dried. Not so many by me. I explained to Li that my system was now delicate and my good health of supreme importance to some eight hundred men. Actually I had about forty

180

patients, but you know how it is the first year. "Very wise," he said. I belched, Aeolian, sforzando. "Good, good," he said. "A compliment to the chef." I smiled weakly and patted my mouth with the back of my hand. Soup was served. Delicious, intoxicating, utterly new to me. "Walnut soup," Li said, "for extraordinary occasions."

"It's very good," I said uneasily. I was a penniless diner awaiting the bill, the crisis. What did they want of me?

Nothing. We babbled, some in Chinese and some in English; spoke of the war, the warm spring, Mao Tse-tung's plans for flood control, the TVA. A love feast. I was frightened. But also full. My God I was full. On a bowl of rice and a mouthful of fish. A little drunk too. Foreign guest. Big nose. Invader, rapist. What next? Honorary citizenship. Exile. My interrogator friend asked me if I knew a place called *The Blue Note*. I did not. Great place, he said. Hawkins, he said. Tatum. I told him that I had once met Tatum but that I was a fiddler. Heifetz, he said. Paganini. Tomorrow they would clap someone into solitary and tonight we ate and drank and chattered of Shakespeare. They did not look at all alike. One of the interrogators was my idea of Genghis Khan: squat, powerful, a mustache. Another was a beardless Confucius, skinny, ascetic. One was walleyed. Ou-yang was jovial and hostly. The war was discussed again, the inevitable victory of the Chinese. Of the Koreans, someone corrected, and they all said oh yes, yes, the Koreans. Asia for the Asiatics, some-one said, and Ou-yang spoke swiftly in Chinese, a rebuke. A brief silence. More gossip. Li was lecturing on blood types, geographical distribution, many races, religions and blood types, and I was nodding, wearied by café society, when a rush of sound jerked my head erect and stopped my breath. Ou-yang smiled.

"What's that?" I was trembling and in pain.

"Radio Peking," Ou-yang said. "Does that surprise you?"

"No," I said. "*No*. That's Haydn."

I stood up; they fell silent. I choked, in my excitement gasped and hummed. I knew the quartet, the movement, three-four; my pulse beat in threes, and the music soared, quavered, hovered, swooped. I sank back heavily, stupefied. I let go then, and sat weeping, and wept to the end. When it was over Ou-yang handed me a cigarette and said I had better go now. It was obvious that I was tired. As I left a waiter came in with a stack of hot towels; I paused, and watched them wash their hands and mouths, fastidiously, like so many satraps.

I told Kinsella that a Chinese doctor had arrived and we had talked about medicine. He smoked the cigarette and told me to be careful.

Too late. Anyway the careful man dies of bedsores. Within a couple of days eight hundred prisoners knew that Doctor Beer, that prick, had caroused with the enemy. Roast duck, whiskey, cigars. Conversations dwindled at my approach. Kinsella drew me aside. "I want the truth." I told him the truth. He astonished me: "Oh what the hell," he said. "Christ, I heard you had women." I laughed hysterically for some seconds. "I'll shut them up," he said.

But then ten men were rounded up for stealing food, not from each other but from a storeroom near the library, where perhaps a prog had spied and squealed, and Fennimer and his friends were among them. They were taken away for a time and it was announced that their rations would be cut, which was infuriating; they would be denied classroom and library privileges, which was merely amusing; they would receive no tobacco, which was definitely comic; or mail, which was hilarious since no one had yet seen so much as a post card. It was less hilarious two days later when a few dozen men, all progressives but one, received a letter apiece, among them Pfc. Bewley, Corporal Ewald and Lieutenant Beer. That night I was court-martialed by Kinsella, two captains and two lieutenants. Kinsella raged. He had warned me. Stand fast, Beer. Ou-yang had mousetrapped me. The men were saying I had informed on the thieves. "Don't be a fool," I said.

"Don't you be a fool," he stormed. "Of course you didn't. God damn, of course not. Last man in the whole god damn camp to do that. Any of you others think he did?"

The others did not think so.

"But you let them split you off," he said. "Why should the men hold out if their officers betray them? Christ, man, we had little enough left. Why should they trust any of us now?"

I had no answer. Lucky Benny, the man in the middle. Gloomily I considered Ou-yang. He would not force me. He would isolate me and tempt me with Haydn and fish. Why? Why should he want me? What could I give him beyond doctoring, and he knew I'd give him that gratis. Cosmic forces at work, galactic intrigue, my soul at stake. "What does he want?"

"Not you," Kinsella said. "Not one officer more or less. He wants converts, but mostly he wants to demoralize us. He wants to show the world a lot of

183

reformed sinners. Show the slant world and Africa and all them. It stands to reason.''

We were sitting on the dirt floor, all but Kinsella; he stood, feet apart, shoulders square, chin high, a general chewing out a whole division.

''Okay. What do I do?''

They debated. I could stay with the Turks, or the British. No; they too knew. I could rebel and have myself popped into the hole. No; they'd say it was a trick.

''I could cut my throat,'' I said.

''You may yet. God damn you. What kine of puppy dog are you? You like everybody.''

''That's a hell of a thing to say about a man.'' The letter was in my waistband, between my shorts and my belly.

''Anyway,'' Kinsella said, ''you're confined to quarters. We'll try to square you outside, but stay put.''

It was from Carol. Often I could not remember her face. Joseph was well. Joseph would be a year old. ''What about doctoring?''

''Forget it.''

''If they send for me?''

''You have to go. But you won't doctor.''

''Shucks,'' I said, ''that's what I signed on for.''

''You signed on to fight for your country.''

''I didn't sign on. I was drafted. To doctor.''

''To doctor your own.''

My own. ''A doctor's like a virgin. He is or he isn't.''

''Sonny boy,'' my major said, ''you just lost your cherry.''

● ● ●

184

I followed orders and remained in the hut. Ou-yang sent for me and I explained that he had his own doctor now, and more coming, as he had told me, and that it was not seemly of me to neglect my own patients for consultations with the, ah, adversary. He discussed humanity. Doctor Li clucked and mentioned my duty to mankind. "Yessir," I said. Ou-yang informed me coldly that I must no longer use the library. I must understand that there were difficulties with the mail, both incoming and outgoing. I was marched back to my hut. "Ewald's cut another record," Kinsella said. "I supposed it was him informed."

"That may be my fault too," I said, and when pressed could not explain.

Carol loved me. I read her letter many times a day over the next two months. In the morning I took light exercise. I ate properly. I talked little. It was a time of unflagging stupor. The Chinese disliked me and the prisoners despised me. My roommates were cordial but remote. Often I lay awake at night. Often I remembered Carol's body, but not with my own, with my mind only. Doubtless a failure of the imagination, emotion disconnected in this infinite tranquility. I meditated various young ladies, including Ho Wen-chen and finally, dismally, Nan. I wondered if I would ever love anyone again. Love. I pondered the eating of rats. I pondered war and decided that men liked it. Statistically. In a large population the number of men who love to kill is sufficient to form a modern army. War was here to stay. If men would die sooner than eat rats, then surely they would die in droves, singing vigorously, for any higher reason; would die willingly, proudly. Proud to die! Unspeakable. I was too inanimate for disgust and simply contemplated the obscenity; men were proud to die. And how much prouder to kill!

And what was I proud of? Once upon a time, making love. Once upon a time, healing. Shameful admission: I had been proud to be what I was. Schmuck! No despair? Four walls, silence, Benny the nothing. I was not angry and not sorry for myself. I was in limbo and it seemed not unnatural. Normal. A room. Food. Warmth. Doubtless I would be expelled in time, into a new and strange world.

Ewald was now a librarian, they said, living it up in a prog hut. Trezevant and Cuttis were well; so were Mulberg and Collins. Auld lang syne. Class of 1950.

In June I sat outside and was tanned.

We went swimming in the Yalu. My fellow officers were a guard of honor. Solidarity. Benny is one of us. Kinsella swam, dived, spouted spray. They laughed and ducked one another. They returned to the hut much cheered. In the bay our navy patrolled. Later I sorted the dead men's dog tags, a form of higher crossword puzzle. Many races, religions, blood types. I read Carol's letter. Jacob was well.

One day in the middle of July I was squatting, hunkered down like an Oriental peasant or a toad, except that with my face to the sun I was wondering how it was to be a turtle. I remember that: it would be good to be a turtle, I thought. I had seen them, brown and orange and green, lying on rocks in the sun, and it was a good life, free of malice. My eyes were shut against the hot yellow light. I was waiting for a princess to kiss me. I heard men shouting, playing a game perhaps, and I opened my eyes a slit to look at them. We were at the crest of a slope and I could see many huts, and men were piling out of the huts and congregating where they could, a mass of agitated blue beetles, and the shouting rose and fell against a wash of voices, like a crowd at a game, so I knew that the world had changed.

I stood up. My fellow officers came to stand beside me. We looked at one another and were puzzled. And then a squad of Chinese marched toward us, along the wire, and Ou-yang was in the midst of them, striding importantly like a prince among courtiers. They came to our hut, and Kinsella stepped forward. The squad halted, and Ou-yang pushed between two of them and stood facing Kinsella. All over the camp men were buzzing and hollering. I decided we had bombed Peking.

Ou-yang said, "Major Kinsella."

"Colonel," Kinsella said.

"I am happy to inform you, officially," Ou-yang said, "that this week, along the thirty-eighth parallel, there was a meeting of Chinese, Koreans and Americans at which negotiations began for a truce."

We were stunned. Shocked speechless and groping. His words had a meaning but we could not grasp it. The sun was intolerably bright.

"You may join your men," Ou-yang said.

After a breathless moment Kinsella said, "Thank you," whispering, "thank you," and stepped around Ou-yang, floated, tiptoed around the squad, and flew down the hill in long, ecstatic, gliding strides, and the others flew leaping after him. I stood where I was, and Ou-yang and I locked eyes, a peculiar exchange, smoldering, outlandish, monstrous, homosexual, secret understandings. Causeless and bizarre: it smote me.

187

Again across centuries and continents. Linked, wedded, a common ancestor: ponies, flocks, stars; the passionate doomed unity of human blood.

I heard my name shouted. "Benny!" Kinsella called. "God damn it, come on. Come home, Benny, all is forgiven," and he stared into the sun and laughed, and the others whooped and yodeled, and I ran to catch up, screaming and yipping, jumping and skipping, and then we were all hugging each other, all races; religions and blood types.

We waited two years.

14

DEFEATED, CORNELIUS CHUBBIED and drooped; tilted far back in a swivel chair, he revealed the angles and swells of mortality, also an incipient pot. "At least we're on the way home. Otherwise it's a bust."

"Not for us to decide," Fontaine said briskly. "Be a year before we know anything."

The black lieutenant said, "You're going to jug some of these men because of what I say. What we say."

"You may jug me," Benny said. "I gather there's been talk."

"I doubt that," Parsons said. "Couple of fellows said you ought to have a medal."

"Good God, who was that?"

The lanky corporal—Benny thought of him now as the cowboy—widened his eyes in mock homage.

"Can't tell you that," Parsons said comfortably. "Be nice, a medal, wouldn't it. I mean because you come from a long line of military folk."

Benny laughed outright. He enjoyed the laugh and went on laughing for some moments, younger every second, goofy, warm and alive, suddenly ardent. There was possibly something to be said for mankind; the species was by now a stale joke but perhaps better than no joke at all. He sat voluptuously and allowed his body, his reprieved flesh, to mediate between past and future. He sighed aloud. "Some of the starch is washing away."

"That's how I feel," the older corporal said, almost resentfully.

"Let yourself go," Gabol said. "Don't fight it."

All these gleaming chairs and table-legs, minutely tooled portholes, sockets, speakers, switches, lamps and panels! A palace. And some day soon Benny would drive a car, clamber aboard an airplane. Practice the medicine he knew and loved. With instruments! with thermometers! with nurses! A fleeting vision, bobbling breasts, pink tones. A brief spasm shook him. "You must have quite a file on us," he said. "Between the army and the FBI."

"We have," Parsons said. "You were exposed to a heavy dose of commie propaganda."

"Commie," the black lieutenant said. "Tell me why I hate that word."

"We were also exposed to a heavy dose of life on the ragged edge," the cowboy said. "What you folks need is a file on everybody who was *never* in prison."

"Who never had to just hang on," the smallish cook said.

"All you nice clean antiseptic fellows," Benny said, "unreliable and unpredictable."

"Right on up to the President," someone muttered.

"That's the real bitch, isn't it," Cornelius said. "You men are proud of yourselves. You, Beer, the way you fought to keep that chop, that souvenir."

"No. That's not the way to put it." Or was it? Possibly. Had he been purified? Deprivations, saint in the desert, fasts; had his soul been rendered translucent and supple, open to blood truths? "Maybe." What language did they speak, these creatures of comfort? "Because of what he said," and Benny gestured, "the ragged edge, real life. I hated it," he burst out fervently, almost rapturously, "hated it, but I can't help a . . . a kind of . . . acid gratitude. It was real, it was real, it was realer than this boat or you people or the war itself. I'm only sorry we never ate rats."

"Listen," the cowboy told Cornelius, "you never lived that way." He jammed a cigarette into the corner of his mouth and struck a wooden match with a sharp sweep of his right arm, and Benny watched the cigarette tremble, the flame shimmy, and was not surprised at the hoarse, urgent tone: "It's not like waiting for a bullet—bang, you're dead. It's not even living each day thinking it may be the last, like an old man afraid to go to bed. It's the feeling that the rest of your life— no, the rest of time, *forever*—is going to be like this."

"It's a different kind of day," the lieutenant said, "a different kind of hours."

"The gut goes tight," Benny said. "The fat melts off and every little choice is like walking a steel wire."

"Right," the cowboy said. "What you do is what you are."

"No disguises and no pretties," the lieutenant said.

Gabol scribbled.

"All right, you were surviving," Cornelius said. "The whole war was for survival, your country's survival."

"Country!" Benny grew hot with outrage; it was a

191

reflex, and he would do better to control it. "Never mind," he said. "I earned food and medicine by fraternizing. Did I betray my country?"

"No," Cornelius said firmly. "You're a special case."

"Ah yes. Yes. I am. Was. Will be. Lucky, different. Okay. I knew that. Oh hell," he almost hollered, "I knew I'd survive too. Way down deep I knew it."

"Me too," the cowboy said. "Even when I told 'em to go shove it I wasn't worried."

Murmurs and nods. Heroes all. Yet some in this room had been weak, had been human, had acquiesced.

"And why," Cornelius asked patiently, "did you say no?"

They were silent.

"And why did some say yes?"

They were silent.

"Then I'll try it," Cornelius said. "You won't like this: it was because they were spoiled. They were never properly disciplined. Never an army. Hence misconduct."

A tattered cheer rose, and a crackle of applause; Cornelius was stunned. Gabol blinked, and left off writing.

"You mean you agree?" Cornelius was all but petulant.

"We do indeed," the lieutenant said, and the others murmured with him. "You're *learning*," the lieutenant said.

"Because they set their own survival above the survival of their country," Cornelius went on.

A groan rose, hisses and boos. Cornelius grimaced.

"Now you sound like a newsreel," Benny said. He

192

contemplated these officers, inquisitors, tanned, firm flesh, toothpaste, liberty.

"But you just agreed with me," Cornelius complained.

"Those napalm photos. Were they real?"

After a moment Gabol said, "You know they were."

"That's war," Cornelius said. "It's not an excuse for misconduct."

"You're insane," Benny said soberly. "If we could do that, why weren't we taught to eat rats? To tear out a Chinese jugular with our teeth? Survival? Good God, no!"

"Listen," the cowboy said, "these kids were brought up to think they could be President some day. Their mommy told them."

"Their god damn mommy in curlers," Benny said, and winced in shame; insane, he too, he too, "hugging them and kissing them and making daddy pretty miserable. Her little boy was a winner, and he was going to be just like her. Wholesome and all."

"Christ sake," the black lieutenant said, "they started *out* better than everybody else. And they get sent out here to kill gooks, animals, wogs—shit, it was like hunting—and then surprise! we took a little beating. Listen, any man in the world fights like hell on his own turf, but you want to send men ten thousand miles to fight gooks on gook street, you better send killers."

"What you did," Benny said, "was you told them all men are created equal, and if we have to we can burn gook babies to prove it."

"Christ," the cowboy said, "some of those kids never been laid. All they know is the flag and mouthwash and necking after the god damn prom. They're not so good at burning people alive in the name of democracy and justice."

"Easy on the profanity there," the lieutenant said, and a few laughed.

"Then they're caught," Benny said, "and flung into prison, and they whimper some and where the hell is mommy? And the mail and the weenies? And why shouldn't they cut a record if it means the kind of food and privileges superior beings are entitled to? And if survival's the goal, why shouldn't they kill their own men to survive?"

"Personal survival isn't a soldier's goal," Cornelius said.

"I never heard such bullshit," Benny said, "and you a major. Listen, the other guy's survival doesn't even matter at *home*. Up the ladder, right? Look out for number one, right? Business is business, right?"

"Future supermen of America!" the cowboy declaimed. "And you want 'em gung ho. The doc's right. You're crazy."

"You tell 'em, cowboy," Benny said.

"Cowboy?"

"What'd you used to do?"

"Soda fountain fixtures in Florida."

"My mistake," Benny smiled.

"Look here." Cornelius was trying to be emphatic. "The whole purpose of military training is to make every man responsible for every other man in his unit. Ultimately, in his company and battalion and regiment and division and country."

"Well then *do* it!" the black lieutenant wailed. "Man, I'm a regular. This is my army. And *nobody* got trained like that, *believe* me. You made an army out of

194

boy scouts with a complaint department and a suggestion box and god damn *merit* badges. I mean it, I mean it—we had a *suggestion* box. Christ, when I was a sergeant I had to watch my *language* around them, or they'd report me. But you just let me train 'em right and I'll *flog* 'em. I'll tell 'em: you kill who I say or I'll kill *you*. And these gooks are *not* human, just do your job, and if you get captured you remember that what they do to you is *nothing* compared to what I do to you if you fuck up."

"You're preposterous," Cornelius said.

"That's the *facts* of things," the lieutenant said, "so why not make it the theory of things too?"

"We weren't trying to destroy an inferior people," Fontaine said. "That's nonsense. I don't like to hear a Negro officer say that."

"Oh shit," the lieutenant said.

"We don't mean there was anything *personal*," Benny said. "But we'd wipe out Asia tomorrow. Or Africa. For business reasons. To bring them the benefits of used-car lots and luncheon clubs, or to save their immortal souls. God almighty, man, where you been for a hundred years? But we can't do it with boy scouts toting candy bars for the orphans they make."

"Then you favor a tougher army," Cornelius said, "like the Turks."

"I need a drink," Benny said. "I am beginning to think the only way to talk to you people is drunk."

"We favor no army," the black lieutenant said softly. "Sooner or later this army, *my* army, is going to wipe me out too."

"You're crazy," Cornelius said.

"You wait," the lieutenant said.

"I sure favor no army," the cowboy said. "I favor

195

setting every general and politician in the world to work. Let 'em dig ditches and build houses and carry bedpans. Bounce 'em off the free ride and make 'em pay their own bills and leave decent people alone.''

Benny said, "I favor letting no general or politician make a war until he has personally bayoneted a pregnant woman in the belly."

"That's disgusting," Cornelius said.

15

TWO YEARS.

Two years.

In first hope we lounged and chaffed, awaited word, a suit of civvies, twenty dollars and a train ticket. Kinsella demonstrated leadership by allowing us some days of unrestricted joy and speculation before announcing that truce negotiations took time, and these in particular would prove troublesome, and we should resign ourselves to a delay, perhaps as much as six weeks. Cheerfully we resigned ourselves. We swam. The progs cut class and also swam; they were still segregated but would look across at us sheepishly, like vaguely remorseful Auschwitzer peasants just learning (surprise!) what the souvenir factory was. No one bore them ill will, as Kinsella explained. Contempt yes, but we were all Americans here, or Allies, and any rebukes or punishments would be administered by the proper authorities at the proper time. So we waved back, or ignored them, and sat in the sun, needing only a cracker barrel, and swapped tall stories. The summer suits were blue cotton, comfortable, even racy. We sprawled like lizards and blinked heavily.

I remembered Ou-yang's fervid glare, his warning, and did not kneel to hope; but the food was richer and the sun was sweet and juices circulated, life beckoned. At night I lay tense, beating back optimism, quelling reverie. Carol. Others. Her. I opened my heart to memory and loss, punished myself with a thousand unforgettables; cheered up and grinned hysterically, subsided and bit the flesh of my own arms.

I made my rounds. I suppose they— "they"— allowed cautiously for an end to the madness; they let me rove the camp, issued alcohol and dressings. Humanitarians now, all of us. Much of my work was useless, or simple therapy; nothing could be done here about badly set bones or flagrant scars or obscure internal pains. Or even athlete's foot: fungicides were scarcer than homicides. I prescribed exercises for limpers, kept close watch on stumps (limbs, digits), treated conjunctivitis and prickly heat. Once I saw Ewald, across lanes of wire: he waved, sketched a smile. I too waved; he looked friendly and apologetic, an air of weakness about him, the last downhill run; he was less round, pale, his eyes pouched. I was disturbed, and shivered. Omens and auguries again, clouds no bigger than a man's heart.

What we needed was an epidemic to restore our hard-won despair. So—presto!—we got one. Far beyond the poor powers of your umble physicker: bleeding at the orifices, chills, fever, headache, vomiting, muscle pains. "God damn," Kinsella cried. "They're pissing blood. They got swollen eyes and blood in the nose and mouth."

"There must be fifty," I said. "I don't know what it is."

"You don't know!"

"No. I never heard of anything like it. Bewley says it's a punishment."

"My God, my God," he moaned. A real moan, a wail, a keen. Kinsella too had his limits.

"Pray," I said. "Keep clean."

"You've got to do something. Pretend."

"Tell me what. I need blood counts and textbooks."

A very few died. The fever went down in five or six days but a few died anyway. Some suffered urinary retention near the end, and died hurting. Some just dozed off. Most just got better. Mysteries. I dreamed of a lab, tests, kidney function, urinalysis, spinal taps, white cell counts. By the middle of a hot August the scourge had passed. The Chinese too had suffered, acupuncture or no acupuncture. Doctor Li fretted.

In late August they delivered the mail. We buzzed, a swarm of hope and joy. Near as I could tell, everybody got a letter. Variously dated. No newspapers. No magazines. No books. Not one, ever, the whole time. Only these scraps of paper months apart, decades. Stunned, we retreated to corners to be alone with the news, the words of love, the peppy assurances and exhortations. Someone guessed that the war might be over, why else this generosity, and in an hour we all believed it, but as the days passed we fell silent, then sad, then bitter.

"There's birds, anyway," Kinsella said. It was true. They had settled on us in spring, blackbirds and sparrows and little red and yellow ones, chirping and stunting, sifting their limy blessings on master and slave alike; there were geese, ducks and cormorants on the river. "Those are eider," Kinsella said. "Listen when they go over, whoosh-whoosh-whoosh." Spring had been green and brown, a vasty blue sky, and in summer flowers blossomed, specks of red and white pricking out a lush hillside.

Then the petals fell. I saw Ewald again, and Bewley, in an outdoor class, sprawled on the grass like college kids, the instructor lecturing, spectacles, minatory finger. One evening I came home—home!—for chow and found a book on my bag of bandages. Kinsella wanted to know where I'd got it. I didn't know. No one knew. It was *Les Misérables*. In French. So at last I read *Les Misérables*. Long stretches of it bored me. There were words I did not know.

Ou-yang told us that the peace talks had been suspended.

Kinsella fell into a depression.

Cuttis was walking. He was tanned.

I wondered how my General Motors was doing, and my Standard Oil.

Later I wondered this: if we had known that it was to be two years, would any have killed themselves, defected, or tried to break out? Or would they have felt relief that it was not to be ten?

The days grew short and the birds fled. V's of eiders whoosh-whoosh-whooshed overhead, darted south, wheeled, streaked north, free. North? More madness. Geese honked at dawn and arrowed south. Smaller birds stuck around and scrounged, but soon they too deserted us. The guards came for Kinsella, and he was away for two days, and came back to us untouched but exhausted. Other officers also. Not me. The progs debated, and more of us joined them. A gang of guards tramped up one day, so we fell silent, and then we saw that they were carrying a burden, and then we saw that it was Trez. They shoved him our way and he staggered and strained and kept his feet and swayed. We moved in. "Trez." The guards about-faced and trotted off. Kinsella took him under the arms and held him up like a lover, face to face, close, and said almost tenderly-,"Did they torture you?"

Trez blinked several times and hoisted a small smile. "No sir," he whispered. "Never laid a glove on me. And I didn't have a lot to say to them. But," and he drew in an endless, epically weary breath,"they sure made me tired." The smile broadened, like a small boy's, and he held out a hand to me, closed his eyes and collapsed. We lugged him to his pallet and laid him out comfortably. "Good man," Kinsella said, feisty. I wanted to knock him down. "Good man. God damn. Give me a hundred like him."

One of our corporals suffered a heart attack and died. In November, a time of dust and frost and sudden yellow winds from the northwest, the issue of winter clothing was a sad event, and we all quit hoping then and cursed the government, ours and theirs, all governments everywhere and at all times. "I quit," Kinsella said.

"Quit when you're dead."

"I'm dead," he said. "Look at that."

It was Ewald again, distant but recognizable with his yellow hair. He walked as if entranced—repeating lessons? arguing with himself? penetrating the dialectic? He suggested some early Swedish saint meditating among the stalks, sauntering under God's eye, murmuring verses and blessing crickets. Bringing word of Bewley the black Christ.

"Poor guy," I said.

"Hell with him," Kinsella said. "No more ducks. I used to shoot ducks. And geese."

"City boy, myself."

"Used to fish too. You ever tramp across a field of corn stubble in November?"

"No."

"Kick up a pheasant," he said. "Wham, like an explosion. In that nippy air, and your breath white. Jesus. I had a double once, it was so sweet, so perfect, left and right. I took them in and had a glass of whiskey I can still taste. Second one was a hen, illegal but what the hell. Benny," he said, "tell me the truth. Is this war going to end?"

"Yes," I said. "How would I know?"

"Doctors know everything," he said.

"Jesus," I said.

"I better get a grip on myself," he said. "It looks like a long hard winter."

That it was. The imminence of death had driven us to the wall; a hint of life had raised us up; now death-in-life palsied us. We moved like shadows, spoke like ghosts. I did my work mechanically and returned to the hut to sit in mourning. To sit through endless hours of space, endless leagues of time. Waves of bitterness, of hate. And then irrepressible waves of grief; sitting there like a dummy and suddenly tears in the eyes. You can't know. If you've done time, maybe, or been gut-shrinking poor. Prison. An indeterminate sentence. Endless. Consider. You who are without sin.

Christmas.

I remembered the story of the old Chinese philosopher who dreamed that he was a butterfly, and when he woke up he wasn't sure if he was a philosopher who had dreamed that he was a butterfly or a butterfly dreaming that he was a philosopher. Was I a free man dreaming that he was a prisoner, or a prisoner who had dreamed that he was a free man?

Ou-yang invited me to sit and said, "They are talking *again*, at any rate." He was sullen and pasty: he too. What I felt was more than sympathy; it was kinship. Sorry. Mark that down. When he said "they." We all had our they. Somehow the same they.

"About what?"

He shrugged. He blinked then, and made a sad neighing sound, and tossed a file folder to me. I opened it. Photographs. Photographs of children with their eyes burned shut and their noses and ears burned off. Children without arms. A mother and child welded together. A boy whose face was a mask, a horror, two tiny eyeholes, no lips. My stomach bucked; dimly I remembered Rospos retching, and before that, years before, other photographs.

"Always," I said.

"Not in your country," he said.

More photos. After a dozen they numbed.

"I want you to broadcast as a doctor," he said.

"I can't."

"A request for peace only," he said, "to hurry the negotiations."

"No." My answer was a reflex; I had chosen my way and was beyond reasons. And I was angry, sick: so blatant, these photos. Do something, as a doctor.

"What's holding them up?"

He shrugged. "Many things. Mainly that the Americans want time to *convert* their prisoners."

"Unlike you."

"They have many thousands. They will not return

them but insist on letting them choose. So they indoctrinate."

Wearily I said, "I hear we have a choice too."

"You could speak as a doctor. As a doctor only."

"If I really spoke as a doctor both sides would shoot me. No. I'm sorry."

"It could do no harm."

"We never know that. Not the simplest consequence of the simplest choice."

"Ah yes," he said. "An ancient Chinese fable. The farmer who found a horse."

I waited.

"And his neighbors came to *congratulate* him, and he said, Wait, wait. And his son was riding the horse and fell off and *broke* a leg, and the neighbors came to *condole*, and he said, Wait, wait. And the duke's captains came to take all younger men for the army, and the son was *exempt* because of his leg. And so on and so forth."

"Yes."

"So you will not broadcast."

"No. Medicine, any time. Diplomacy, no. Show business, no."

"Would you like to write to your family?"

"Oh not that, please," I said. "Only if everybody does."

"Such heroism."

"God no. Not even patriotism."

He snorted. A big man, bowed, hostile, the enemy. "I could make you trouble," he said.

"Don't make me trouble," I almost fell asleep then and there. The weariness was an ache. It was not sleepiness; it was a way of life. "Listen to me. I had a friend, a Chinese, in New York. A rich boy, from a rich family, and one day I asked him where he would spend his life. China, he said. They won't have you, I said. China, he said. He said even if there was a *Japanese* in charge," and Ou-yang went gratifyingly popeyed, "he'd still go back to China. Do you understand?"

"Of course," he said.

"Not patriotism."

"No, no. Much more."

"Much more." I was out of it now, slack, even sleepier. "So much of what a man was, and is, and will be. The landscape, the language, the color of the sky and the rhythm of the rain. Virtues and defects. You understand me?"

He nodded. "Give me the pictures." I pushed them across the desk. "I will not make you trouble, Diefoo."

"Ding how," I said.

"Ding how." He smiled, I smiled.

On the way out I ran into Ewald. He was reading as he walked, and his lips stirred. It was earnest and rather touching. "Well, where you off to?" I asked.

He was startled; thoughts and words pushed at him. He licked his lips and said, "I'm glad to see you, Lieutenant."

"Been a long time since we talked."

"Yes."

"Heard from home?"

He nodded. "They're okay."

"Good. Take it easy," I said.

"Lieutenant," he said, so I stopped. "I'm beginning to understand. A lot of things."

"Well, that's good."

"I mean about the war."

"You're a better man than I am."

"And that time, when we were captured."

"Forget it," I said.

"Well," he said, "I just wanted to tell you."

"Sure," I said. "Listen, watch your step. Someday the others—"

"I'll take care of myself," he said. "I've got the will to live."

The will to live. This innocent. This squarehead. This eminent philosopher. "So did Jack," I said.

"Who?"

"Just watch yourself. I mean it. Don't move around alone. Stay with your progs."

"You can sneer," he said, "but we could end it. All of us. If we—"

"Go to hell," I said.

The interrogations resumed, ceased, resumed again. No one was injured but the pressure was constant: what next? when? New prisoners came in, a trickle. The food improved again but there was no mail. No reading matter but Lenin and Hugo; I tried reading aloud to my bored fellows, translating as I went, but kept falling asleep. My audience made no protest. When I was not working or extending the previously recorded limits of torpor, I made an effort to think about sublimer matters. Tried to find, for example, an absolute. One. To hang on to. Deduce from. You may have one. God. Country. Wife. Husband. Lucky you. For us sad skeptics it is not easy. The closest I managed was the sanctity of human life. No two human beings are alike—an axiom, biological differentiation—therefore every life is unique and no man is expendable. Not even the enemy.

Corollary: therefore every man is absolutely alone at all times. Contradiction: we all die, so are expended after all. Important to ourselves but not to the universe; yes, man's whatness and nature's so-whatness. Then I wasn't sure, so returned to simpler matters. You will not mind. Short attention span. I wished for paper and pencil but they would not have helped. I hummed themes until rudely silenced. We improvised a chess set but energy failed. Kinsella caught cold and blew his nose through his fingers. Jacob did that in the wash-bowl every morning, while warm water ran. "God damn. You know what I miss, I miss handkerchiefs. Got this little polyp or something too."

"I'll fix it up free when we're home."

"Nah. The army'll do it."

"That's right, the army," someone said. "Where the hell are they?"

"They'll be along," Kinsella said in an invalid's voice.

I thought of Jacob, who might be suffering more than I: and about the history of my obstreperous sect: and about the existence or non-existence of chance and fate. I decided that I was an atom, possibly even an electron, possibly one of the more mysterious particles, certainly a negative charge, capable only of weak interactions, a bit of mass, a bit of energy, hello and goodbye. Unprofitable but time-consuming ruminations: I omit detailed fantasies, laments and whimperings. In the end I was grateful for work and devoted myself to public service. Dropped in on my platoon. Fennimer and company had joined them, replacing departed shades. Good tough bunch now: Cuttis was a baby boy still, but the others were mean and raunchy. Except Trez, who had not condemned earlier and did not toady now.

"Lieutenant," he said. "How you doing with the nurses?"

"Killing myself. How's the Marianna flash?"

"Hard as nails," he said. "Two hundred pounds of dynamite."

"About one fifty," I judged. "Anybody sick?"

"Not my boys."

Fennimer said, "The major escape yet?" They snickered.

"What's the gossip?" Trez asked.

I told them what I knew about the truce talks. They all cursed. That was as far as we ever went, jokes and current events, but they shored me up. Some days it seemed we were the only Americans in the whole camp who planned to survive. Turks and Greeks and Englishmen, sure; they were real people, but many of my compatriots seemed insubstantial. To identify them you would have to examine their dog tags. They did not wail and gnash teeth; they faded. That second winter was deadly in subtler ways: the unexpressed sense of permanent servitude, of life foreclosed. Plus the oft expressed sense of betrayal, or at least criminal horsing around, by generals and politicians. Yessir. Oft.

We survived, and spring came again. What a simple statement! You will draw an approving breath and think, thank heaven, our boys certainly deserved survival and springtime. Ah, to hell wid all o' yiz. I had a rebuke building here, sharp, savage, memorable. Forget it. We survived, and spring came again. (All the same, what were you doing that spring, or a dozen such springs since? I know: paying taxes. Accept this fig, one and all.)

Kinsella survived his cold. I chatted with Ou-yang. The truce talks were in full swing, one millimeter each way. Early birds fluttered in, the ice on the Yalu floated out. One night, late, dark, I was trudging homeward, my mage's rounds accomplished, and the air was sweet, moist, the stars icy and reassuring, and I was a shaman, possessed of intimate powers, tuned to an eternal animism, immune to the wrath of capricious gods. I was, for reasons still beyond me, sanguine; had survived an unnamed plague; felt a bit more like Benny Beer, condottiere, scion of the eminent buttonhole merchants, lover, financial wizard and glass of fashion. This war would end. I visualized the brass band. The Irish queen . . .With whimsical excitement, almost aroused, I remembered a legend: Cuchulainn? Brian Boru? His men won a great battle for a great queen, and when they marched back to the queen's castle her women had lined the road on both sides, and as the warriors tramped by, the women raised their skirts to the neck, every last one of them. Keep your brass band. Give me Kathleen O'Toole every time. So I trudged, musing upon that mossy allée of noble shrubbery, when I heard a moan. I thought it was myself moaning, but when I heard it again I halted.

I found him quickly, with his belly cut open, one good slash and the blood welling. I looked around like a cat; we were alone. I ran, shouting, momentarily mindless; then doubled back, still shouting, and padded the wound, awkwardly, an amateur. A guard called. "Diefoo," I shouted. "Kwai kwai," which meant quick. I heard commotion. I felt for a pulse. Perhaps I caught the last flutter, the last desperate message. I crouched, cold, cursing Fennimer and his cronies—unfair, it could have been anyone.

The guard ran up soon, Li behind him. Ewald was dead. He could not have been saved. He was dead. That poor baby butterball. Dead in a far place. I sat down and raised him, to look into his face by starlight. It was stubbled and drawn but it was the face of a chubby child, dust on a country road, the old swimming hole, apples. Men gathered around me, and no one spoke, and I cradled him in my arms, and rocked him, and wept dry tears.

No one was questioned or punished. What was Ewald? Dirty prog. Two more dog tags on the heap. I bore them to Kinsella, Ewald's final expiatory offering, like the testicles of some sacred bull.

Well golly folks I wish they'd crucified somebody, Bewley maybe; nailed him to a wooden cross and left him to hang for a day, and then in the morning we all gathered, all eight hundred, and Kinsella and I took him down gently, and Trez wiped his face with a cloth, and the sky darkened and a great cry went up from the people, and the Chinese wept and turned away. How it would round out this blockish account! How it would lend meaning to all that happened!

No. What happened was meaningless. A dreary succession of minor episodes in the subhuman comedy. You want more. You insist on significance, affirmation, a chronicle instinct with life, informed by morality. Okay. First they had a hunch about that crazy epidemic, the bleeding and fever: ticks, they said. So we declared war on ticks. We worked at it. Nothing inspires a man to virtue like the fear of bloody urine. Sure enough: only two cases. They survived. Then one day they said we could all write home, and they supplied paper and pencil. So we all wrote home. Briefly, but to the starving man an egg is a chicken.

A week later—it was August of 1952—we were swimming in the Yalu under a molten sky; we played, splashed, rolled sensually in the girlish waters, about twenty of us, and on a friendly eddy there sailed to us a sheet of paper. "A message!" Kinsella cried, and we laughed boisterously, urging ribald suggestion, and he stroked out to it and bore it in. "More," I called, and pointed; behind that first message sailed a flotilla, some crumpled, some soaked, some like toy boats or paper hats. The men cheered and thrashed to the rescue. Then the laughter fell and the sun went black: they were our letters. All of that same date, all in those flat formulas. Angered and silent, we stood in the shallows. A few more letters floated past. Deliberately timed? An accident, just a day's garbage like any day's? How's that for significance, affirmation and morality?

We could not tell now whether the planet outside existed still, and that night we sat upon the ground and told sad stories of the end of the world. Suppose we had dropped the big one, and the Russians had done the same, one for one, and then two for two, and New York was gone, and Moscow, and Peking? Kinsella scoffed and ordered a change of subject. But the thought was almost cheering: imagine *other* people in trouble! Entertainment. Flights of fancy. Modern art. The difference to us would be slight: our letters would never be mailed, therefore the outside world did not exist. The seminar proceeded: it exists objectively, one said. Then why did our letters come back? Weird sense, but sense. Suppose a visitor came and reported all well outside? Then for the space of his narration it would exist. Then it must exist now. Why? Why does existence have to be continuous? "God damn," Kinsella said. "Shut up," Very high-class stuff. College level.

"Your wives and kids exist," Kinsella ordained. "Now shut up." I wondered.

Vignette. October, 1952: Doctor Beer has just conferred with Doctor Li about a Chinese private who seems to suffer from Raynaud's syndrome. Will wonders never cease. Chiefly in females. Is the private perhaps a female? No. Numb fingertips, swollen, painful. The man is obviously neurotic. But neurosis does not exist in the Chinese army. Perhaps, says Li, acupuncture. A transfer to Canton, Doctor Beer suggests, warmer climes. That, says Li, is merely treating the symptom; acupuncture treats the whole organism. Doctor Beer admits defeat and slinks off. Outside he takes a good lungful of crisp Manchurian air, turns a corner and finds himself face to face with a Russian officer; squarish face, farmer's jaw, broad pug nose, blond hair, blue eyes; all this absorbed in a blink. The Russian is escorted by a convoy of Chinese officers, and for a moment no one moves: the Chinese seem to retire, to subside, to vanish, ectoplasmic. The Russian and the American stare, spark, and for the space of a weak interaction a new bond exists: white proton plus white electron equals racial flash: what are we doing in this Mongolian madhouse? (He felt that; I swear it.) Doctor Beer breaks the crust of a smile; the corner of a Russki mouth wryses. Doctor Beer steps aside; the convoy of officers stamps past. Cossack! Anti-Semite! (But I felt it too, Cousin Vanya!)

Ou-yang sent for me again, more sociable now, to tell me that General Eisenhower had been elected and had promised to come to Korea and end the war and all sorts of fine things. For an insane moment I thought he was saying that Eisenhower would come *here*, and that we must prepare for an inspection. Ou-yang was displaying good will. I had no idea what I was expected to say, so I said that I would miss him, and that we must have lunch some time when it was all over. No. These pleasantries whizzed through an exhausted mind, but no sound issued. I shrugged. A year and a half ago there had been talk of a truce. Now there would be more talk of a truce. It was the prisoners' equivalent of the Christian heaven, the Communist utopia: later, always later. The smart ones, the tough ones, knew that there was no such thing and never would be. We were all lifers.

And yet we hoped. Damn, *damn*, we hoped. Even the best of us. The most brutal, obscene epithet in the English language is "optimist," and yet we hoped.

Listen, if they'd crucified somebody, if there'd been any sort of grand finale, bugles, showgirls, we'd have had a right to hope. To infer a rhythm, a beginning, middle and end: here, students, after a long and some may say tedious development, the pace quickens and the themes converge to be resolved in a thunderous climax, after which a brief anti-climax and the show is over; the audience strolls home, the actors remove their masks and are revealed as healthy and personable young men, while the echoes of bravo fade. Nah. Nothing.

I'm not sure. Maybe in fifty years I'll see a rhythm to it. Stalin died the first week in March, in 1953, and it made no apparent difference; the Chinese announced the event with solemn sorrow, and we milled around wondering what they expected us to do or say; should we cheer or look gloomy or what? Nothing. But in a queer tickling way it did make a difference: the passage of an age, the final laying of some ancient curse; the world was infinitesimally but truly different, and any

213

difference was to the good. We were only phantoms by then but that day we thickened slightly, grew a layer of skin, took on a misty, flesh-colored outline.

So that when, a month later, the gods commanded us to live, it was not too late. Strong men wept, you bet. It was called Operation Little Switch, the exchange of the badly sick and wounded. I had only twenty-odd of those, but the exchange itself, the event, was overwhelming. It was like thick meat soups and platters of spiced fish, fowl and beef in rich sauces (some of the men vomited the day after the announcement, as if to mark by an act of violence the precise moment of belief); like a trainload of fancy whores suddenly, whoopingly, attacking us (talk of women began immediately: projects, fantasies, minutely detailed descriptions). Anger blossomed, and affection; we cursed the progs, and slugged one another lightly on the arm in greeting. Ah, it took damn little! Hell, I got excited too, wise old doc, intimate of morality; for a while there I simply forgot to be lugubrious.

It was our turn in July, and there were no sentimental farewells. Von Ou-yang and I made no plans for a cigar at the United Nations tearoom, where we would pursue our discussion of Nietzsche at leisure. Hell, I never even knew if he had a wife and kids. I suppose if I'd done what he asked I could have come to know him better, and maybe made more sense of the whole two and a half years, the whole century; but the price was too high. I'm not talking about the political price; I hope you understand that by now. What they were— communists or vegetarians or technocrats, utopians or sensualists or lovers of wildlife—was not the point. I had to say no; *that* was the point. I say no to you too, so as to remain myself, which is little enough.

They signed the truce on July 27, 1953. Operation Big Switch followed. It took us some ten seconds to pack. Yes, Ou-yang sent for me. His office was full of Chinese; I was the only Occidental. Which reminds me that in that whole damn war I saw hardly any Koreans. I stepped in and he said, "Well," and there was a murmur of greeting. "Well," I said. Failing altogether to seize the opportunity. Think: I could have been cold and unforgiving. Could have extolled my country. Could have spat. Could have threatened to report them to the proper authorities. Could have laughed or cried or wet my pants. I just said, "Well." Then Ou-yang said, "Here is a man who wishes to *meet* you." An officer smiled warmly. "He speaks no English," Ou-yang said. "Chang Ting-hua. Pee-joe Die-foo. "

The officer stepped forward and held forth a hand. I took it. Why not?

"This is the man," Ou-yang said, "whose life you saved. Before your capture."

Chang Ting-hua spoke.

"He asks me to thank you," Ou-yang said.

"Thank him for the cigarettes and the food," I said.

"It was a bad time for us, and the dried peas saved lives."

Ou-yang did so, and Chang nodded some more. He spoke, and handed me a small cloth-covered box, about four inches by two by one.

"He would like you to have this," Ou-yang said, "to thank you and to hope that this will not come again."

The box was fastened by two little ivory teeth that passed through loops in the cloth. I disengaged them and raised the lid. Inside was a tiny covered dish, of porcelain, and in the dish a gummy red wax; beside the dish was a square-sectioned shaft of ivory, with characters in relief on one end. Awkwardly I dipped the end in the wax and held it up. Chang smiled. Ou-yang braced a small pad of paper and I stamped it. The characters were delicately carved; they might have been dragons and birds.

"It is called a *chop*," Ou-Yang said, "and that is his name. Chang, here, and ting, and hua. He wants you to have that."

"Well," I said, "I'm grateful. It's very beautiful. I'll take good care of it, and I'll keep it all my life and give it to my son when I die."

Ou-yang translated, and Chang was pleased. I covered the dish and laid the chop in place and closed the box. What the hell, I thought. I remember grinning, and I remember thinking that: what the hell. I reached inside my collar and tugged the necklace of dog tags over my head, and offered them. It was clearly a classic and refined gesture: the exhalation of approval was celestial music. Chang beamed and accepted the tags. The officers were murmuring, "How, how," which meant good, good, and a patter of applause rose. Then Chang began to laugh. He laughed loud, in great booming gusts, and his eyes sparkled at me, and I figured I knew why he was laughing. These damn fools, he was saying, these imbeciles, every damn one of them, yours and mine, these *shits*—and then I was laughing too. The others fell silent and then giggled politely. Perhaps. Perhaps not. Perhaps Chang merely thought I was funny-looking, with the big nose and the round eyes. Anyway, we laughed for some time. Then we shook hands again and I said, "Ding how," and he said, "Okay," and we laughed a bit more. I waved a silly salute at the company and said, "Good-bye." They nodded and cackled. I shook hands with Ou-yang. "Good-bye," I said. The impulse to say "thank you" was very strong, which made me feel foolish and angry and moderately demented, but I smiled and smiled. "Goodbye," he said. "Good luck." I nodded and backed off, bowing and ducking and waving, and shot a last wink at Chang, who also winked, and then I was outside and shortly on a truck for Panmunjom and later Inchon and you know the rest.

16

"No HARD FEELINGS," Cornelius said angrily. The bridge sailed by above them. Benny contemplated San Francisco with no great emotion.

"Colonels and up," Benny said.

"The more I know the less I know," Cornelius said. "There was one man who thought the Chinese were protecting him from the North Koreans."

"No escapes," Benny said.

"Not one. Not one in the whole war. And as far as we know only nineteen prisoners died after that first July. Only nineteen in two years."

"What happened to Yuscavage?"

The question was for Alex, who shook his head cheerfully. "Classified."

Secrets: good guys, bad guys. "Who killed Ewald?"

"Classified."

"Yes. Poor kid. Thousands like him."

"You said it was your fault."

"I gave him ideas," Benny said. "I saved his soul. I set him a good example. Never set a good example. It may kill somebody."

Soon Gabol said, "San Francisco. How does it feel?"

"Never been there," Benny said.

"See the world."

"Benny," Cornelius said,"I still think it was a just war."

"There are no just wars," Benny said. "There are only dead people."

"Your country matters," Cornelius said.

Country matters. Do you think I meant country matters? "On your own turf, then," Benny said. "Otherwise you have to believe that everybody in the world is your enemy. Gabol can tell you what that's called."

"Do me a favor," Alex said. "Stay out of the army."

Benny laughed ungrudgingly. "I promise. What about you?"

"Oh, there'll be a place for me somewhere," Alex said.

A bank of fog thickened astern and flowed silently toward the hills. It blotted out the bridge. The hills of San Francisco stood bright, busy, unpocked. Benny weighed one seventy-five and was still hungry. Not a mark on him, not a scratch, no stories for Joseph. I was kicked once by a Chinese guard. I ate walnut soup and belched. "And you do me a favor," he said. "Don't give me a medal."

"It's not up to me," Alex said. "If they give you one, you'll just have to put up with it."

Melancholy stilled them; they leaned upon the rail—officers and gentlemen, ignorant, useless, mortal—and were borne home. An hour later Carol's miraculous face rose to meet Benny's, and he knew he had learned something about love.

The
Oldest Boy
in the World

17

It is no small thing for a man of forty-six to be roused at dawn by colic; so it befell Benjamin Beer, M.D., on his very birthday. He emerged from yearning infinities and pawed the telephone, remembering almost immediately who he was—existence precedes essence, but only by a second or so. His ''Doctor Beer speaking'' was grave, sympathetic, unresenting; he heard the complaint, prescribed, comforted the young mother, and rang off. Gray light, mizzle: six o'clock. He rose ponderously, a bear at winter's end, and sprang the shades; the lake lay gray, pocked by raindrops, treetops poking up, gnarled diluvian hands; on a black branch a kingfisher ruled.

Benny stretched. He inhaled strenuously. He touched his toes, again, again. He twisted his torso left and right. He scraped his coated tongue on furred teeth, and resolved again to resist cigars. Barefoot he padded to the bathroom, answered other calls, showered. He shaved, whipping a bowl of soap with a badger-hair brush. He scoured his perfect teeth. He combed his undiminished hair, modestly shaggy now in the new

223

fashion, edged artistically in silver. The finished product, naked, groomed, pleased him. Presentable and racy still, though graying much within.

He costumed himself in shorts, a T-shirt, dark brown woolen socks, tan corduroy trousers, a shirt of wide brown and white stripes, and a classic, ageless brown jacket of herringbone tweed. He thrust his feet into ankle-high brown suede shoes. He filled the customary pockets with the customary minor baggage, including a monogrammed handkerchief, gift of Joseph Beer on a previous birthday. He passed quietly through the hallway, with the customary bittersweet glance at Carol's door, the customary twinge of mad, melancholy lust for that dearest of dolors, and stole successfully downstairs.

Outside and squinting, spattered by rain, he paused for an invocation: "Wheat and soybeans," he told the sun god, "closed higher." He dashed for his car. He had told Jacob it was a Fiat luxe, and Jacob had believed. He peered out over the new lake at the roc's nest, barely visible in the rain, a tangled mass of twigs and withes woven patiently by a thousand years of auks, dodos, moas, phoenixes and pesky crows. For fifteen years Benny had wondered what secrets its prickly bowl cradled, what riddles universal and eternal lay raveled and revealed within: riddles of spring, of migration, of survival, of love. Tomorrow he would see; he would row to that nest in his own boat, and the man-made lake would be, at last, high enough. He assumed, always, that he would be present tomorrow.

He had thickened with the years and now trudged through his days heavy and sad, though still a handsome dog and shamefully susceptible to the tawdriest impulses. Within him there dwelt a raddled, stunted monster, rearing hoarsely to ogle and scratch. This fiendish skink inhabited a small but growing void at the center of Benny, and was perhaps a native of Korea. Once a year or so Benny let him out for exercise.

Fifteen years Benny had driven this road! He drove toward town, crossed the wooded ridge, admired the undulating fall of a dozen dingles behind the scrim of rain; he let the road carry him downhill, and left the dam behind, and the drowned houses. Fifteen years. His vision had blurred a bit, a recent annoyance, but otherwise he lived in a serviceable body, its tone maintained by recurrent orgies of rage, despair and romantic fizz: he had committed himself to the preservation of a species he despised.

"Man is the only animal that commits moral nuisance," the old doctor had pointed out. Bartholomew drove slowly, with kindness and deliberation, as if the comfortable automobile were a friend, a partner; Benny sat loose and unworried beside him and admired the fine fluffy white hair, the sharp blue eyes, the tangled white brows. Bartholomew wore a white linen suit and a blue denim shirt, and his hands were light on the wheel, the pink nails shiny. Benny, restored to fighting weight, felt gross.

"We can see it all from here," Bartholomew said, and drove onto the shoulder and let the engine die.

They contemplated many miles of green valley, and dots that were dairy cows, and a thin winding line of blue river. The lighter blue sky was cloudless and endless. Two hawks hovered a mile apart. The two men sat for some time without speaking. Birds sang, twittered, chawked. Grasses rippled. "Indian country," Bartholomew said. "The names. The river's called Mill River, but it used to be the Misqueag. That hogback, above those red barns there, that's Quaggin Ridge. See a nose now and then, among the farmers, like that fellow on the nickel.''

"It's beautiful," Benny said. "I don't believe it."

"You may be bored here."

"Not for a while," Benny said. "and maybe never."

"Got a few weekend commuters. They liven things up. Your neighbors, some of them, if you take that house. Got a painter too. Fuzzy squares, orange, yellow. Not my style, but then I go back some."

This valley too went back some, this pastoral Eden, macadam roads and eaved roofs. The shadows of mastodons, and files of phantom redskins. "That's a sawmill."

"Yes. Westerdonck's. A lot of Westerdoncks around here. Thrown out of Holland for horse-thievery about Rembrandt's time. Been a Westerdonck killed in every war we ever had. Got a little museum down there, and talk your head off if you let them."

"Healthy-looking place," Benny said. "Long life."

"Long life. Tough winters, but they're good for you. Don't feel much over twenty-one myself."

"Lazy summers."

"No such thing. Baby doctors are always busy, and then I'm the only doctor in the village proper. Young ones like to be up to Suffield with the electronics and the new machines."

"Not for me," Benny said. "Just a quiet time with some nice people. I just want to be left alone. Not vote, even."

"Nice people. That's a tall order. Been a doctor for

almost sixty years and if I had it to do again I'd be a veterinarian. Better class of patients.''

"Strong talk."

"I get fed up with them," Bartholomew said. "They breed like animals and drink themselves to death and then tell me human life is sacred. I take a little bourbon myself from time to time."

"For the circulation," Benny murmured.

"Exactly. And I have nothing against sex. Beats hell out of television. Old enough now to appreciate it. But—oh hell, I don't know, no style any more."

"My father talks like that."

"A doctor?"

Benny shook his head. "A tailor. A little Jewish tailor from the big city." He stared off at the dairy cows. "I meant to ask about that. Certain troubles I will not take lightly."

"I wouldn't worry," Bartholomew said. "Times change. Anyway the Jew they had in mind is about four foot six with horns and a tail. Hell, boy, I suppose you're some sort of hero. Any trouble, spit in their eye."

"By God," Benny said. "A hero."

"Anyway they've got the Negroes to worry about now."

"Are there many?"

"About fifty families, over in Suffield. Some of them work at the hospital. No better than anybody else, no worse. Christ, boy, we've got some Mayflower families here I wouldn't pee on. Don't worry about that kind of thing. Look out there to your right."

They had rounded a long curve and Benny could see back to the upper part of the valley.

227

"Back of that notch," the old man said, "that's where the house is. If you come here, grab it. Highest house in a beautiful bowl, birch and pine, maples."

"It looked pretty."

"Pretty, hell, it's beautiful. That bowl is God's own south forty: deer and woodchucks and foxes, possums and porcupines. Every five years or so a bear passes through. Fool engineers want to put a dam in the notch so some monopoly can make a fortune selling power to the big city. Been talking about it ever since the WPA, but it won't happen. A little farther back there's a lake about half a mile across, bass there, perch, lots of little ones."

"It's all too good," Benny said. "There must be something wrong with it."

"Well, there is. One movie. A rundown high school twelve miles off. No music or theaters or anything like that. For that you take a couple of days in Sodom and Gomorrah. You said your kids were about five?"

"Five and four, boy and girl. Never even saw the girl until she was two. Never even knew she was coming until she was there."

"They're years from high school, and the grammar school's good. Small. Basic. Time they get to high school there may be a better one."

"One thing at a time."

"Good sense," the old doctor said. "There's our little town again. You want to visit the hospital now?"

"If you have time."

"Time? A man of eighty has all the time in the world."

They drove cautiously through Misqueag and Benny noted again the drugstore, the general store, the hardware; people waved, and Bartholomew waved back, and Benny found himself waving and wondered if this were a mirage, this exotic world of slow-moving giants, of calendar babies and catalog overalls. Saturday night drunks? Would a figure pop out of the barbershop, masked and feathered, rattling gourd and pointing bone, shouting "For Christ!"? Were there Kallikaks? Antique and mysterious corruptions of the blood, foot-long earlobes? Old Doc Beer on the courthouse steps, sipping Agri-cola. No French movies, but a town whore.

The Misqueag Diner was open for business, Sylvester Burris a hustler, a black capitalist, no illusions, life is travail, and Benny scrunched across the wet gravel through a cool white morning, mist and cloud and the light rising, Benny drifting between dew and rain. The diner was classically meretricious and one of the few commercial structures Benny could abide: not an old railroad car, but chrome and fluorescence and red plastic, and honest-to-God imitation linoleum on the floor. He clumped up the cement steps and inside. Sylvester Burris, black and round, the Pinsky of a new era, suspended his sunrise ritual—slicing, dishing, setting out—to smile and say good morning. "Coffee is ready."

Benny swung aboard an unstable stool and set his palms flat on the cool formica. Finally he lied: "Good morning." Burris was sixty-some and they had been friends for twelve years. Burris was a widower with two grown children, Artie and Mary, and they too were Benny's friends—he thought, he hoped; Mary and Artie, it was not easy these days.

Burris set coffee, sugar and real cream before him

229

and said, "How about ham and eggs? I was about to, myself."

"Good."

Burris bustled. Sounds arose, sizzles, odors. Beyond the panes light thinned, trees loomed. "How's your boy?"

"Just fine," Benny said. "College boys. Blue jeans and no underwear. How's Artie this grand morning?"

"My son the labor leader," Burris said. "Well, they won't strike today. I tell him not to strike at all, but they will—tomorrow, more than likely. He's got the orderlies and the janitors and some of the practical nurses, and the painters and plumbers will go out in sympathy."

"Hallelujah," Benny said. "Solidarity forever."

"You may not laugh when they have you toting bedpans."

"True. Not many patients, anyway."

"You wouldn't refuse?"

"No," Benny said. "Artie does his thing, I do mine."

Burris nodded. "God bless fresh eggs! Don't think Artie isn't grateful."

"Just keep quiet and give some decent service," Benny said.

Burris laughed softly. "He thanks you all the same. Just doesn't know how."

"Oh, what did I do," Benny said in minor but real annoyance. "Stop being grateful for nothing. What good was it? All those damn Westerdoncks and other such Calvinists. They won't even C.O. white Quakers, much less big black Artie with that fat ass in those tight black pants and those nostrils like wastebaskets." Burris jiggled with laughter and Benny grinned. "I don't know why you laugh. He almost went to jail."

"That's why," Burris said. "That *almost*."

"It was none of my doing," Benny said. "It was those smart lawyers from the big city. Hebrews and Ethiopes. So now I have to run my own bedpans."

"Mary'll work twice as hard."

"Now there's a girl," Benny said lightly.

Burris set platters on the counter and doffed his apron; he stepped around to sit beside Benny. "Oh that smells good. Oh my God that smells good! Some days I can hardly eat breakfast. But when I am hungry in the morning, food smells better than any other time."

"Morning is the pure time," Benny said, "before you ruin your senses. Morning's like being a virgin."

"Son," Burris said solemnly, "I lost my cherry in nineteen hundred and twenty-four and you cannot expect me to recall the previous state." In some gloom he added, "I suppose I'll find it again soon."

"A transplant," Benny said.

"Wouldn't that be something. Well. We sure got to the subject early in the day, for a couple of old bucks."

"We have no morals," Benny said. "No morals."

Sylvester mopped orange yolk with golden toast. "Ah. Morals is just when you want to and you don't."

Momentarily Benny was breathless, hot, tremendous; he sipped coffee.

"I held my breath for a bit," Burris said. "It was about as crazy in all respects as anything I ever heard of."

"You never said a word. Or did you talk to Mary?"

"What word?" Burris chewed, old and tired, perhaps wise, tall and black and capable of scorn, pride, the wounding shaft.

"I'd have given almost anything," Benny said. "There's that almost again."

The mizzle persisted beneath a white sky; Benny belched, and drove respectfully on the slick blacktop. The sea hissed and boiled; at the bow Nan shouted and waved and he made out Rarotonga rising from the mist. He halted behind a school bus and peered in sleepy curiosity as Frank Cole in the police car raced toward them and past. At seven-thirty. Crime knows no season. Or Cole had a girl friend. Behind him the siren howled; he cringed and then craned: Cole semaphored. Benny sprayed gravel, swung about and followed. Cole was small, dapper, military, bald beneath the campaign hat; with hostile eyes and thin lips he was perhaps ideal, the passionless enemy, everybody's perfect pig, by the numbers, crack shot; yet in small, indolent Suffield he was an exaggeration. Furthermore, he suffered ulcers and was persuaded that these caused chronic and inexorable bad breath. In moments of drama and glory he ducked and mumbled. The siren again: Otter Branch Road. Benny experienced a tremor, a premonition, goose flesh. And this his birthday. Signs and portents. "One of these days," he said aloud. "Hell and damnation. Death and other inconveniences." Frank Cole skidded; Benny heeded, and rolled on slowly. He had once believed that nothing important could happen before luncheon.

He was not astonished when Cole roared into the Coughlins' driveway. Cole ejected himself from the police car and dashed for the door. Benny followed with the black bag. The storm door slammed. The house smelled like a summer camp; the washing machine was in the living room and on the mantelpiece stood a rank of tin trophies. He crossed to the bedroom. Rosalie Coughlin sat blubbering; Frank Cole was livid and furious, and jerked a thumb at the crib. The baby was named Roland after Walt Coughlin's father, and there was blood on his mouth, the lips smeared and the classic trickle at one corner, vivid crimson against the chalky skin. One eye had started from its socket. The head itself was misshapen, lopsided, and one arm was obviously broken. Benny was quite weary, and closed his eyes.

Rosalie sobbed and wailed. "Oh, Benny."

He spoke to Cole: "Have you called an ambulance?"

Cole was outraged: "They were out. I left word." To Rosalie he said, "Where is he?"

She shook her head.

Benny asked, "Are you all right?" She nodded. "He's alive," Benny said. "Let's be quick." The bag was open and he was performing. Hey, presto! Salve on the gauze, gauze on the eye, a quick strip of tape for light pressure, voilà! the deuce of clubs. He felt the head, soft, impossible to say, perhaps a fracture and perhaps riding up over the fontanel. With two tongue depressors he splinted the arm. He wiped the mouth. The good eye was closed but the baby was breathing. "A blanket," Benny said.

Rosalie sobbed. Cole pushed her away and stripped the bed. The two men folded the blanket, an army blanket, like soldiers retiring a flag. "Rosalie. Put on a coat, quick." Rosalie sobbed. Benny slapped her lightly, a token, and cupped her cheek in his hand. "Yes," she burbled, and rose. Benny and Cole paused to observe; yea, on the brink of death, god damn it, she was twenty-three years old and for a season had been Miss

233

Misqueag. She wore a sheer short nightgown doubtless mail-ordered from a dubious magazine; her nipples stared, immense, and her navel completed the triangle, and below it the darker triangle flourished. "Hurry up," Cole said regretfully. "Damn that man." The woman rummaged in a closet; Benny and Cole shook their heads. Benny set the baby gently on the blanket. "Christ what a piece," Cole murmured, and Benny remembered her on another day, a dopey broad but incandescent. "She'll carry the baby," he said. "Go fast. I'll phone ahead and be right there." Rosalie returned in a raincoat and harem slippers, and after a moment of utter desolation, the doc and the cop and the broad staring down at the future of the race, Benny shooed them out.

They beat him to the hospital by ten minutes; Benny ran inside. "Good," Cole said. "You don't need me, do you?"

"No," Benny said. "Go get him."

"I'll find him," Cole said. "I've got the state troopers out."

"Drunken bastard," Benny said. "I'll call your office when I know."

"How's it look?"

"Bad."

"Good luck."

Benny nodded.

"Why'd she ever marry him?" Cole asked.

"Don't ask me," Benny said. "You're his cousin."

"Oh hell," Cole said. "With a hundred Westerdoncks in between."

"She wanted fun," Benny said.

"Christ, we all want fun," Cole said.

"Amen."

"Heartbeat's all right," Bobby Grentzer reported. "Setting up a cardiogram now."

The child was pale as death, still but for the slight, regular rise—barely more than a throb—of his frail chest. "Respiration?"

"Regular. Very shallow. Do you want a tracheotomy?"

"Not yet. I want a chest x-ray. Rod Cohn in yet?"

"On the way."

"The eye has to go, I'm afraid. X-ray the skull. You touched?"

"Yes. Nothing obvious. You want a tap?"

"Not yet. Blood pressure?"

"Sixty over forty."

"Damn. Could be low normal, could be low. We'll see. No i-v. Blood pressure every half-hour. If it drops to forty start an i-v and call me. Motion?"

"A twitch now and then. Head rolls a little. What happened?"

Benny told him.

"Ah Jesus," Grentzer said. "I wish I had him here." Grentzer was an athlete; the new breed, he had doctored in Vietnam, cursing; he wore striped bell-bottoms but had kept his sanitary crew-cut; as if in apology, he wore a peace medallion. "Previous history?"

"Previously," Benny said, "he only beat his wife. Where is she?"

"Ward six. Bruises. Otherwise all right, I think. Iacino's looking at her."

"Good. There was blood."

"Lip and gum."

"All right," Benny said. "Take care of the arm. And I want a blood count, and schedule another in six hours. I'll be back in fifteen minutes."

Bedded, sitting up in a hospital gown, her hair brushed, light lipstick, Rosalie seemed fifteen, and Benny, already glum, grew murderously sad that he was not twenty-five. He sat on the bed and took her hand. Nurses marched, patients gossiped, a janitor swept; those were the snapping twigs, bird calls and soughing breezes of Benny's life. "He's alive, and we'll know a lot more in an hour."

"Oh thank God for that," she said, as if she had been taught to say it.

Yes indeed. Thank God for a one-eyed baby with possible brain damage. Benny subdued faint nausea. How old was baby Roland? A year? Fourteen months? The oldest boy in the world: he might be dead tomorrow.

Benny smiled at Rosalie as he had been taught to smile. Her father raised hogs and sat on the school board to keep sex education out of the classroom. He contemplated this piece. Damn Cole. She was not a piece now; wondrous how breasts could vanish beneath a hospital gown, gender itself diminish. And this was a bad day, a worse day than she knew. He saw her old at forty. She would never read a book, and would shop in plastic curlers, and the estimable breasts would sag and wither, and he saw her at sixty in a trailer camp.

A hand touched his cheek and a voice said, "Hello, Benny," and his heart lifted as he said "Mary" and touched the hand. "You're lucky," she told Rosalie. "You were late, so we boiled the eggs fresh. They're hot." Rosalie smiled briefly; Mary Burris made her comfortable and set the tray before her. Rosalie exclaimed in a baby's voice, and carefully set the fork to the left, and the knife and spoon to the right. Benny's glance was neutral, and Mary winced: in the presence of a patient's relatives, no news was bad news. Delicately Rosalie achieved her preparations, and Benny could see her laboring through an article in a young-marrieds' magazine, frowning, her lips stirring, the ponderous, inching effort to accomplish ladydom. He cursed himself for a snob. He had not seen her for a year, perhaps longer. He had known Rosalie for seven or eight years and remembered the adolescent, the pale blue eyes, the precocious bust, the cheerleader. When he was tipsy he believed that a great love affair awaited him, and when he was drunk it looked a bit like her. A pattern it was, a bad habit, and he accepted it as others accepted red hair or a squint.

"That's what started him," she was saying, talking with her mouth full. "The baby woke him. Then he wanted to make it, but I had to feed the baby and he got mad and made a drink, and then he started to talk, complaining, he's always complaining and all he ever wants to do is make it, and he talked himself into a fit and then he hit me. Then he drank some more and I wouldn't, I hate liquor, and he went and made faces at the baby and then he spit on him—spitted—and then he slapped him. So I hit him and he knocked me down and began hitting the baby. Then the baby—" She sobbed, and cried out.

"Stop it," Benny said. "Finish your juice. It's all right now." It was not all right now, but he had treated babies for fifteen years, and parents too. "Then the baby passed out and he got scared and ran off."

237

"Yes."

"You told Frank."

"On the way. I wish I could have married somebody like you." A bolus of egg white had lodged in the corner of her mouth; Mary handed her a tissue.

"Sure," Benny said. "I'm like all the rest."

The baby was in x-ray and Benny, a bad taste souring his mouth, retreated to the staff room for coffee. "That's a real man," Iacino said. "Who is he, anyway?" Iacino was a female intern, or a lady doctor, or whatever the approved phrase was; in Benny's presence she was shy and attentive, which pleased him.

"Ah, you're new here," Benny said. "Walt Coughlin. Scion of one of our oldest families. The last of a long line of cousins."

Iacino grimaced.

"Possibly the best mechanic in the world," Benny went on. "Ace stock-car driver. He races. He plows your snow, and sometimes your wife. He drinks. In his own phrase, he plugs a lot of broads. The salt of the earth and the backbone of America. I'm tired."

"She's pretty," Iacino said.

Benny wallowed in a leather chair and gulped coffee. "He's got pale blue eyes like hers, and light blond hair like hers, and pale, pale skin. The eyes are flat and his reflexes are perfect and he's a famous hunter. S.S. incarnate, and he's one of us."

"What's S.S.?"

"Never mind," Benny sighed. "You young folk. Anyway, he's only medium size. I could take him in ten by leaning. If he was six-four he'd rule the world. How's the Vannep kid?"

238

"Fine. That's young for a hernia."

"Hell," Benny said, "they grow up fast these days. He'll be back at thirteen with the clap."

Iacino thought that funny, but she was an intern. "Do you want a central venous pressure?"

"Not yet."

"I've never done one."

"Don't train on this one."

Iacino glanced away. "Sorry."

Benny hauled himself up and kissed her on the cheek. "Stop that," she said. "Pig. I'm not one of your grateful mothers."

"You wrong me savagely, ma'am," he said, and then gravely, "I never in my life touched a patient's mother."

"I'm sorry." She was visibly embarrassed. Benny thought she must be sorely ashamed of his maudlin puerility, until she said, "You're just so damn warm and wise, and everybody loves you."

"That's awful," he said. "I'm a mess. I'm almost psychotic." He went on awkwardly, and could not help himself: "That's why I never—the mothers, and all. Everybody needs one absolute. Everybody has to start somewhere. I have to keep it separate. Some people don't eat meat. It's—I—sorry." He shook his head deliberately, like a man sobering up. "I'm forty-six today. Perhaps I shall run for mayor."

"Many happy returns," she said.

"I don't know if I could stand another one," he said.

"It has to be removed," Cohn said. "No question." Cohn was tall and pallid with long straight black hair and a dash of mustache; he reminded Benny of Dreyfus, or for that matter of the Bourbons. "I trust the happy father will be castrated in public. Does the mother consent?

"We have the release," Benny said. "Listen, this baby may be dead by tonight. No sense telling the mother about the eye."

"You're a gentleman," Cohn said. "Like to meet the father. An eye for an eye, isn't it? Well. I'll calm down. Steady hand. Nerves of steel. Ah, God."

"I'll prep him," Bobby said.

"His father prepped him," Cohn said.

"His father had a bad time in Vietnam," Bobby said.

"I see. And returned inured to violence. Not his fault. The country's fault."

"No," Bobby said. "Merely an observation. I had a bad time in Vietnam too. So did a rather large number of babies."

"We must be the only species," Cohn said, "that bothers to produce an equal number of males and females. We'd get along fine if it was about one to twenty. Let's stand by with everything. We may need it. Levophed, plasma, the works."

Benny left them to their work and made his early rounds, snooping and prying; busybody, he visited all wards. His children sat playing, or lay frightened: poor anemic Hale, with a knot of brown hair like a Seneca chief; poor Wanko, seven years old and freshly deprived of tonsils; poor Amberly, an excess of hydrochloric acid in the stomach, "may be a manifestation of neuroticism," at five! All of them, a half-dozen, innocents in this torture garden. He clucked and chirruped and grinned. Ah, what one saw, nature's failures! Omphalopagus, he had seen that once, dead, a twin mon-

240

ster joined at the umbilicus. In thine image. Here was Hirschberg, with cystitis: a bladder infection at three. Not to mention simple deformities. Always, on rounds, he thought of Joseph and Sarah, breathed mute thanks: mumps, measles, chicken pox, colds, bruises, scratches—how simple, how peaceful. Though other wounds prevailed: Joseph lost, flailing, fleeing to sulk in college; Sarah living happily with a lout, a bankrupt composer, unpublished, of bankrupt songs, thirty-two and illiterate. That, at any rate, was past; Sarah laughed about it. And himself: forty-six and a vampire. Basilisk and gryphon, potential molester of sweet young things. He paused to cheer Vannep, wan Vannep, snatched from home and mother, dispatched to the dark regions, restored to life neatly hemmed and patched.

He prowled the wards; all was quiet. Many empty beds. At Ward 9, west, he paused: twelve beds for terminal cases. He passed it by. Sufficient unto the day. He went to his office and studied charts. A signature for commitment: Jean Diehl, poor lady, McCook's patient. A note from Taubeneck: can we see you at three. Ah yes, that. A strike tomorrow. What next? Communists. Lysergic acid in the reservoir. He stepped to the hallway and hailed an orderly; it was little Crewe, shiny black, Afro'd. They exchanged good mornings. "Just wanted to know," Benny said, "you going out tomorrow?"

"Depends on Artie," Crewe said. "But it looks like yes, you dig? You hear any new buzz from upstairs?"

"No. They want to see me at three."

"Well you tell 'em no more bullshit," Crewe said.

"I may do that. Is Artie around?"

"Nope. Be along later, maybe."

"Thanks. I'll look for him."

Crewe grinned happily. "He's a *mean* man."

"He sure is," Benny said. "Good luck."

"We could use that," Crewe said. "A little good luck is about due."

"It went fine," Cohn said, "but the poor little Cyclops is half-dead. I tell you, I'm not even angry now."

"It passes and we forget," Benny said. "Every day."

"I just want to go into some other line of work," Cohn said. "Cop, maybe. In a dictatorship. None of this nonsense about lawyers and trials."

"All right," Benny said. "Let's keep him alive."

" Antigonus Cyclops," Cohn said, "a Macedonian king, one of Philip's sons, one of Alexander's generals. Lost an eye. Lived to be eighty."

"The things we know," Benny said.

"The things we learn," Cohn said.

"Here's the plates," Grentzer said, and they huddled to look.

"He's no worse," Benny told Rosalie, "but you're in for a rough time."

"Oh Benny," she said. "Oh Benny."

"Don't talk about it."

"No. All right." She smiled. "I feel better. It's so nice just lying here, and everybody waiting on me. Will it cost a lot? If I stay over it will."

"Don't worry about that. Just relax." And prepare for the death of your first-born, and maybe your husband will draw five-to-fifteen, and you can go to the big city and be a call girl and read magazines.

"You're such a marvelous man," she said passionately.

242

He dropped in here and there and distributed good cheer. He walked among his people, his troops, and waved and smiled, a pompous fool, Agamemnon inspiring the ranks before Troy, fine figger of a man, glassy smile. He conferred with Mrs. Mackey, supervisor of nurses, almost deaf, who had once, to his knowledge, misheard instructions and caused, or permitted, a death. "She's not to know anything about the baby's condition except from me or Grentzer. Got that? *Nothing*." He moved on. He blew a kiss to Eleanor Chandler, dietitian, winked at Iacino, goggled at a gaggle of student nurses, and walked away, hand in hand, with Mary Burris. So strode straight-shafted Benny among the hollow vessels. Melancholic, he drove home for his office hours.

18

HE HAD BEEN unfaithful to Carol a dozen times, at decent intervals, and often this drive from the hospital, rousing memories and skirting landmarks, became in his mind a historical pageant, scenes and acts better forgotten but unforgettable. A public park: here his imminence randy Ben Beer had sat with her prominence dandy Madame X, he growing every moment more prominent, she more imminent. The summer air musky, the shrubs a jungle. Deutero-Benny lapsing and backsliding. And older, thirty-five then. Her husband a selectman. Benny not even ashamed, merely weary. But even now, on his forty-sixth birthday, observing traffic signals, he lusted in memory and cranked up a small smile. Benjamin Beer, M.D., hardened ex-con, and always this deplorable tendency to moon and gargle. Well, bless her substantial shade. Were his needs ignoble? Unlikely; he was, after all, a prince. But he too harbored a hollow that wanted filling, deep within, a spherical hollow, cold and dark, that awaited some finishing touch. The angel of death's meat hook perhaps. Work could not fill it, or card games or bowling or memories. It was perhaps connected to the navel. It was perhaps the skink's lair. That tiny arctic void. In the beginning was the void.

He crossed Huddleston Memorial Bridge. The bronze plaque, dead heroes, flagless today in the drizzle. The Westerdoncks had not yet lost a son in Vietnam and were growing nervous. Everywhere the dead, the dying, Hiroshimas, Biafras, Vietnams: why save Roland? Penny wise, pound foolish. Save Joseph, save Sarah, lose a million elsewhere. Where was Lin? Where was Ou-yang? Should Benny abandon these pampered babes and minister to Asians? Yet he paid his taxes, in sorrow and wincing guilt; signed his returns, affixing Chang's chop—bold gesture!—and killed children. He should go. He knew he should go. God of Abraham and Isaac. Slaughter of the innocents.

A billboard: porkettes. These existed: porkettes.

He grimaced as the brookless conviction gripped him again, goading, the prick of madness: there was yet love to come, passion, annihilation. He blinked at the blurred road, slowed, halted at a stop sign: his car stalled. He revived it, raced the engine, proceeded. And passed the slave quarters, Suffield's small black enclave, roads without names: Road #1, Road #2, Road #3. Where he had met Sylvester. A better memory if not a happier. A house call, at Mary's request, Benny driving slowly into the compound, Burris waving from the doorway, their first moments of conversation courtly, Oriental, stately honorifics. An old black man with swellings in the groin, nodes. Benny asked, "What have you got on your foot?" and Sylvester said, "My sock," which sufficed; they laughed and bantered. Benny examined the blistered foot. "Fungus." He prescribed. "Four a day for ninety days."

245

Burris nodded, hmm'd. In the silence Benny swallowed, smiled miserably, wished he were other, elsewhere, a progressive, scientific, humanistic country doctor in Dostoevsky, wringing his hands and polishing his pince-nez. But he was an ancient Hebrew bringing bad news to a clapboard house on Road #3—a house which, he now noticed, smelled faintly of alien meats—and he could only blink, scowl, ignore a twitching muscle in his upper arm and hope that within the next few seconds words spoken by one of them would assemble themselves into decent meaning. Burris obliged. "That stuff costs. Fact is, I have no money."

Benny said, "That's no problem."

Burris cocked an eye.

"The drug companies," Benny said, "give me all sorts of free samples. Advertising. I have cabinets full of stuff."

Burris accepted, nodded; a little luck was every man's due. "Can I handle food? I'm trying to make that diner pay."

"Yes. Just wash after you medicate. Change socks every day."

"I always do. Now, the matter of your fee."

"The matter of my fee. It was on my way."

"No," Burris said.

"All right. I'll check you once a week, you feed me once a week. What time do you open?"

"About seven. I like that."

"Sometimes breakfast is a problem," Benny said. "It would be a help."

"Done and done," Burris said. "All frying in butter. Heavy cream."

"No jukebox."

246

"I suppose you want fresh eggs."

"And back bacon."

"You'll ruin me," Burris said.

"I'll give the stuff to Mary," Benny said. "Ninety days. Don't cheat," and they moved to the door, chatting, and he left, feeling foolish but not irredeemable.

Now he crossed Bigelow's Creek. Biglow's Crick, b'gosh. In spate, white water, a screen of rain, another spate in another year, repeated attempts, unsuccessful, parents weeping silently, she in curlers, the swimmer-child pronounced dead by Doctor Beer. Farther up, in still another year, he had fished Bigelow's Creek. Bartholomew reclined on the mossy bank and discoursed quietly. "Don't know about color perception, and I don't believe it matters. Trout ain't mammals. The right fly, in the right season, they can't *not* strike."

Which year? Bartholomew seemed eternal. Now Benny was driving through the rain on his forty-sixth birthday and resisting rushes of mortality, and he thought of a photograph in his desk drawer, a night-club photograph taken, he remembered, by a half-naked female all legs, teeth and business cards: three couples plus Benny in—*where*?—Harrisburg, Pennsylvania, the festivities following hard upon a pediatrician's powwow. But the odd man out was not Benny, ah no, it was the owlish drunk beside him, the aged pixie, name long forgotten, freckled and wrinkled, rendered comatic by sour mash. Between him and Benny sat a happy memory.

"Nor will I forget," a drunken Benny later told an alarmed seatmate at thirty-five thousand feet, "a certain yellow-haired Amazon from Harrisburg, a gorgeously fair-fleshed mountain of custard, a Mont Blancmange for my Matterhorny moments." He had encountered this blond phenomenon in the cocktail bar; if conventioneer he must be, conventioneer he would be, and the third vodka was cascading down his gullet when she breasted the swinging doors. He glowed; in his finest redskin baritone he spoke: "Time . . . plant . . . corn." "Nasty," she said, and dashed imaginary ermines to the tabletop. "Bourbon and ginger ale." He retched briefly and issued commands. "Working girl?" "Sir," she said severely, but he was grinning; "Well, yes." Drowning in chicken fat, he exulted foolishly. Miserably. Ecstatically. God save us, her name was Laverne. Tawdry! Sordid! Motel! Two squids. Lovely. The old joke: asked to describe in one word the worst sexual experience he ever had, the fellow thinks a bit and then says, "Marvelous." Deutero-Benny, rooting and snuffing, the truffle king. "Young man," she says sternly, "would you do that at home?" Benny chokes, cachinnates, roars jubilee. Hee-hee-hee all the way home. Hooting in relief, joy, hilarity, love, yes damn it love, driving sedately, MD plates, a madman at the wheel. For years he glowed at the memory, fingers and toes tingling; as he had tingled and glowed in that happy bed, the two of them like frisky particles in some pornographic atom-smasher, wham! matter and anti-matter! obliteration! The blast was heard in Philadelphia. Later, a littered inscape, soul's trash, remorse; he pondered submission to the proper authorities for commitment, gelding, lobotomy. Anneal one duct, perhaps, dredge out a new gap. A simple paper-clip in the proper place. He had once been charged with "violating a stop sign."

He swung off the old road now and up the hill, on the gleaming wet year-old blacktop, and a slight skid startled him; he had judged the turn badly. He let the car drift to the grassy shoulder, accelerated, and drove on. To his left the dam loomed; he averted his eyes, as always here, fleeing its faint, massive malevolence, as if hard-hatted witch doctors bestrode its catwalks pointing the bone at unwary strangers. He drove on, ignoring the lake, the submerged old road, suburban Atlantis; what dead sneakers, abandoned kennels, discarded hibachis lay drowned? No more neighbors, only Benny, and he too restless and itchy.

Choices drummed at him. Grentzer thought he should go to Vietnam. All murthers past do stand excused in this, he had said. Children. Hundreds of thousands of them, the unlucky undead, whores and pushers, armless, paraplegics, rickets, beggars, blind, flippers for legs, Grentzer had said, phocomelia americana; he had seen it, done what he could until his own vitals rebelled and he was sent home shaking, gagging, cursing the God he had loved. Choices. Ghetto medicine. Donaldson in Texas, with the public health people, assured by the county medical society that no health problem existed. He looked, he noted, he reported: malnutrition, rickets, tuberculosis, trachoma, leprosy. "Gentlemen: as doctors in a free society you may choose to ignore this. I simply remind you that these children go to school with your children." Shock, profanity, disbelief, portly indignation; then a program, clinics, posters, a mobile diagnostic unit, and six months later nothing, nothing, the unit sold, the posters tattered, stout fellows assuring all that no health problem existed.

Like Carol: "No problem. We get along fine. You're just overworked, and you take it out on me." Possibly. Many nights he veiled mad eyes. Did the children know? They frightened him. They sensed.

Mutely they reproached. Mutely Carol reproached. Mutely Benny reproached. "We spend," he had almost said, "less than a tenth of our lives together." Beady-eyed, cramped, shuffling, a drop at the end of his nose, he had kept miserly count one year: "Three hundred and thirty nights a year," he had almost said, "I might as well be sleeping alone." He knew then that he was sick. "Never," he had almost said, "do you lean over to kiss me good night." "Always," he had almost said, "you edge away from caresses. These empty hands." "When you kiss," he had almost said, "you purse your lips and close your eyes." "Never," he had almost said, "do you wake me with a lewd surprise." We have so much," he almost said, "and so little; it is all so right, and all so wrong."

Other things he did say: witty endearments, lascivious parodies, accented invitations. But only once; they were not, it seemed, funny. Long ago, it seemed, they had been funny. "I am getting the hell out of here," he almost said, but never did, not that. Perhaps he would now. Joseph in college, Sarah officially at college but one never knew now. One was not meant, not entitled, not expected to know. The tide at high stand: marriage over, children grown, house too big. Forty-six. Imagine.

Now the rain fell thicker, in splats and blobs, and his wiper labored. He edged along the ridge and down into what remained of the bowl, the once-green bowl, once glades and glens and apple trees, black willows and alder and choke-cherries, woodchucks and muskrats and foxes, squirrels and chipmunks, and the graceful, vicious deer. Also graveled drives, boxwood, terraces, split-rail fencing, a paddle-tennis court, a paddock. All vanished, drowned. Entering his own drive he slumped, and for an instant again saw double; as he crackled to a halt he let his head bow and shut his eyes and was old. He remembered Bartholomew and said, "Let them die."

And he said, "I will gird my loins." He straightened, and only then saw the scrap of paper on the seat beside him, a note. Later; he jammed it into a pocket. He slammed the door behind him and tilted his face to the cold rain, enjoying it. He trudged to the rowboat and tugged at the painter; it was secure. He walked back to the front door, passed gravely between two saluting arborvitae, and attacked the keyhole. The key slipped and scratched, and he bent to peer. Yalu lock, he read. Preposterous. He inserted the key and entered. He trod his own carpeting, admired the halltree, the Victorian looking-glass, the graceful, operatic center staircase, curved above like rams' horns. He stood alone in his wholly owned home, wifeless, childless, unemployed. He fumbled for the note, brought it close. It was a parking ticket. He smiled like a maniac, once more goofy and unhinged, and spoke aloud to the vacant house: "I am guilty of pride, avarice, lust, envy, gluttony, anger, sloth and double-parking."

Mother Vogel fretted. If he would only look at Michael's tongue. He looked at Michael's tongue and saw the thick, tight frenum. "He has trouble with his l's," Benny ventured. Mother Vogel was astonished and delighted. This genius. "It's very simple, and not at all dangerous," Benny said. "I can do it here in the office." He heard his voice, saw his hand draw the explanatory diagram. Mother Vogel and her Michael swam to and fro. Amenities.

Next. Three patients waiting, three mommies. He

chatted, reassured, smiled, distributed a sugarless equivalent of candy, like the packaged pellets expelled by green machines in progressive zoos. Manikins, girlikins. Homely, resentful, growing into sorrow, pain and betrayal. "We want a moratorium," Bartholomew had sighed. "I save lives against my will. Wonder I haven't gone crazy. Maybe I have." Benny had been appalled at first. Not now; now he missed the old bastard. "A lie for a lie and a truth for a truth," the old man said. "In a world of horses' asses, manure is scripture." Benny heeded, and grew in wisdom.

At eleven he called the hospital and Grentzer said, "The same," and Benny thanked him. By then there were new arrivals in his waiting room. Lester Rosen, asthma; two minutes with the mother and you knew why. Repeated wounds, inflicted with love. By love. He too had inflicted a few. Lester's problem was simple. "It's called a chalazion," he spelled it for her, "and Doctor Cohn's your man. He'll do it in his office, fifteen minutes, scary but absolutely no trouble. The eyes are always scary."

"Doctor Cohn." Mrs. Rosen sniffed. "He's anti-Zionist." Benny let his vision blur and she became a dark continental beauty of the '20's or '30's, and the caption always said "disappeared during . . ." or "now in Harbin." "Not anti," Benny said. "Just non. He thinks it's none of his business."

"Well it *is*."

"But there's so much," Benny said gently, "so much wrong," and rose, initiating the tedious process, the excavation almost, by which he would rid himself of the Rosens' presence and rejoice once more in solitude.

● ● ●

In the performance of homely acts he found footing. Glumly considering Baby Roland, he stacked dishes, looked for a note from Carol, found none, and felt hunger. He spread chopped liver on Portuguese bread and poured milk. The refrigerator hummed merrily. The breakfast nook. From here he could see the rain lashing down upon his private lake. He could see the old maple and the crow's-nest, a man's height now above the surface. He doused the light and sat in the pleasant midday gloom. Solitude had its uses. He fingered a slight swelling on his chin, an ingrown hair perhaps. Perhaps cancer. He must have a checkup soon. Heal thyself. Years of good health, complacency. Strong as a bull. Ox. Only the tight chest. Cigars. He chewed, and found the taste good. He drank off the milk and poured again. Benny lives, he said. Withered and staled, but Benny lives. A rainy noon, minor key. What could he have altered, ever? Knowing that it would come to this, would he have fled at eighteen? And missed it all? 57359. Where was 57359? Pinsky was dead and his delicatessen was a stereo shop. Karp too was dead; nephritis, complications. Jacob thought Benny was on top of the world and made suits for him, elegant, fitted, Italianate. He would call Jacob tonight. Old father, old artificer.

He went to his room and sprawled. He prescribed naps, and saw no reason to except himself. Sometimes he slept. Often he lay hazy, cataloging small patients, reminiscing, seeing Bartholomew again, Ou-yang, Nan. He could not remember Nan's face but that was to be expected. There had been other faces. Others because he did not keep that deep-sworn vow. Benjamin Bull, feeling a feathery tickle now between his legs.

He wondered if Nan was happy. Or even alive.

He wondered if Prpl had married.

He wondered if Lin had found a home.

He thought of a woman named A— and a woman named B— and a woman named C—, and he mocked himself. He remembered a girl named Irene. He remembered Union Square on winter nights. "I never really knew a woman in my life," he said aloud. "A pig and a fascist, I am." Too late now to map his heart, bluffs and streams and eroded hills, and the one grand canyon. What's past is prologue! Prosperity is just around the corner!

He stripped and showered, very hot, very cold, and thought of long drinks, dark rum and water, and the white sailboat. Perhaps. Perhaps now was the time. He could do it; he had the money. But that spoiled it, having the money. Sailing off in his dhow-Jones. No no. Still a child. Crew of four, round maidens, comely, skilled and grateful. He remembered a woman with bright red cheeks in a padded, bulky blue suit. He remembered Ewald. And Parsons. Life had rewarded him to that extent: never again the merest hint of Parsons. Parsons would arrive tonight and arrest him for double-parking.

He dried on a fluffy towel longer than himself, and dressed. Champagne tonight. Romance. Phony male stuff. Did liberated women shriek and bellow at the little death? Did they tip a quarter? Everybody liberated into equality. Like to be liberated out of it. Like to be special again. Corporal. Whoa. Very special in Korea. Can't have that again.

His work at least had gone well. Bartholomew rested, advised, shifted the load. "Damn new medicines come too fast," he'd growled. "Old Finlay

254

has a shelf full of antibiotics worth about five thousand, and they're half of them obsolete. Damn detail men come in every week with some new miracle, soothes the breast, calms the bowels, makes childbirth a pleasure. You, sir. Large bottle? One thin dime.''

Benny reported that one of the countless Westerdonck wives had produced her ninth, a boy, healthy and normal in all respects. ''I'm just too tired at night to keep that man off,'' she said. Briefly Benny envied him. She had heard that tubes could be tied off. Enough was enough. She was thirty-three ''and not even Catholic.'' Bartholomew groaned. ''I once loved humanity. But I went into practice in nineteen oh four.'' Benny was uneasy; within him too a small executioner resided, and stirred now: massacres, seas of blood, cities destroyed, later a manageable world. But the survivors would be Westerdoncks. He suffered a premature nostalgia for vast bays, broad western uplands. ''We can advise her to do it,'' Bartholomew said, ''and maybe even talk that horny husband around. We're all doomed, boy. They're putting up those cardboard-and-horseshit houses over on Turtle Lake, and a little electronics factory. More damn women in bullfighters' pants and men's haircuts. More damn bowling alleys. Chewing gum. And those god damn plastic curlers in public places. I tell you, these politicians ought to have their brains in a bottle at Harvard.''

''Chewing gum,'' Benny said. ''I always think of tired girls on buses and subways.'' A light ache, the merest throb.

''Don't know what got into me,'' Bartholomew apologized. He started a cigarette, and blew smoke darker than his hair. ''Getting old. Pay no attention. Keep the faith.''

"Never thought of myself as a man of faith," Benny said.

"You'll lose it," the old doctor said.

But he lost Bartholomew. The old man died, not quickly as he had wished but over several days, a general but unhurried vascular collapse. Benny tried but could not see it as the death of a man; Bartholomew had lived almost ninety years and had earned his rest. Instead Benny saw it as his own loss: another era, country, limb detached from him and restored to eternity. "They" had taken the old man away from him. The surviving doctors insisted on every technical refinement, and long after Bartholomew had lapsed into coma they were feeding him, cleaning him, plugging him in, monitoring awesome machinery; the dying man was like a spaceship, with fuel and arithmetic and little red lights and telemetry. Benny kept remembering a line from some protocol—religious, medical, perhaps the Pope, he could not recall—but the line, yes, pure poetry: "There is no obligation to use extraordinary means to keep the person alive." He wanted to shout it; he said it quietly instead, and earned scowls.

He went to the old man's house and found suits, shirts, shoes, a large stamp collection, many books, most of them history; on the walls reproductions of Constable and the rural Dutchmen. He sat in a plump armchair and married himself to the silence, tried to be Bartholomew, and for a moment succeeded. He sensed in himself much of the old man's grudging and sullen rectitude, and was pleased; also a cheerful pessimism. He remembered the silvery hair and the sea-blue eyes as if he had lost a lovely woman. Then the housekeeper arrived weeping and evicted him, so he returned to the hospital.

Bartholomew had not come to, and Benny knew he never would. Later they found that he had left everything to a niece in Vermont, and had explicitly ordered that his body be defended from quacks and haruspices and bound over to the nearest Episcopal church, the higher the better, for decent burial. Benny emitted one bawl of absolute mirth, earning more scowls. Even at the funeral he suppressed loony laughter, as if only he knew that Bartholomew was not really dead, just Sisyphus taking a little time out for that restful walk back down the hill. A week later he wept, like the heroine of some Scotch romance, wept as if his heart would break, yes, because he had lost a friend and he was lonely.

19

HIS AUTOMOBILE he decided, was contemptible and malevolent: he must be a whoreson buggy doctor. He almost smiled. He was tired of the shuttle, the one road, toing and froing past the innumerable milestones of his own rut. He remembered earlier days, he and his buggy spanking new and the morning itself of breeze and brass, Benny avid, diamond-eyed, gleeful and catchy, making his rounds, saving lives and the surf roaring . . . Yes, we were all young once and sang aloud. Now he drove through whiffs of petroleum, cigarette smoke and stale sweat, riding sullen between ribbons of roadhouse and restroom, no Irish princesses to do him homage. Just once. Once before he died he would like to see that. Principally brunettes. Only for remembrance, nothing personal, you understand, an anecdote for my grandsons.

He entered the hospital and found himself smiling at strangers, who made way with the utmost deference; he tried to look grave, sagacious and respectable.

No change. None of his pint-sized charges had swallowed a thermometer or savaged a nurse. None had died, not even Baby Roland, who lay comatose and untroubled. A rare moment of peace: at the nurses' station no bustle, no clatter, painters, plumbers or janitors; only the occasional pad of a ripple-sole, or a lost visitor doing his righteous best.

"Management summons me," Benny boasted.

"Ah so," Grentzer rejoiced. "Remember: up against the wall. We shall overcome."

"My God, I forgot about Rosalie. How is she?"

"Checked out."

"I don't believe it," Benny said.

Grentzer shrugged.

"Citizen Grentzer," Benny said, "it becomes more and more difficult to love the common people."

"The baby has brown eyes," Grentzer went on, "or *a* brown eye. Notice that?"

Benny said, "Bobby, today's my birthday. Do me a favor and stick to fruit flies."

Grentzer laughed. "Many happy returns. How old?"

"Forty-six and fading fast."

"Old Doc Beer. I hear you're going to run for mayor."

"Gruff, kindly old Doc Beer, chuckling merrily at gleets and buboes. Who's on tonight?"

"Dembo and Hines."

"Good. Good. There isn't a damn thing I can do, is there?"

"Nothing."

"Then I can go home and enjoy my birthday."

"Absolutely."

"And the baby won't ever know that nobody cared."

"Never."

"Terrific," Benny said.

He strode the wide corridors like a ghoul, Flying Dutchman, Wandering Jew. Behind every door a malfunction mocked him, a clot or lost limb, tumors, bloats. Sobs. Radios. Orderlies, interns, nurses, housekeepers, like floorwalkers and salesladies. The team, as Taubeneck said while underpaying all. Benny had intended a quiet private practice, occasional visits to the local pesthouse, pomander ball well in hand; he had been tricked, edged, elbowed and betrayed, euchred by history and politics: medicine was hospitals now. A bright expensive machine for every cheap dull ailment. Here at the end of the corridor, a solarium, standard irony on a day like this, and a couple of tables, cards and checkers, forlorn plants. The panes were streaked; beyond, gloom and cloud. A woman wept. He hesitated. Rosalie? He peered cautiously within. Mrs. Diehl. The melancholy Mrs. Diehl. She glanced up; he smiled. "Is anything wrong?"

"Oh no." In her forties, frumpish and silent, short curly brown hair and insufficient chin, she endured in sempiternal depression. Her commitment papers, complete, lay on McCook's desk. "My medicine," she said.

"Oh? Are they late with it?"

"I mean will they let me have my medicine in the other place?"

"Of course," Benny said.

"I'm running out," she whimpered.

"I'll tell the doctor."

"No. I mean my own." Tears welled.

Benny sighed, sat beside her and patted her hand.

260

"Spring's coming. You'll cheer up." They shared a flaking trailer on the shore of a large lake. It was one of many hundreds of flaking trailers, occupied by retired couples, mainly Baptist and overweight. Mrs. Diehl gathered wild onions while Benny, in dirty khakis and a tank-top, smoked a nickel cigar and fished from the bank. The fish he caught were diseased, coated with sludge, trapped in plastic loops or used contraceptives; they seemed stone-eyed and prehistoric and could not be eaten. But Mrs. Diehl smiled, and gathered wild onions, and cooked stews, and adored Benny. No one else in all her life had let her be.

"Oh yes." She strained at a smile. "It's just my hands. Without the medicine I hurt all day. I can hardly pick things up, or play solitaire."

She was not his patient, and he recalled nothing of this. "What kind of medicine is it?"

"Pills. White pills."

"What's it called?"

"It's cortisone. You know cortisone."

"Yes, I know. How long have you been taking it?"

"About a year. I don't know what I'd do without it."

Benny patted her hand again. "Don't you worry," he said. "I'll see about it."

"You're a gentlemen," she said.

"I'll stop in later," he said. How many times had he said that? Five times a day, or ten, for fifteen years. As needed for chronic fear and acute disillusion. "You take it easy and don't worry."

She smiled, a tear-stained mask. Benny rose. There but for the grace of God went a human being.

At his knock and entrance they said "Ah." Smiles bloomed, papers seemed to skitter, they stared like the

Syndics. Benny nodded; Taubeneck, chipper, indicated a chair and said, "Tea, Marcia, if you will." Marcia Hargum, president of the garden club, whose husband raised Brown Swiss, offered a silvery smile and darted up. Benny sat between Finlay the pharmacist and Runge the oil dealer, Finlay thin, gray and dapper, Runge balding and rumpled. Mrs. Lacey winked; her late husband had been mayor and real estate. Drs. Bolden, Thilmany and Lindahl sat glum. Cassini the bank manager, young and groomed, strove for dignity.

Taubeneck was a lawyer, a large man and bluff, with hairy ears; toward Benny he affected the plain blunt camaraderie of aging warriors—intended also, Benny knew, to convey righteous fraternity, all races, religions and blood types. Benny visualized him at the country club: "That Beer is a Jew and a fighting man." These directors were of all shapes, and they all had money. When Benny stepped into this ducal room—oak and leather, deep armchairs, an ostentatiously simple conference table, oil paintings by local landscapists, the colonial tea service—he thought of cash. Sometimes he even saw it: fat piles of green bills, chamois bags bulging, louis d'or, a litter of finely engraved securities.

"Well," Taubeneck began, "we've got our hands full this time." Benny did not answer; he accepted tea. "A bad business," Cassini said. "A disgrace," Bolden said. They waited.

"You own a share of Finlay's store," Benny said, or wanted to say, to Thilmany, "which is highly unethical and maybe illegal." Outside he saw hills, houses, moving vehicles, the drab setting of a rainy afternoon.

"The disgrace is here," he said, "and not out there.

Any one of us spends more in a day than they make in a week."

"Good old Ben," Taubeneck murmured.

"You know how I feel," Benny said.

"That's not the point, comparing like that," Finlay said.

"I'm just a witness," Benny said. "I have no vote."

"Well now," Taubeneck said, "*that's* not the point. The point is, we've got to keep this hospital running, and make them see reason."

"The working conditions are admirable," Mrs. Hargum reported. "They have a cafeteria."

"This is a private hospital," Lindahl said sourly. "We don't have all the money in the world."

"We have the glaucoma clinic for children," Cassini said.

"And therapeutic abortions for rich ladies," Benny said, or wanted to say. And tea and cookies at board meetings.

"Back to the point," Taubeneck insisted. "We all know the hospital's history, and the good work we've done. Question is, what do we do right now about this particular problem. Benny?"

"Give them what they ask. It's not unreasonable."

"We can't," Lindahl said. "Can't give in just like that. They'll come back for more."

Marian Lacey said that there was a question of principle. She was pleasingly plump, prematurely white-haired, surely corseted. Benny's tea was hot, tasty and invigorating. Taubeneck reminded them that the hospital was run at a profit. Droplets of mist condensed on the shiny panes. Thilmany spoke of a costly computer. Benny drew forth a leather cigar-case and extracted a breva. "Your permission," he asked the ladies. They nodded. He clipped the cigar while Finlay spoke of health insurance and communism. The cigar was as rich as chocolate; Benny saw a finca on the Cabo de Viñales, all green and gleaming brown in the Cuban sun, his ketch lying offshore. Nan sipped red wine. He thought it was Nan; her face swam and shimmered, out of focus.

"That cigar smells good," someone said.

"Honduras," Benny said. It was a fine Havana, colorado. "All I can tell you is what I think," he said, "and some of it you've heard before. But people don't listen to me. I'm not very forceful."

"Just a moment," Taubeneck said. "We're particularly interested this time because you know some of these people better than we do. I think you know that we all have the greatest respect for you, and if we don't agree with you—well, it's an honest difference of opinion."

"Right," Benny said. "That's what it is, all right. I know some of these people pretty well, right you are. Marcia," he said, sunny, "a bit more tea? A spot, I believe."

Alarmed, she sprang to serve him, frisky little Brown Swiss, udders bobbing, dark eyes moist. Marian Lacey smiled primly and winked again. A conquest. The widdy-woman, so chic, blue suit, Liberty scarf, chiming silver earrings. If they two were younger. That lovely tension: he with his fingers crossed, she with her legs. Finlay blew his nose. Finlay's left hand was cramped and arthritic.

How to begin? When I was in Korea. Yessir. They would be attentive and respectful. The way the Chinese army handled this. I think we should ask Frank Cole to shoot them down, and start fresh. Unemployment is

264

high. Perhaps the board too. He thanked Marcia Hargum. He sipped; he blew blue smoke. "First," he said, "this hospital is not run at a profit and never was. It was built mainly with federal money, and if you had to pay that off you'd never see a profit. Second, the place does half what it could. Twenty years ago they pumped all that money into the countryside because that's where we had no hospitals. Then everybody moved to the big city, and big city hospitals are a mess now, and all over the country little rural hospitals, much like ours, are turning into nursing homes and such. We run at about sixty percent of capacity, so you jack up the prices, and people who can't afford it don't come, and pretty soon it will be fifty percent, health insurance or no. Now, by the terms of that federal grant we're supposed to give at least ten percent of ourselves to charity, more if we can—free clinics, beds for indigents, emergency care for poor people. We don't. The glaucoma clinic, for God's sake. Two hours a week?"

"If they don't pay," Bolden said, "they don't appreciate the care and they don't follow instructions."

Certain elegant crudities, the relics of a distinguished military career, leaped to Benny's tongue and expired there. He tugged grandly at his lapels instead. "That's absolutely not true in my experience," he said. "And how would you know? You make them pay."

"Medical care is a privilege, Benny, not a right," Lindahl said.

"Ah yes, I've heard that," Benny said. "And the doctors who favor free care are always the doctors who wouldn't make it in a competitive situation, we've all heard that too; and if we treat the poor we only assure the survival of the unfit, we've heard that too; and anyway we have no health problems around here, and if

265

we give out a free aspirin it's the end of the American way—"

"It's no sin to turn to profit," Finlay said.

"Maybe it is. We sell life, not gaskets."

"What's your point?" Taubeneck asked.

"Hell, I've got a dozen," Benny said, with a patrician wave of his cigar. "A strange day. My birthday, ladies and gentlemen. Upon this day in nineteen twenty-four—" They murmured felicitations. "I have premonitions and tremors. Firedrakes and aerolites tonight. Mars in the house of Venus. An Aries trembling on a sharp cusp."

"There he goes," Thilmany said.

"Nay," Benny said, "I do but begin. I mean, take this tea set. Eight hundred bucks, I believe. And half your hospital was contributed to start with, the Westerdonck Pavilion and the Schirmer therapy room and the Lazenby staff room, television and pool, and for all I know the Agatha Mergendahler Featherstonehaugh duckbill speculum. And on Elm Street there are no elms, and there's TB, rickets, anemia, honest-to-God malnutrition. What kind of health boutique are you running? You took the federal money and then broke the contract—that's what it amounts to. You're liars and cheats and possibly murderers. Other than that I refrain from moral judgment."

Taubeneck said sternly, "That's enough, Benny."

"No. It isn't enough." He hitched himself higher in his leather armchair. "What's my point, you said. One: give in on this strike. Just give in. What they want is pitiful. Don't make it a matter of principle. Two: put some blacks on this board and some poor whites too. You people have no idea what this county needs. A computer, for God's sake! Do you know how many

266

outpatient visits a computer would cost? Why not a hyperbaric chamber to use twice a year, or an open-heart unit to use once? Three: preventive medicine. A free checkup once a year for everybody in the county who makes less than a certain amount. Four: take Bolden and Thilmany and Lindahl and Finlay off the board—nothing personal—or at least make sure that a majority of the board, a working majority, is at all times non-medical. Why should us docs make policy and lay down priorities and set fees; who checks on *us*? We're prosecutor, judge and jury. We're the only industry in the whole damn country with no quality control, no cost control and no inspectors. Five: when people like Lipscomb try to set up a prepaid group practice, or any damn new thing whatever, don't keep denying them hospital privileges. We're going to need a whole lot of new ways. All you free enterprisers—any kind of competition comes along and you call out the cavalry. This isn't a hospital, it's a club."

"All very generous," Taubeneck said. "Do you suggest that we abolish fees altogether?"

"Why not?" Benny was delighted. "We're all rich. Right, Cassini? Cassini knows. I've been here fifteen years and I'm fat as a hog. Wheat and soybean keep closing higher, though pork bellies are lower. Tell you what: you're making socialized medicine the only alternative. Won't be the hairy radicals bring it in; it'll be you."

"Not immediately, I trust," Taubeneck murmured. "This is all very idealistic, Benny, but we have a practical problem too."

"You sure have. I suggest," Benny said formally, rising, "that you consider Comrade Beer's five-point program. Otherwise you may have to melt down that

267

tea set for bullets.'' He paused for a general view of his colleagues: the men barbered, concealing bad hearts, livers, arches; the ladies lacquered, bewildered—he was mystically aware of straps and harnesses, unguents and mascaras, tiny pads within tight shoes; and Finlay wearing a truss. He stared, fascinated, a trifle wild-eyed, at the complex reticulation of minuscule capillaries on the wings of Taubeneck's nose.

''Benny's right,'' Runge said.

Startled, Benny sought irony, but Runge meant it. His muddy hazel eyes, pouched above a fat nose, held steady on Taubeneck; with full lips, a wide mouth and an irrepressible black stubble, stolid Runge sat like a champion bull about to bellow. Benny admitted hope, and modest affection: Runge the voice of America, the good honest dealer whose men turned out at four of a winter's morn when the burner broke down.

''My boy says the same thing,'' Runge added. ''People are talking against doctors—and not just poor people.''

''Against doctors!'' Lindahl glowered. ''We gave them health insurance.''

''Hell you did,'' Runge said. ''They took it. You fought it every inch of the way for fifty years. And as soon as they got it we doubled our prices. Soon as we knew the money was there. Doubled in five years. These orderlies and all, their pay went up about ten percent. If that. Can't blame it on them.''

''He's right,'' Cassini said. ''My last baby cost so much I almost sent it back.'' They laughed, relieved, the strain diminished, a neutral unfunny joke.

''You should have brought figures,'' Runge said to Taubeneck. ''You ought to bring figures and sit down with that Burris fellow. Or I will if you like.''

"Who elected Burris?" Bolden complained.

Benny said, "His colleagues elected him. Who elected us?"

"God," Taubeneck said, and grinned. "I was brought up to think so."

"I don't like any of this," Bolden said.

"That's not the point," Benny said.

Marian Lacey said, "I just heard you were going to run for mayor."

Jean Diehl's chart. He rooted among files, extracted one and made himself comfortable, sucking pleasantly at his cigar. Sad biographies, facts and figures, pompous comments. Psychiatric reports. He read carefully, replaced the file and said, "Damn."

Coughlin nagged at him: the uncontrolled particle, smashing arbitrarily through random chambers. Tanking up; Benny hoped that he was drunk, unconscious. The deranged were unknowns, eerie. From a booth in the corridor he called Frank Cole.

"Here and there and around and about." Cole was exasperated. "But in the neighborhood. Not doing any of the smart things you might expect. Quite a boy."

"Quite a boy," Benny said. "If the baby dies it's manslaughter."

"At least," Cole said.

"Rosalie's gone home. Can somebody check her house now and then?"

"Yeah, sure, no problem. We'll find him, don't you worry. Any trouble at the hospital?"

"The strike, you mean."

"Yeah."

"No. No trouble and I don't think there will be, and I

269

think Don Runge agrees with me. Can I ask you to go very easy? Forget it, unless we call?"

"That's not what Taubeneck said. We've got a man there now. Peattie."

"Taubeneck. Well, my advice is to call him off. Nothing's going to happen before morning, and don't forget Artie's a pacifist. Strictly non-violent. He's also smart."

"Yeah. I'll think about it."

"Please. I mean it."

"Well, I'll try, doc, but it's my job to keep an eye on troublemakers. We haven't had much of that here, and maybe the best thing is just to come down hard the first time."

"No guns," Benny said.

"Oh now, doc. Can't send a man to do a job without tools."

"What job?"

After a silence Cole said, "We'll keep the peace."

Benny surrendered. "Good luck. I'm off tomorrow but if you need me call me. Blessed are the peacemakers."

Cole chuckled. "That's what they used to call the old forty-four."

"If you find Coughlin let me know."

"You'll hear," Cole said.

"McCook," he said, "can I see you?"

"Doctor Beer. By all means." McCook gestured grandly toward an armchair. "How's the youth of America?" Crinkly graying hair, modeled features, about the eyes an impressive air of sanity.

"They're all fine," Benny said. "It's one of your patients."

McCook had caught his tone, and fell solemn: "Oh?"

"The Diehl woman," Benny said.

"Ah yes. Damn shame. Husband and four kids and she just can't make it." McCook was dashing. He sported half-spectacles and wide ties with sunbursts and Fibonacci spirals.

"How come?"

"Tight as a drum," McCook said. "Conflicted to the core. Upbringing, sex, God, politics even. She needs a long stay in good hands."

"Well," Benny said, and chose clemency, "I've found something new."

McCook chuckled. "It's late. She's due to leave tomorrow. I have the papers here."

"It's not too late."

Warily McCook raised a brow. "You've got a theory. You're going to give me hell about something."

"I'd like to," Benny said, "but I could be wrong."

More cheerily, McCook sat back, tapped at the edge of his desk with a golden pencil and assumed an aspect of intelligence. Benny was incredulous. Perhaps the man practiced before a mirror.

Benny strode hunched and fretful toward the heavy glass doors; somewhere out there Coughlin marauded. Or lay in ambush. He paused at the doors and rocked on his feet, planted them wide and gauged the afternoon like a sailor; the rain had slacked, the wind had backed, to the west the skies were lighter. Behind him footsteps whispered and he knew as he turned that it would be Mary; day's end, going home. Sadly he scanned her black face, the soft dark eyes, the wide nose, the full

271

lips, all in perfect round, crowned by a flocculent Afro. They flew to Cuba, and in a white frame clinic on a green mountain they healed little children, and at sunset they drank coconut milk and made love while the distant fringe of sea turned purple. "Want a ride, little girl?"

"Have to ask my daddy."

"Leave him alone. His feet hurt." Benny held the door against a warm breeze, and refrained from taking her hand.

"What's this about Diehl, Jean?"

"Diehl, Jean." Why should his heart be heavy? Carefully he collected thought. "Poor lady. She's been on cortisone for a year and McCook never knew, and it may be only cortisone depression."

"Dear God," Mary said.

"Anyway, we caught it."

"Thank heaven. Hard to get into that place and harder to get out. What now?"

"We'll take her off it and see."

"How'd you catch it?"

"I stopped in to say hello, and we chatted."

"Yes. Old Doc Hello."

"Don't make fun of me. Damn." Pull yourself together, m'lad. "I'm a little depressed myself."

"Baby Roland?"

"Among other small matters."

She touched his hand. "Dear Benny."

"Did everything right," he said, and a tremor shook him. "Should have known better. It all turns to shit. You get old and it all goes away."

She was silent; they paced along, and gravel crackled. "You need a vacation."

"I need . . . God knows what I need. Mary,

272

Mary!" he burst out. "I'm forty-six. Today. And I don't love anybody."

"Happy birthday," she said. "I'm thirty-two and nobody loves me."

"We sound like a bad movie."

"Yes. We run off together and get killed in a car accident."

"I have just the car for it," he said. "It's in worse shape than I am. Where would we run off to?"

"Algeria."

"Grentzer thinks we should all go to Vietnam. Expiate. Salvation through works."

"China," she said. "I'd like to see China."

"Peking. Those tile roofs, and temples. I'd like it," he said, cheery for an instant.

"A fantasy."

"Well," he said weakly, "you're fantastic."

"Why, Doctor," she said. "How gallant."

Ou-yang smiled broadly. "She is a *lovely* girl. I never thought to *see* you again."

"Are you in real trouble?" she asked.

After a moment Benny said, "No, I just don't like myself much. I keep wondering why I bothered. Why I bother. Life is a dull, chronic pain in the ass. And when I think what else I might do, it's always something childish and shameful."

"Like running off with me."

"You wrong me savagely, ma'am. We've been circling each other for years."

"For the wrong reasons."

"Yup."

"At least you know."

"At least *we* know."

He drove her home and kissed her gently. "Why do I

kiss so much?'' he asked suddenly. "Why do I bother you with that?''

"Why not?'' she said. "And why talk about it? Come in handy when you run for mayor.''

"Sorry,'' he said. "I guess I'm not very good about women. Never grew up. Do the same again, too,'' he muttered.

"They all think you're beautiful,'' Mary said.

"I turn into a great hairy spider at midnight. The things I like to do,'' he said, "used to be sins. Now they're social errors or political tyranny. All the fun is gone. I used to think of myself, years and years back, as a good lover distributing joy. It turns out I'm an exploiter. Admire the female form; turns out I'm an exploiter and a voyeur. Like to live naked; turns out I'm an exploiter and a voyeur and an exhibitionist. I don't know where I was headed but I got sidetracked. And *years* ago. Why can't I grow up and forget it? You think I would have been happy as a stud? A dumb paid stud?''

"You men are all alike,'' she said. "All you need is a good fuck.''

He laughed through shock and anger. "Don't be bitchy. I don't talk that way and I don't think that way.'' Half a dozen superspades ringed him, smoke eddied, a piano tinkled. "What you doin with that sister?'' one of them asked softly. "What you doin here anyway?'' and they ringed him closer. Just found joy, the piano said. "Art Tatum,'' he said. "I once shook hands with Art Tatum. He was blind and he had stubby little fingers.''

"Niggerlover,'' she said.

"Oh shut up,'' he said. "I was a prince.''

"Now what does that mean?''

"I was a prince," he said stubbornly, "and a famous violinist. From high notes to middle, from middle to low, you be my fiddle and I'll be your beau."

"You're fun," She giggled. "You're a beautiful man."

"I'm glib," he said. "It's not the same. Hell, you've got troubles too and all I do is talk about myself, and I suppose I like you as well as anybody I ever knew."

"Ah," she said. "That's dangerous. Good day, your highness." She slipped out. "See you to-morrow?"

"I'm off. Day after."

"I'm off day after," she said.

"Three days," he said. "Can we make it?"

"If they go on strike I'll see you tomorrow. You're not too old, you know. You're too young."

He was miles down the road and framing future replies when he saw Walt Coughlin. The red car whipped toward him, and past, and for a split second they clashed, the white-gold hair and the ice-blue eyes looming at him; his heart thudded, and he pressed down on the accelerator, but Coughlin vanished behind him, unswerving.

20

HE CROSSED HIS doorsill at a quarter of five, and announced himself to his answering service. For years he had done so with barely suppressed hope tingling in his fingertips: "A Miss Swinburne will call back," they would say, or "Doctor Lin called." More likely Parsons. Often it was "Mrs. Untermeyer," sometimes "Mr. Jacob Beer." Tonight a miracle: no messages whatever. He left Iacino's number, and called Frank Cole. "In the red car, on the Misqueag Road. Headed for Suffield. Driving fast and looked a little wild."

"I don't know what the hell he's doing," Cole said. "We keep missing him by fifteen minutes. Drunkard's luck."

"Let me know."

"Doc."

"Yes?"

A silence. Benny grimaced. Imbeciles. "Would he have any reason to bother you?"

"None at all," Benny said.

"Okay."

"Can you keep a man at his house?"

"Haven't got that many men. If we had any kind of decent police force. I told her to call me if she heard anything—a car, footsteps, anything. She's home, you know."

"I heard. Good luck."

He changed to woolen trousers, flannel shirt, work shoes; he zipped himself into a windbreaker—ah, foul-weather gear!—and let himself out the back door. The sky was still pearly but clearer, and glints of white light rippled off the lake. He went to the rowboat; it was floating free, and the stake was low. Grunting happily, he levered the stake from the damp earth and with a small rock pounded it home a few feet farther up the receding bank. Bizarre landscape, treetops alien, rising like skeletons from the water, rootless and trunkless. The crow's-nest huge in the late light. Tomorrow. If they had miscalculated? If the waters rose and rose, and Benny too went under? He looked back at his house, masonry and brickwork and timbers, wide windows, and watched the water rise, flooding the basement, blowing the furnace, dissolving away his carpets, furniture, diplomas, bed. But they had not miscalculated. They were professional men, with slide rules, unsmiling men. Benny would have his private lake. Lucky Benny. And his private house and his private car and his private joys and private woes. Like to have a few public joys. He sold out next day and went to join a commune in California, where his skills made him welcome. There were thirty-odd communards; Benny was the oldest, but they tolerated him and would like him in time. The young women were splendid, tanned and buxom, and they ground flour and baked bread, and no one slept alone.

He left the lake and trudged among his limp shrubs.

Crocus soon, and daffodils, resurrection and head colds. He sloshed through puddles and rivulets, circled the house, slogged up past the south chimney, headed for the front door and saw the woman, the suitcase, the rusted, dented foreign car. His breath was stopped, but briefly; he walked on, faces and names thronging, and when she heard him and turned, he saw with sudden, immense, unmanning love that it was his daughter.

Early in the day, he cautioned himself, preparing two whiskeys, but a special day and tomorrow off, and how often do I drink with a maiden of nineteen? Maiden! More jokes. Shoeless he shuffled to her; she blurred, hazed to Carol, Carol at nineteen. God, these carbon copies! He missed Joe: a pang.

Sarah raised her glass: "Love and luck."

"Love and luck." They sipped. "Tell me all."

"I will not."

"Good girl. I couldn't bear it. Are you pregnant?"

"Oh God," she said. "My father is a male chauvinist pig. Why not ask me if I have a job, or what am I doing about capitalism? No. I'm not pregnant. My mother is a genetics counselor."

"Keeps my work down."

"Ah. Say on."

"Nope. Never discuss your wife with your girl friend."

"Oh dear. You're quarreling."

He shook his head and smiled for her; why break good habits? "No. Life is sweet."

"It's a bloody bore," she said.

"Oh come on! You're nineteen. You're supposed to be out there screwing and yelling bullshit and having a high old time."

278

"You don't think that's boring?"

He shrugged. "Never bored me. Naked on the beach." A faceless woman stretched and blinked luxuriously in the molten light; oily, she gleamed. The ketch bobbed offshore. "Anyway I'm supposed to be learning from you. That's what all the papers say."

"No way," she said. "You don't groove on rock."

"I like the Beatles."

"You would. How's Mom?"

"I thought you'd never ask. She's absolutely fine. Misses you badly. Alone, the two of you gone, the two of us working; she bustles and makes cheerful noises, but I think she'd love another family."

"Oh, how funny!" Sarah sparkled. "My God, if she had five more."

"You jest." Benny drank, comfortable and happy. "You and Joe were plenty. I used to lie awake dreading disasters. Auto accidents, dope, rape. We were lucky. A little of each, but no harm done."

"We were lucky. How's Joe?"

"Okay, I guess. I wish I knew more about him. What kind of trip did you have?"

"Good." She too drank, and tucked up her feet, and smiled Carol's heartbreaking smile. "Good. Skied the whole way home, almost. Stopped off everywhere, then moved on. I couldn't stay in one place because I didn't have enough clothes. Clothes are very important."

Benny clucked. "False values. Bourgeois society."

"You bet," she said. "It cheered me up after Lonnie. All those apple-cheeked boys breathing frost and lusting after me."

Apple-cheeked boys. Benny felt himself glitter slightly, an old goat's last caper. Would you start

279

again? Give them up, annihilate them, exchange them for the gift of the gods? Be an apple-cheeked boy with an old goat's art? Carol, Sarah, Joe, obliterated in an instant, painlessly of course. Faustus. The God of Abraham and Isaac glared. Yah. Who can you sell your soul to these days? "What now? Or shouldn't I ask?"

"Home," she said, and mouthed a kiss. "I'm going to go on a diet and read elevating literature and bring my daddy his slippers at night."

"Godsake," Benny said, popeyed. "Just what I always wanted."

Again she disconcerted him: "Is it?"

After a friendly moment he said,"No. You're too young to know what I always wanted."

"You're a terrible man."

"Nonsense. I'm a pillar of the community."

"Oh that," she said.

"Oh that," he said. "Want another?"

She rose and stretched; he observed with more than interest, and mocked himself again. "No thank you," she said. Her black hair fell to her waist, to the label on her jeans, as she pirouetted; it swirled, floated, fell to rest. "I'm going to shower, and anoint myself, and get out of this leather shirt and into a sexy little dress and drive you crazy."

"A fine way to treat your spiritual adviser," Benny said sternly, and she hooted merrily, and plumped into his lap, spilled his drink, kissed him soundly, leapt up and pranced out of the room.

Later he stood naked at his own window, old goat, gazing drowsily at his own lake. At the knock he called "Come in," who could it be but Carol, and she did

280

come in, his Carol, home from the office. He stared. She was two Sarahs. How, when, had that happened? A rich, round fertility goddess; he saw Sylvia suddenly, and remembered Sylvia once, diamonds between two rubies. Carol blurred, then flowed back into her own ample contours; she closed the door carefully and gazed upon him in pity. "Let me guess," she said. "Mahatma Gandhi."

"It's my birthday suit," he said lamely, and they laughed; Carol said, "Happy birthday, old man. Here's a kiss," and her arms wrapped him about. "By golly," he said. "Good thing we don't stick out in the same place." "You have less character than any man I know," she said. "Furthermore, you've lost your pants again." He squeezed her plump behind, and she moved away. "Are you through for the day?"

"I am. Iacino holds the fort. I was planning to take a drink or so." A quiver of lust tightened his flesh and passed; inwardly he frowned, and was defeated. He sat on the bed and rubbed his eyes. "You're tired," she said. He nodded and opened his arms; she moved into the embrace and stroked his hair. Her breasts, his temples. Holding her, he loved her. "Lie down a little," he said. "My prowess is legendary."

"Later," she said. "So is your prow."

"It isn't lust," he said.

"No?" She tilted his face and scoffed. "Prostate."

"Oh go to hell," he said, but he smiled. "I have a serious case of adolescence. They said I'd outgrow it but it keeps getting bigger."

"So it does," she observed. "The fact is, lover, that I'm tired too, and hot."

"A long hard day."

"The usual. Diaphragms, IUD's, abortion referrals.

281

Oh, I get tired of it. We ought to go away. It's been a gloomy winter." She released him and went to the mirror.

"Good idea," he said. "The islands. Season's about over." The ketch flew, wing-and-wing; the keys were deserted, and the sooty terns swooped and shrilled.

"Whose car is that in the driveway?" she asked. "Some patient dead in the office?"

"Surprise," he said. "A house guest."

"House guest?"

"Right. Young, sensationally beautiful, a hot number. Likes older men."

"Benny! Oh Benny! Where is she?"

"Why don't you light up like that when I come home?" he asked, but she was gone.

He lay down again, and astonished himself by sleeping. He was awakened by the telephone. "He's got a pistol," Frank Cole said. "Just thought you ought to know. A dozen streetlights, and two embarrassing holes in that Miss Milk billboard."

Not fully awake, but perceptibly if inexplicably more cheerful, he arrayed himself in conventional flannels, a flashy blue shirt and moccasins; he stood at the window again and watched evening gather above his lake, and the long gothic shadows of the crippled trees. Spooky. Gods. Silently he padded to the hall and crossed to the front window to watch the light fail farther up, on the high ground, the wooded hills. Often he had seen deer from this window, pricking brittle through the brush; once, browsing on the rough lawn, a lone buck, wary and almost final.

Now Benny was alone, and the shadows gathered, and he recalled Germany. A limousine purred into his drive, gleaming softly in the gray light, and Lin emerged in a dinner jacket, and behind him Prpl in Balkan dress, embroidered, a blue bandanna. The two joked and drifted toward Benny's door as the second car drew up and a liveried chauffeur stood at attention while 57359 sprang out, portly and bald, a gold pincenez, a gold-headed walking-stick; he turned and offered a hand to Kinsella and Trezevant, Kinsella older but still starchy, Trezevant still tough and stocky. From the third car Ou-yang descended regally, tugging his Mao jacket into place, slicking down his straight black hair; he and Lin eyed each other, bowed slightly, did not speak. The knot of shadows flowed houseward. Voices rose: a working girl from Harrisburg. Music: he would play the Haydn for Ou-yang, the quartet, soaring and swooping. 57359 walked briskly, chattering, reminiscing of Berlin and Heidelberg; Prpl quoted Heine. Kinsella smiled fiercely; he and Trezevant wore green uniforms and each sported six stars on gold epaulettes. Nan took Prpl's arm, and Benny snorted.

"About time," Carol said, rising with a smile to kiss him; she pursed her lips and closed her eyes and Benny wondered again what might happen if he declined to kiss; would she remain forever frozen in that attitude, unfulfilled, all gesture and no substance? He kissed her; she relaxed and withdrew. He kissed Sarah, who said, "Happy birthday, mon vieux." Carol asked, "Scotch?" Benny nodded. Sarah said, "You look terrific." "For a vieux," he conceded. Sarah grinned: "A sale vieux." "You're not supposed to know that," he said. "Thanks, ladies. It's a warm room and a good evening." On the hearth a fire blazed and snapped, the brown beams were ageless against the beige walls, and all was harmony: the tweed-covered couch, the leather-covered couch, the venerable carpet, the black piano, the hospitable upholstered armchairs, the lambent shimmer of hooded lamps.

Carol served him whiskey; he raised his glass. "Many more," Carol said. "Hear hear," Sarah said. Benny wondered if he were a problem drinker. Ten minutes and amiability would take hold. "To Joe," he said. Thank God! The Lorde was with Joseph, and he was a luckie felowe.

"How I wish he were here," Carol said sadly.

"Hell," Benny said, "I'll buy you a shaggy dog. All Joe ever did was grow hair and ask 'When's dinner?'" He heard another car and was momentarily bewildered —who could this be? Parsons? Trezevant. Old Trez. He was amazed when Carol rose and said, "Who's this?"—a real car!—and then he thought of Walt Coughlin, set down his drink and hauled himself to his feet.

"Sit down," Carol said. "I'll get it."

"No you won't," he said, "I'll get it," and saw, as he passed, her startled eyes. He heard the metallic slam, and at his own door took a deep breath; blood running quicker, he pulled the door open, and shouted with pleasure as he saw Jacob and Sylvia and Amos. "For God's sake, *a party!*" He thrust open the storm door, gathered his father to him, and pushed them inside one by one: hugs and kisses, voices rising, Carol and Sarah coming to help, coats, hats. "The heater broke!" Sylvia cried. "A six-thousand dollar car and the heater broke!"

Benny said to Jacob, "That's a beautiful coat." He stroked the cloth.

Sadly Jacob nodded, but Amos too was stroking the

cloth: "That's right, that's right, it is. Never noticed in the car."

"A gift," Jacob said. "You remember my Thursday nights."

"Pinochle."

Jacob nodded. "And only three of us left. Years ago we were eight." They manipulated hangers and buttons in a sluggish, dawdling ballet, the three little tailors; Amos's glasses slipped comically and perched precariously. "So about a month ago," and as they sauntered toward the living room Jacob's eyes grew moist, "Itzkowitz and I were waiting for Mendel, but it was a messenger with two boxes. No message, just two boxes, with our names. Two topcoats, the richest cashmere, you saw, a perfect fit, each one. Next day we heard. Mendel went to a Turkish bath, the works, rubdown, and then took a nap with a whole bottle of sleeping pills. Cancer of the prostate. Undignified, also painful. So no more pinochle. A mean man, Mendel, but all the same."

Amos, a man of culture, stood before the fire, turned his back to it and thrust his hands under imaginary swallowtails. After a moment he faced the flames and rubbed his hands, saying "Aah."

Benny turned to Sarah, and his eyes widened. "My, my," he said. "I really hadn't noticed," and his daughter sealed his joy by blushing. "You *are* a piece," he said softly. "Spin around." She spun slowly. "I'll take a dozen," he said. "There's only one," she said, and he sighed. Jacob clucked: "What they wear these days." Amos came to life: "For God's sake. Is that legal?" Benny said, "Among consenting

285

adults." "She's only a child," Amos said, and Benny's eyes met Sarah's for a hot, funny, lovely instant. He laughed aloud. "A nice birthday," he said. Carol came in with a tray, and after a moment's rumination set out strategic heaps of hors d'oeuvre. Benny pictured her in Sarah's dress and jiggled his brows. "What will you drink?" Carol asked, and the flames danced merrily, and everyone was all right, a little stiff here, getting old there, a miserable winter, but everyone was all right.

Before his third whiskey Benny prudently called Iacino, to hear that there was no change. "Blood count's the same. Everything *regular*. But I'd love to hear him howl once, or see his eyelids flutter."

Benny nodded, translated the nod: "Yah. Me too. Always that . . ."

"That what?"

"Permanent damage. To me too, half a dozen tiny strokes every minute—"

"You're drunk," she said firmly. "We have more important people to worry about."

"You are all affability and condescension," he said. "I'll call again about midnight."

And did he care? He stood, his hand still resting on the receiver, a yawn building and thoughts exuding painfully. Do I care. Wanko or Roland or even Sarah or Joe: is there not a manikin, cunningly ambushed in the hem of a ventricle, or lurking back of the spleen, who gives not a tinker's dam for anyone but me? If they all dropped dead tonight that alter ego could survive it. Hearts do not break. Fortify the spirit with that truth: hearts do not break.

● ● ●

"Cigarettes," Amos commenced, "pollution, the pill, permissiveness." Sarah vanished into another world. Benny glazed slightly. "I don't mind living," Jacob said, "and I don't mind dying, but I hate being sick." Dope, Sylvia said, a nation of addicts, and Sarah smiled politely. Into a silence Benny belched; he tried to retrieve the moment by intoning "Evil spirit depart" and Carol groaned and rolled her eyes: "My barbarian." "Strictly speaking," Sarah said, "the barbarians were Persian." Benny looked the question. "The Greeks made fun of the language, bar-bar, bar-bar, and it became the name for rude strangers, barbaroi, the barbarians."

"Or Berbers," Amos said. "That's a smart girl there."

"No, no," Benny keened; he saw Rospos and Demavin, inseparable and laughing, Beer, Beer, bore bore, bar bar, and saw Lin and Prpl, plain as the full moon, and that plump usherette, and oh God what a year! Sid Berger's. Oh god of appetizers and side orders! His eyes shuttled, Amos to Sylvia, Carol to Jacob. Sarah: take heed! Beware!

"No what?"

"Nothing. A memory."

"Some girl named Barbara." Carol smiled, all toothy mischief, and Benny winked. Ho ho. There is no man that sinneth not.

He lapped up his soup and noticed that Sylvia had aged and was no longer voluptuous; she was, in the words of Benny's favorite masseur, "a fat Yewish lady." Amos said, "The wine, the wine! You girls clear these bowls. I'll do the wine." He scurried plumply, his glasses winking and glittering. "Ah," he said. "Ah." Wine plashed happily, gift of Amos.

Amos sniffed, tilted, poured and swirled. Choirs sang. Benny throbbed with thirst. Amos had poured a mouthful for Jacob and the two old men sat wrinkled, judging solemnly. Amos puckered, and somehow kissed his own tongue. "The bouquet," Jacob said. "The color," Amos said. "The body," they said. In desperation Benny lunged, snagged the bottle, and poured for the ladies and himself. This was no time for sobriety. "I have thought," he announced, "of running for mayor."

Pulse thudding. Benny sank deeper into his dinner, and into his bottle. Dimly he recalled a tale of homunculi. Homunculuses. Bottled, pickled, rising and falling with seasons and storms. So Benny one day, holding his breath, semaphoring from a Margaux of 1959. For now, at his own table, he felt that traditions were being observed, their importance affirmed, the seating arrangement perfect, and out of six lives and so many decades, the proper level of anecdote. Amos at Carol's right, Sylvia at his own, Sarah at his left and Jacob at Carol's, and still the strength to chaff and laugh, these survivors, intimates of Bach and Pinsky. It was mess in a crack Jewish regiment, banners and shields on the wall: Masada, Cologne, Auschwitz, Babi-Yar, Bronxville. God must have loved the Jews; he made so few of them. And there was plenty of wine yet. Carol looked fine, rosy and busty. How long had it been? Never look back. Nose to the west wind, all upon the hazard! A cabin in the mountains, stream, lake, sunrise, a blond squaw contriving sourdough pancakes. In the pink light a bass broached. Far across the lake, below a vast stand of spruce, the telephone rang.

"Let me," Benny said, pushing off. He blinked

powerfully and flowed to the hall, sure that it would be Frank Cole, but the operator chanted "I have a collect call" and he was saying yes, yes, of course, resisting a gorgeous burst of boozy tears. "That's what I call good manners," he bellowed. "You learned something after all."

"You betcha," Joe said. "Ancestor worship." Questions tumbled, answers flew. Weight steady, grades good. Benny wanted always to ask the eternal questions, Got enough money? and Got a girl? But he was learning, slowly and painfully, to subdue his own neuroses in the presence of youth. "I'm strong as hell," Joe said. "Been lifting weights. How you feeling?"

"Good," Benny said. "Slowing up a little but acquiring brains." At the sound of the doorbell he prickled. "Damn," he said. "All I wanted was my dessert." Joe said, "I can call back." Benny said, "No, no. Not you. It's the doorbell. Hold on, will you," and as Carol passed he cried, "No. Don't go. Here." He thrust the receiver at her. "It's Joe. Talk to him. I'll go."

Carol showed puzzlement. Benny said, "Ah, there's trouble out of doors. Maniacs in the night. Werewolves. I didn't tell you." He would open the door and be shot to pieces, and if this were any other woman he would touch her one last time, in all the secret places. "Here," he said. "Talk." He went to the door on wooden feet and opened it a crack, holding his breath. The front light fell yellow on Rosalie. Benny said, "Faugh."

"I'm scared," she said. The sound of a car faded. "I took a taxi." She trembled.

"Of course," he said. "Come in. Where's your

husband?'' He closed the door behind her and pleaded with Carol. Rosalie wore jeans and a brown leather jacket. Carol nodded bleakly; her earrings flashed. ''He called up,'' Rosalie said. You can't stay, Benny almost said. All I want is to be left alone. ''Where is he?''

''I don't know,'' she said. She had wept and her make-up had run. Absently Carol spoke to Joe. ''I tried to watch television and I tried to sleep but I got the shakes. The real shakes. I heard noise and I couldn't breathe and my heart was pounding.'' Beneath her eyes blotches of black and blue.

''Carol,'' Benny said,''help me.'' He aged, bowed under innumerable atmospheres. ''Hold on, Joe,'' Carol said, and covered the mouthpiece. ''What is this?''

''Rosalie will tell you,'' Benny said. ''It's pretty awful. Please.'' He took the receiver; it squirmed in his hand. ''Joe,'' he said. ''Sorry. A patient.'' Carol brooded at him, and led the girl off. Joe, he wanted to say, I'm sweating. Close to the line, Joe. An old sack of tripes, blubbering and leaking. ''I'm innocent,'' he said.

''Who asked you,'' Joe said. ''Innocence is another name for ignorance.''

Benny focused. ''It is unbecoming for young men to utter maxims.''

''Your old men shall dream dreams,'' Joe said,''and your young men shall see visions.''

''By gosh,'' Benny said,''you've been reading that book.''

''It's on the wall of this booth,'' Joe said. He spoke of a trip by sea, down the St. Lawrence next fall. Benny said,''Great.'' What else? Advice? Teachings? Example? Preposterous! Different planets. Rosalie here! Happy birthday!

Sarah emerged, wagging her tail. Gently Benny suffocated while Joe babbled on. He made answer. Sarah hovered. Joe wished him many happy returns. They exchanged avowals of affection and nostalgia. "Call again," Benny said, "and here is a surprise." He handed the receiver to Sarah, imbibed a huge breath, wiped honest sweat from his noble brow, and shambled to the dining room.

Amid the black bears Rosalie sat like a baby rabbit. She had told them at least part; Jacob sat shocked, and Amos was furious. "You said nothing," Carol objected, queenly and angry.

"What for? To spoil everybody's evening? Rosalie, have you been drinking?"

"No," she whispered. Benny pushed his bottle along. "Amos, pour for her. Give her Sarah's glass. Anything about the baby?"

"No. It's just him." She quaked a small smile, not now the blond goddess, and Benny breathed easier.

"Him. Well, you're all right here." The laws of the tribe. He remembered his first sight of her, miniskirted and braless on a summer's day, glorious, the evil delight, and the memory merged with other memories: the sunny canyons of the great city and he too treading pools of light, the world his oyster which he with sword would open. He was some pounds heavier now and carrying considerable wine.

"How can it be?" Amos asked, a white-haired fool but in his voice iron and rich sorrow. "How can men do this?"

No one answered. Soon Rosalie said, "He called up.

I told him the baby was in the hospital. I said that the baby might die. He said goddamn and hung up. Then after dark I kept hearing noises. I thought about calling the police but it didn't seem right. I mean, I don't like him but he's my husband." Benny stared. It didn't seem right. He drank. "I got scareder and scareder and I had no place to go, and when I couldn't stand it I called a taxi and came here. Can I stay? I can sleep on the floor."

"You should never have left the hospital," he said.

"I can't afford the hospital," she said. "He'd just get madder."

"And had suffered many things," Benny said thickly, tired and tipsy and his bones heavy, "of many physicians, and had spent all that she had, and was nothing bettered, but rather grew worse." He hoped his chest would not tighten. This was his birthday and he deserved a fine cigar. He had begun to feel like another man and a worse: the drowned sailor perhaps, sights and sounds approaching him slowly through a vinous murk. Lover or liver. Please espleen. Mussily he stared at Rosalie; she sat straighter and an odd spark leapt the gap. The wine, he decided, had restored her color. A merry-go-round jingled in his head, rages and lusts, sprays of life's shrapnel, old photos, victims, but instead of horses and swans they were riding limbless babes and blinded crones. "You can stay here," he said.

Carol started to speak, but held off. Jacob said, "Of course." Amos said, "A sleeping draught." Benny had not heard the phrase in years, perhaps ever. Sarah was with them again and said, "Walt Coughlin. He was something."

"He's still something," Rosalie said, "but not the same thing."

Sarah said, "Oh," and then to the others, "Joe sends his love," and to Benny, "Where's Walt now?"

"Around and about," Benny said. "Drinking a bit. I may do the same." There goes the birthday ball. Why is this night different from all other nights?

"I remember Joey," Rosalie said. "He was nice."

"I'd like my dessert," Benny said. "Dessert and coffee, and pass that bottle back." Maybe I could sleep with Rosalie. A deep inner logic there.

"We can put you in with Sarah," Carol said to her. In a dark blue cardigan out at the elbows bald Benny sold bubble-gum.

The cake was almond mocha and a lone candle burned bravely. No song was sung. Properly doped, Rosalie slumbered upstairs. "So, happy birthday," Jacob said softly, "anyway." A mazel tov here, a l'chayim there. Benny's fumy mind pinched tiny thoughts: the baby would die; Joe might be a father; where was Coughlin. "Hell," he said. "I was going to have a good time and drink. When I was drunk enough I was going to play the fiddle."

"Life is too dramatic," Amos said.

"Life is a farce," Benny said, "played by understudies." Carol's eyes held his, a long look. "I'm sorry I'm a doctor," he said. And sorry I married, and sorry I fathered. A lie for a lie and a truth for a truth.

"We're all sorry at times," Amos sighed.

Benny sipped coffee and resolved to cheer up. "Brandy," he said. "Sarah, m'love. The good stuff, and the clean glasses."

"She's a pretty girl," Sarah said. "She told me she loved being a cheerleader, and she was a drum majorette, and when she won the beauty contest she hoped she could twirl someday on television. She wanted to win a national title."

"Marchioness," Benny laughed, and was ashamed. And your own vie de bâton, old sport?

Later they were happier and the party was almost a party. Benny smoked a cigar and rolled his shoulders when his chest tightened, but a third brandy eased him and his mind recommended its familiar race. Jacob reminisced about 57359, and Benny told them that life was like that. He told them about the soldiers he had survived with, and about Lin and Ou-yang. He did not mention the girl from Harrisburg. "Even the people I see every day—we don't connect, they hardly exist, it's all bits and pieces, loose ends, unfinished business. Nothing ever . . . *coalesces*."

Never mind. Tomorrow they would see his lake, and they could fish. He did not tell them of his other lakes, the savory trout sizzling and pink mist rising off still green waters, or about his ketch or his variable crew. He agreed not to fiddle but riffled sleeves for the old quartet, and Sarah mocked him, and they sat heavy with food and drink and the past while the German dance soared and swooped. Benny thought he might like to die listening to it, and Sylvia was almost asleep, and Carol kept her own council, pensive, and Benny thought again that she looked well—no, she looked good, worthy of love. That tore his mind from the music, and he tasted the familiar bile, the old, ferocious, bitter rage of sheiks at defiled wells, at poisoned oases, the desert of his sex life, mile upon mile of gritty respectability and all the starry dead nights lost forever. Whose fault? He knew: no marriage is singular. And no

294

one would ever hurt her, no one, he would see to that.

He poured a brandy, knocked it back, said "Ah" and poured another. "Easy there," Amos said. "Once a year," Benny said, and Carol hm'd, and he dispensed the jolliest of smiles. "It's beginning to feel more like a party," he said. "You know, I may retire soon."

"We all should," Jacob said.

"I mean from medicine," Sylvia came awake and stared. "I don't really care any more who lives and who dies. If half the world dropped dead tomorrow, I wouldn't care. I might even rejoice."

Jacob asked gently, "Which half?"

Benny grinned and cringed. "All right. The other half. But I'd still like to take a few years off. Read. I'd like to read. Good stuff. The Bible. The Iliad. The black ships, and the straight-shafted spears. And the Greek plays. Not to be born is the best for man. That's Carol's racket, right, baby?"

"Shut up," she said. "I'm a technical adviser and not a commissar."

"Ah, there's the rub," he said, but Sarah fought back: "What's so great about the Iliad and the Bible? I mean with Vietnam and all."

"Ha!" Benny cried. "He that begetteth a fool doeth it to his sorrow. The Iliad, my girl, is all about Vietnam."

"A lot of good it does," she said, and once more Benny was alone, too old to be young, too foolish to be old.

And then, as it will, the doorbell rang, and this time he knew it was for him, knew too that he was somewhat drunk, and sniffed up a great cool breath, felt his nostrils flare, his eye gleam, the blood beat hard—Cuchulainn! Cuchulainn, with the one eye staring out of his face and the top of his head a mass of flames, and he was twenty-two again with all to win and all to lose. "Sit still," he said, and sprang to his feet; "keep out of it," and he stretched, stood tall, smiled fiercely, and strode forth haloed by fire. Snarling aloud as the door clapped to, he crowded Coughlin back along the walk, hustled him hard, whacked, walloped, thumped and rammed him, swatted the revolver free with one hairy hand, plucked it from flight with the other, cold-cocked and pistol-whipped good old Walt Coughlin, blacked the eyes, broke the nose, split the lip, boxed the ears blowing the drums, dodged a shower of straight white teeth, inverted the son of a bitch, bounced him thrice on the spattered flags, ripped off the ears and scaled them across the lake, and panted for a moment, intoxicated, licking the taste of salt from his own lips. Then he drained the man of blood, gave the liver and lights to charity, flensed and rendered him, and ground the bones for good light bread. Immediately the war ended, the sick were well, and lovers were not separated.

He opened the door boldly enough, and peered out into the moist night, and yessir it was Walt Coughlin, red of eye and weaving in place but the pistol was a fact. It blurred, twinned; Benny scowled. Godlike he advanced. Truth to tell, he slipped. With sacerdotal dignity he flung the storm door outward and strode, and his heel skidded cleanly on the worn aluminum sill. Flailing backward he groped for the knob, which evaded him; as his left hand slapped the floor, the storm door sprang back and bruised his shins. "Ow," he said. He swore, and bulled himself upright. He fought his way out and glared at Coughlin. What to say? Coughlin, you are under arrest? He sensed that Coughlin was
296

drunker than he was, a minor but appreciable blessing. The evening rocked gently.

Baleful, squinting, Coughlin peered back, swaying; khaki trousers, denim jacket, a swatch of white hair silky limp down one temple. He spoke in a snarling twang: "Is my wife here?"

Benny shook his head earnestly. "No."

"Satchwell said he brought her here." He waggled the pistol and said, "Urf."

"You're drunk," Benny said. Coughlin too blurred and twinned.

"Had a few," Coughlin nodded. They breathed at each other.

"I slipped," Benny said. His tongue seemed swollen, and the night light very yellow. He swayed; so did Coughlin, and Benny was mildly seasick. "Stand still," he said.

"My wife is here," Coughlin said.

"The hospital," Benny said. "We sent her to the hospital."

Coughlin said, "Hospital."

"That's it," Benny said, and nodded solemnly. "Where the baby is," and he showed his teeth. "The baby may die. Roland."

Coughlin grunted and aimed the pistol at Benny's chin. Benny dried suddenly. His bowels moiled, and he clenched. He tried to swallow. The night was altogether still. Too early in the year for crickets or peepers. "I had high school," Coughlin said. "*Finished* high school."

"Football," Benny said. "I remember. Twenty pounds more, you could've been a professional."

"Yah," Coughlin said. "Pretty good. You remember."

"The good old days."

"Good old days." Coughlin frowned. "Where was I?"

"Football."

"Finished high school," Coughlin said. "Four brown eyes do not make blue eyes."

"Backward," Benny said.

"What, backward?"

"Four blue eyes do not make brown eyes."

"That's what I said," Coughlin said.

"The baby may die," Benny said again.

"Everybody dies," Coughlin said. "I seen *girls* beaten to death."

"I have an aunt," Benny said, "with one blue eye and one brown." He felt that he should speak carefully, but also that nothing would matter much. He must not disgrace himself. Style. A time for style. His bowels pressed; also his bladder. Breathing was not easy, but he knew he should be natural if not casual. Even airy. Perhaps help would come. He would spring for a branch.

Coughlin was considering. "One blue and one brown."

Benny tried to remember what one did in these circumstances. Something from the cinema, perhaps. A man of his wide experience and proved courage.

"You," Coughlin said abruptly, "have a Burble Heart. *I* have a Burble Heart."

"Then don't shoot at me," Benny said, profoundly and inexorably logical. It was astonishing that he felt no fear—and with the thought, fear swept him. Fear saturated him. He prickled, and his legs trembled. This had happened before. All of it.

Coughlin squinted at the pistol. "Maybe." He lowered his hand; the pistol bumped his thigh and hung. "Bitch," he said. "I don't even want her."

"It's late," Benny managed. "Why don't you go home now?" His voice, he noticed, arrived, or re-arrived, in tiny wind-borne brassy swells. He shut his eyes and reeled slightly. Tiny tinny tones and double-ments, whywhy dodon't youyou gogo hohome. He swallowed with difficulty, and remembered that he was frightened. Why must he be full of drink at this grandest of life's moments? Nothing seemed *consecutive*.

"I had a good woman in Nam," Coughlin said, and suddenly sniffled. "I was very happy there with that woman. Something," he quavered, "has gone wrong. I just wanted a lil work and a fren or two and some sweet pussy from time to time."

"That's ridiculous," Benny said. "That's insulting to womankind. Besides," he added reasonably, "you have that."

"Wurff," Coughlin breathed. "Buuuull . . . *shit*. Number ten, old buddy. She got it sewed up, old buddy." Tears stood bright. "Gon siddown," he said, and saddown on the blue flags; the pistol scraped and chinked, and Benny hoped woozily that the safety was firm. In the yellow wash Coughlin seemed onstage. "Have to *ask*," Coughlin said. "Have to *beg*." A sob. "Meimei was all over me like the *measles*." Goggling he thrust the muzzle between his lips; he withdrew it, said, "Bang," and snickered. Crafty and confidential, he offered the best deal in town: "How'd you like to buy a slightly used wife? Transmission a lil rough but up, uphol, up*hol*stery good as new. Not sure about one owner. Might have been a demonstrator," he said roguishly, "but low mileage. Real low mileage." Benny heard a crowd at the roadhouse, guffaws and backslaps; dim memories surged at him. Romeo turned television comic, life all gags. But he would not shoot, and Benny took heart.

"You stink," he said. "You stink of drink, and you beat children and women. Don't you even care about Roland?" He flushed, and his skin prickled again; loons laughed in the night and this was not real. Beyond Coughlin the lawn swam, the parked cars undulated.

"You stink too," Coughlin muttered, and flapped the pistol. "Ought to kill you."

"Sure," Benny said. Where was everybody? "Beat up a baby and kill an unarmed man." He shifted a foot and staggered. "Whoo."

"None of your god damn business," Coughlin said. "And it's my baby."

"But it *is* my business," Benny said, "and you just told me it wasn't your baby." Again the words returned from a great distance, slurred and musical, the remote echo of a belling stag.

Coughlin scowled. "Smart. Know-it-alls. Know-it-alls," his voice dropped to a mutter, "twenty god damn thousand years." He brooded, slack and lippy.

Benny said, "You bet."

Thunderously a window clattered open; he gasped aloud. "Benny," Carol called. "Benny?"

"What?" he screeched.

"It's Artie Burris on the phone. My God, who's that?"

"It's Walt Coughlin," he said. "It's just Walt Coughlin." The window slammed. "I'm wanted on the phone," Benny explained.

"Stay put," Coughlin said, and Benny smelled the lake on a sudden breeze, and high aloft ducks were

300

northing, maybe eiders, whoosh-whoosh-whoosh. "Yes," Coughlin said airily,"she's in there, and maybe you are the daddy of that son of a bitch, horny old Jew doctor with—no offense, no offense, race creed or color, a fucker is a fucker, hey, Doc? Hey, I hear you want to be mayor."

Benny weaved in place and understood that all this was possible. "It's my birthday," he whispered.

"A present," Coughlin said, and aimed.

"Don't," Benny cried, full of shame, nausea and infinite regret.

"Last chance," Coughlin said. "She in there?"

"No," Benny said, tasting brandy, and the scene quivered and tilted; he was about to be very sick, but he hung on, he would do this right if nothing else, and for one splendid moment the devil ran away with his tongue: "That, sir," he slurred, and flung his arms wide, "is a question no gentleman ever answers. Or asks." Immediately he felt like a fool.

"First," Coughlin said cheerfully, "we shoot out the brown eyes."

The shot deafened Benny, and he shrieked. Coughlin was laughing. Benny's legs gave way and he sat down like a doll. Bolts of lightning shattered his breast, and his lungs strained.

"That was just for fun," Coughlin said. Benny was faint and weepy; he sucked air, dizzy with terror, defiled by shame. "Don't," he whined from the heart, and then he was angry. "By God. What are you doing to me?"

Behind him the door opened, and he called out, "Close it. Go back."

"Daddy," Sarah cried. "Daddy, what is it?"

Coughlin said, "Hey hey. Looka this."

301

"Oh my God," she said. "Stop it."

It was too late for will, desire or choice. Benny was calm. "I'm getting up," he said.

"Now look here," Amos said. Rising, still dizzy, Benny turned; behind Sarah, Amos and Jacob filled the doorway. "Go back in," Benny roared. "Are you all crazy?"

"I don't know what this man wants," Amos said, "but you can't go around shooting guns on private property. Not at this time of night."

O God of Abraham and Isaac, are these truly thy sons and daughters? Benny straightened, breathing loudly. Amos's hair was sparse and white. Jacob stood sorrowful and reproving.

Coughlin said, "Who're you, there, sweetie?"

"I'm Sarah," Sarah said.

"Sarah. I remember little Sarah. Rich kid. How old are you, Sarah?"

"Nineteen. Just about."

Coughlin rose and waved the pistol. "Can't shoot Sarah's daddy." To Benny he said, "That's a *piece*, man," and to Sarah, "get your coat. Let's go drink."

"Nonsense," Carol said. Carol too. Benny felt rather left out. Perhaps he was dreaming this, snoozing by the fire. Coughlin smiled sweetly at Sarah and said, "Do you fuck?"

Benny quit then, delivered himself into the hands of the God of Abraham and Isaac, and roweled himself forward. He shambled to Coughlin and seized the pistol in both hands; his heart boomed and the light dimmed, his legs failed him again and they fell together; Benny shut his eyes and bit Coughlin's wrist as hard as he could, heard Sarah's scream, and tore at the pistol. It came away; he clutched it; he tried to drive a knee into

302

Coughlin's belly, missed, rolled off and sat up. He tasted brandy and bile, and licked his lips.

Coughlin was laughing. He shouted, "Some other time," and turned to run, slipping and lurching as he moved off. Corporal Beer rose quickly, placed himself sidewise to the target, and sighted along the barrel down the bright tunnel of his own night light. No time now to flip a coin, cast a horoscope, consult the I Ching; his thumb proved the safety off, and slowly he depressed the front sight, splitting the small of Coughlin's back. Carol shrieked, and for the space of two of Coughlin's erratic strides Benny was possessed by faces, voices, smells; men and women, soldiers and children, patients and prisoners, mud, snow, love, pus, chants and orders; and in the next instant, steady as honor, his vision absolutely clear, his heart, sap and sinew thrumming in a wild flood of pure joy, he squeezed the trigger.

Still trembling, giddy, nitwitted, he sat huddled on the edge of a club chair. The pistol lay before him on a footstool. "Don't touch it," he had said. "Maybe one more brandy," he had said, and Jacob and Amos joined him, and the women sat pale and silent. His pulse thudded; the glass shook. "Unbelievable," Amos said angrily. "In a place like this, the countryside. Something should be done about people like that."

"A peasant," Jacob said.

"You're all crazy," Benny said shakily. "You should never have come outside."

"You poor man," Carol said, "poor old Benny, with his wide circle of interesting friends." She surprised him with a warm kiss, and he patted her aft. "That woman," she went on, "slept right through it."

303

"Thank God," Benny said. "All we needed. A cheerleader."

Jacob said, "It took me back. All those years I worried, you'd be killed, or you'd kill somebody."

They considered this enormity.

"I suppose it was written somewhere," Benny said lightly. "I was not meant to do harm."

Sarah said, "You knew it was empty."

"I did not know," Benny said.

A log popped; the room was heavy with peace, and Benny was sleepy.

"A happy birthday after all," Jacob said.

"After all," Benny agreed. "You called Frank Cole?"

Carol said, "Frank Cole?"

Benny set down his snifter. "My God," he said. "You never called?"

"Listen," Sylvia said, "don't get involved."

Do bears sweat? He wondered that, sitting naked, head bowed, on his bed, aware now that he had sweated plenty. The room was warm and he was sober, and the hair on his chest was gray but on his thighs and in his crotch it was dark and springy. The light was golden and pulsed, and his eyes burned; he was overfull and logy, and seemed to jounce with each beat of his blood. Sad body. How romantic to think of himself as a bear, when he was only overweight.

He showered, dried, brushed his teeth. Wearily he donned his new paisley pajamas, and remembered the days of his youth when he had slept naked and hopeful. Abishag, soon enough. Drowsy, he became aware that he was stiff and sore. Fear? Or the brief wrestle?

Carol came in quietly and shut the door. "Hello," he

said. "My hero," she said, in a dark blue kimono, wide sleeves like wings. "You might have sent her to the hospital. Is she a floozy or a slut?"

Rebukes. He did not deserve rebukes tonight, but he subdued unworthy resentments. It could be worse, always: he might be blind, crippled, or dead. A frequent thought. "I couldn't do that," he said. "The baby lost an eye. She'll know soon enough. If he dies we'll tell her then. Or if he lives. But somebody would have let it slip."

"Oh my God," Carol said.

"So it doesn't really matter if she's a slut, does it."

"I'm sorry."

Lazily, love canceling gall so that his tone was indifferently light, he pursued: "Still, you're right; she's a slut. A funny thing," he went on, with an eye for a lie and a tooth for a truth, "but I like her a lot. Most of the women I've ever liked were broads. Warm and giggly. Give me a good round broad who jiggles when she laughs and nurses her baby at the blacksmith's picnic. Those others are killers. I'm a doctor."

She startled him: "Yes. I know. I meet them too."

"Come here," he said. "Lie down. I won't hurt you. We're very different, you know." She lay beside him and he held her close. "Some sort of birth defect, I suppose. I'm a doctor and a lecher, and I hope to live and die doing one or the other. Never really grew up. Never really wanted to."

"You're a slut," she murmured.

"All heart, that Benny."

They lay still, warm and silent, and soon she kissed him and left him, and he slept.

21

HE WOKE AT seven much refreshed, and his blood bated at the memory of that dry, shocking click, the savage disappointment, unjust, unjust, a last stab of frustration racking his body as Coughlin fled beyond the light. "Thank God," he said aloud, and luxuriated in pure, sweet relief, the aftermath of nightmare. "Thank God," he said, and set about his morning's work: ablutions, exercise, clothes. A sunny morn. In the bosom of family and friends. He grunted and hummed, Achilles about to leave his mildewed tent and amble down to inspect the black ships.

Clean and empty, in rural garb, he trod the hallway with a glance askance at Sarah's room and a shady ode to the two cookies therein. Goat-footed Benny greeting the sun, a pinch of incense to the infinite possibilities of every day. Wheat and soybeans. Outside the back door he squinted in the sudden blaze, and winkled off through the wet grass. Heavy dew caught the light and dazzled; he saw two fat robins, and rejoiced. The boat and the stake were where he had left them. The waters had risen, and had ceased to rise, and his lake was breath-taking, silver and gold, green and blue, and the tips of drowned trees waving a welcome. He exulted, and stood on a bank beaded with gems: an elderly party, beautifully tricked out, rich, fat, and about to undertake a voyage of discovery.

He cast off, and rowed with animal pleasure. The house too was handsome, painted last fall, bright and safe in the clear light of a spring day. He plowed a straight wake. When he reached the maple he was warm, and doffed the worn jacket. The nest was head-high; he considered the problem. At the rattle and flash of a blue and russet kingfisher he offered ardent thanks; almost he wept. He stumped carefully to the bow, tied the painter to a low branch and hoisted himself to a narrow crotch. The bark was black and slippery, and a breeze off the water blew his sweat cold; he shivered. The nest was larger than he had though , three feet across, a primeval tangle of twigs, small boughs, dead straw, feathers, hanks of still waxy twine. He wrapped his legs about the thinner trunk, grasped a branch above him and hitched higher. Feeling like a boy, a foolish boy, he peered into the nest. It was empty. He had expected that. No egg, no diamond. No parchment. A mass of dried twigs, the faint rank residue of lake and lime. The secret of life, aha. Lodged among the twigs were the remains of dried droppings. He felt that he should leave an offering, but he had not furnished himself with a suitable ex voto. Reverently he took aim and spat. It would have to do.

He descended with care, freed the painter and wiped his hands on his dirty khakis. He was breathing hard; too much party. He wondered if Coughlin was properly jugged. Must call the hospital. And Cole. And Artie Burris. Well, plenty of time. The true peace of God, he remembered, descends a thousand miles from the nearest land, and he would not admit the day's cares until he was ashore. Rowing back he steered by the maple, and his shoulders ached. As he watched, a patrol of crows swooped down upon the tree and sat; seven crows, like stern pudgy monks. The oars dragged. A foolish old man. But he had waited years to look into that nest, and was pleased with the day.

The prow touched; as he shipped the oars he felt another tug, and looked behind him to see Carol hauling at the painter. She helped him ashore and said good morning. "Good morning," he said, and they shared a swift hug. "Beautiful day," he said. "You too." She was, yes; twenty years now, but given half a chance he would not tire of it. He squeezed her happily here and there. "Oh dear," she laughed, dodging away.

"I know," he said, "I know, they're all lined up at the windows watching." This morning he did not mind. They would catch Coughlin and the baby would improve and soon the family would assemble for a noble breakfast, champagne perhaps, and they would turn down a glass for Joe. Benny thought he might try to be a good doctor and a loving husband.

They walked on the lawn with the sun in their eyes, and Benny slipped into his jacket and blinked cheerfully, and laid a happy hand on Carol's far hip. She slipped her arm inside his and hooked her thumb on the back of his belt, and he bumped her near hip slyly with his own. Benny was forty-six years old and for a moment wanted desperately to be twenty-two. But the moment passed and did not sadden him.

"What was in the nest?"

"Well," he said, "a little fellow in a pointed hat with stars and moons all over it. He said I was going to make a long voyage by water, and at the end of it there would be a beautiful princess with blue eyes and black hair, and we'd have twenty-four children and you'd be a good round woman and nurse them at the blacksmith's picnic.''

Their shoes scattered the dew in tiny showers. They turned up the slope toward the house.

"Benny," she said, "I'm sorry, but I have to ask."

He knew but waited.

Her hand pressed his back, her head his shoulder: "Benny, is that baby yours?"

He smiled upon her with love. "Carol, Carol," he said, "they're all mine."

He stumbled then, and fell heavily, so that the pain was sharp, he seemed to have fallen on his chest, and Carol had gripped his arm, much too tightly; he wanted to call out to her and ask her to ease her grip. His face was pressed into the wet grass, and the blades of grass were gigantic; there was one directly before his eyes, a gigantic bowed blade of grass with a single swollen drop of dew perched upon it, shot with all the colors of all the rainbows he had ever seen. He thought of nothing and no one. He heard his name called, a high, quavering morning cry; and that was all.

Where do we walk? Into the night. How do we walk? Heads up and ready for trouble. (Jacob said nothing, but wept, and rent his garments, and grew small.) Life is a riddle and death is the only answer, and each man dies alone. (Carol raged and ached: "Now what? Now what?" She learned what widows learn: to go on.) Benny's journey took him the road of good and evil, which wizened to better or worse, as love and hate wizened to rue and scorn; he never solved the riddle, but he never quit the quest. (Joseph and Sarah survived.) Benny knew that the answer was unimportant, a mere ceasing, and only the riddle mattered, or the riddling, the seeking and straining, yes, the old word, the striving, the strength to say no, to hold out, to do justly and love mercy, to see your own sins in the sins of others, to resist the strong and succour the weak, and to love men and women and children, the whole miserable, selfish, cowardly, pullulating lot of them, with all thy heart and with all thy soul and with all thy might, because then weeds beat scurvy! and Benny lives!

About the Author

Stephen Becker was educated at Harvard; in Peking, where he lived for a year; and in France, where he lived for four years. He has published eight novels (most recently *The Chinese Bandit*), nine translations (including *The Last of the Just*), biography and history; of his half-dozen short stories and magazine articles, four were anthologized. He has lectured in several countries and once every two or three years he teaches for a term, but he prefers the seclusion of a farm in the Berkshires, where he and his wife Mary raise beef and goats.

BESTSELLERS FOR THE BEST READING!

CHILDREN OF DUNE   (03310-4—$1.95)
  by Frank Herbert

THE CHINESE BANDIT   (03403-8—$1.95)
  by Stephen Becker

FINDING MY FATHER   (03456-9—$1.95)
  by Rod McKuen

THE GHOST OF FLIGHT 401   (03553-0—$2.25)
  by John G. Fuller

THE HOUSE ON THE HILL   (03648-0—$1.95)
  by Jonathan Black

INDIGO NIGHTS   (03629-4—$1.95)
  by Olivia O'Neill

Send for a *free* list of all our books in print

These books are available at your local bookstore, or send
price indicated plus 30¢ per copy to cover mailing costs to
Berkley Publishing Corporation
390 Murray Hill Parkway
East Rutherford, New Jersey 07073

MORE BESTSELLERS FROM BERKLEY